Elton Hall Chronicles:

FIRST SEMESTER

By Sarah Fischer

Elton Hall Chronicles: First Semester

Limitless Publishing, LLC
Kailua, HI 96734
www.limitlesspublishing.com

Formatting: Limitless Publishing

ISBN-13: 978-1-64034-033-6
ISBN-10: 1-64034-033-5

Dedication

I dedicate this book to the girls whose voices have been silenced, to the ones too afraid to come forward, and for those who are still fighting to survive. Also, to Kelsey McKnight who is largely responsible for giving me the confidence to release this story.

Chapter 1

As I was only nineteen, I'd never been to a casino before, but this was pretty much what I imagined. There were waitresses clad in little black dresses bringing multi-colored cocktails to students with varying sizes of chip piles. Shouts of excitement erupted as the roulette wheel stopped and cheers exploded from the craps table as someone chucked the dice.

Looking around at everyone, it was easy to ignore the basketball hoops folded up toward the ceiling and the bleachers pushed against the wall. Annabelle and I swiped our university ID cards and were given the fake money.

"Where do you want to go first, Violet?" Annabelle asked as we looked around Elton Hall University's gym.

I eyed the poker table with a sly look on my face. My dad had always been a big poker fan and had taught my brother and me to play. Mind you, we never played with more than one hundred pennies. Over the years, I had turned into quite the card shark, but I liked to keep that a secret. Half of the fun was in the hustle.

"I know how to play Texas Hold 'Em poker so why don't we go over there," I suggested, and we headed toward a table with several open seats.

My roommate had decided to attend another school last minute, therefore, my double was temporarily a single. So I decided to say hi to the shy girl across the hall, Annabelle. Luckily, she didn't think I was a serial killer and came with me to the university's welcome night event, Casino Night.

As I sat down, I noticed Annabelle didn't. "I am going to watch first. I have no idea what you're doing," she assured me as she slid her Mary Poppins size bag under my seat. Annabelle's dark eyes surveyed the table with fear but for a second I thought I saw a glint of excitement.

"Okay, I can explain," I started as I traded in my fake money for chips. As I was going over the game to her, I couldn't help but notice the sex on a stick sitting two chairs away. He pulled my focus at first, but I didn't want him to see the effect he had on me so I turned to look at Annabelle and avoided his gaze entirely.

I tried explaining to her but it was no use.

"Yeah, I'm still confused," Annabelle complained to me.

"That's okay, just watch a round or two and you'll figure it out."

I looked down at my hand and saw two tens, a club, and a diamond, and Annabelle nodded as I showed them to her. The betting began and I looked around at the rest of the table. Next to me was another guy. He was wearing a superman shirt and khaki shorts. He had thick glasses and unmanageable eyebrows. He also seemed really nervous as his knee bounced uncontrollably and a trickle of sweat slid down his face. Next to him, the sexpot was staring at his hand, looking indecisive.

He was older, maybe around twenty-six or twenty-seven, with a little bit of stubble caressing his chin. He had an angular face with a strong jaw and a heavy brow. His dark brown, almost black, hair was gelled to the side. Big green eyes surrounded by long dark lashes looked up over his cards. For a second, I was mesmerized. Then I realized I was staring for an uncomfortably long time and returned my attention to the game. There was no way I was going to let him throw me off.

The blonde girl on my other side had just placed a bet. It was a small wager and looked more like she was fishing to try to see what everyone else had rather than providing clues to the cards she had. I raised the bet a little to see if I could scare her off. I also wanted to send a little message to the remaining players that I had something. Hopefully, though, they thought I only had a small pair.

The guy next to me folded almost instantly. However, the Greek god next to him looked me straight in the eyes. He seemed to be trying to read my soul he looked so deep. My heart raced as I held his gaze, determined not to be the first one to break the trance we seemed to be in. He smiled slowly, showing his perfectly white teeth. The tooth to the right of his front tooth was a little crooked. Ah, he so he had a flaw! The now almost Greek god called my raise.

As I predicted, the other girl involved folded. So it was just Hercules and me. The dealer dealt three cards, the flop, and I tried to contain my excitement. It was the three of diamonds, seven of diamonds, and the ten of hearts. I had three of a kind.

I showed Annabelle the cards again. She nodded and I used that moment to pull my face together so I could face Hercules again. It was up to me to start the betting and I was determined not to reveal anything to him. I raised and gave him a sweet smile.

"I call," Hercules said as he looked deep into my eyes again. I should have looked away. I wasn't that good at hiding my feelings, and if he kept looking at me, the lust I was feeling for him would be all too obvious. But maybe that was a good thing.

The dealer dealt the next card and placed it with the three community cards in the middle of the table. It was the five of diamonds. I was sitting pretty at this point. From looking at Hercules, I had to think he was sitting on a pair. If he was, then I had him beat. There was another round of betting and I felt my heart pounding in my chest. The adrenaline from the game mixed with the sexual energy flowing through me was almost too much to handle.

The last card, the river, was dealt then placed with the other four in the middle of the table. It was the seven of clubs. I had a full house. I pulled myself together while looking at my pile of chips, pretending I needed to think about what I was going to do. I could feel Hercules's gaze on me and that was really what was making me blush. Considering how pale I was, that was not hard to do. I took a deep breath and raised. Hercules smiled big this time and it reached his eyes. They squinted and crinkled a little on the edge. It was a breathtaking smile. I shook my head and tried to get it together.

"All right. You may know the rules of the game, but I'll bet you don't really know how to play. I raise you two hundred dollars." Hercules threw the chips in the middle and gave me a smug, satisfied look.

My adrenaline really kicked up another notch and I was practically bouncing out of my seat. He had challenged me and assumed he had me beat. I took a deep breath and smiled at him. If I was wrong, then I was going to look like a complete fool in front of him.

"I call." I pushed the chips into the middle and then turned to look at Annabelle. I gave her an excited glance and returned my attention to Hercules. He had a glint in his eyes and it was completely naughty. I felt like he was undressing me with his eyes and I soaked it in. Anyone could see that the sexual desire was mutual.

"Ladies first," he insisted, indicating that I should flip my cards over first. I wasn't one hundred percent sure but I thought he had a British accent. It sent a purr through my body that was not easily silenced.

"I believe my full house beats your three sevens," I said as I flipped over my tens. The smirk on Hercules's face fell as he flipped over his two sevens.

"How did you know?" He shook the hair out of his eyes and looked at me incredulously. The accent was real.

I couldn't immediately look away as he seemed to have me in that trance again. So I decided to play with him a little. "A lady doesn't kiss and tell," I teased as I collected my chips.

He stared back and his mouth slid into a devilishly handsome smirk. "You're not playing games with little boys anymore. You should be more careful not to taunt me."

"I've been looking for a man to play with for a while now, let me know if you find one. I'll be sure to show him a good time."

Hercules chuckled for a minute and wagged his pointer finger at me. "Nicely done."

I smiled at him and then turned to look at Annabelle. "What do you think? Wanna play?"

"I'm not playing! You're like psychic or something. I'm going to go grab a drink. Do you want one?" she asked as she grabbed her bag.

"Sure, I'll take a Coke if you don't mind," I said as the dealer sent me two new cards.

Hercules barely noticed the cards that were dealt in front of him. He was too captivated by what had just happened. Really, I just guessed and got lucky. But there was no way I was going to tell him that. Being a lady of mystery was way more fun.

"All right, let's do this again. I've got your number now," Hercules jeered as he finally picked up his cards and I looked at mine.

I was sitting on an eight of hearts and a nine of

clubs. Not the best hand but I had a lot of opportunities for a straight. I checked. Hercules and the blonde checked.

The game continued as the three community cards were placed on the table. After another round of betting, the blonde next to me folded. It was just Hercules and me again. Annabelle hadn't come back with my drink yet so I had nothing better to do than to look at Hercules's deep green eyes. They dipped down and he stared at his cards.

As he was mulling over his options, I found myself looking at the rest of his face again. He had a straight nose that seemed to suit his face. But what really took my breath away were his lips. They were full and luscious with just a hint of red to them. I began to wonder what it would be like to kiss those lips. How it would feel to have him leave a trail of kisses down my neck. For that trail to drop below my collarbone and inch ever closer to my breasts. To feel those lips caressing my…

"What's your bet?" The dealer had tapped the table in front of me to get my attention. Apparently, the world did not actually stop while I was imagining his lips.

I shook my head and looked at my cards again. After the river card had been flipped, I had my straight. I didn't know exactly what Hercules had but I had a feeling he was bluffing.

"I think you're compensating for something. I raise to two hundred dollars," I purred, staring at him straight in the eye.

"You have no idea what I am working with." Hercules laughed. He had a deep laugh that tickled parts of me that had been left dormant for too long. It was intoxicating.

"I call." Hercules tossed the chips in the middle, as if acknowledging that I had just called him out.

"Ladies first, I assume?" I asked as I flipped over my cards. I had a smug look plastered on my face because I was sure I had him. When he flipped his cards over, he confirmed I was right.

Hercules shook his head at me and smiled. "You are really a hustler, aren't you? Coming in all innocent but really knowing exactly how to play the game," Hercules commented in that rich accent as the dealer took the cards and began to shuffle.

"Sweetheart, I have always known how to play the game." I looked up at him through my eyelashes. His voice was melodic and stroked my inner animal. It was gentle and dangerous at the same time.

"Oh, I am sure you do." He held my gaze for a second too long. Then he gathered his rather small pile of chips up and walked over to the roulette table.

"I think I'm done too," I said as I grabbed my chips and walked over to meet Annabelle at the concession table. She was busy talking to a gorgeous man with thick blond hair and blue eyes. His muscles were instantly apparent and he oozed confidence. He should have left me panting like a puppy but I couldn't help but notice that he didn't have the same effect as Hercules had on my system.

"You won all of that?" she asked as the guy left. But it took me a second to hear her. I was too focused on the fact that I noticed Hercules had been watching me from the roulette table. I tried to act cool, but inside I was bursting. He seemed to ignite something inside of me that I was not quite ready to explain to Annabelle yet.

"Yep. My dad, brother, and I used to play poker together all the time when I was young. I picked up a few things." My mouth had gone dry so I took a long drink of the soda she'd given me. I was sure it was just from the game, though, and not him.

"So, do you think you're going to join any clubs?" Annabelle asked, apparently oblivious to the internal struggle I'd been having.

"I'm not sure. I think I may look into pledging a sorority. My mom was in one and she had a really good time. But I heard you have to wait until second semester to pledge." I hadn't really thought about clubs. Since I didn't really know anyone, it was probably a good idea for me to look into it. "What about you?" I asked Annabelle.

"They have this club where they plan for concerts and comedians to come to the school. They also put on smaller events throughout the year. That guy, Trent, was telling me before he had to catch up with his friends. It is called EET, Elton Entertainment Team. They have an interest meeting tomorrow at one. I think I'm going to check it out."

"Yeah, that sounds fun. Do you mind if I come with you?" I asked as I tried to keep from searching for Hercules.

"Nope! Sounds good. Want to meet up and then head over?" Annabelle asked.

"Awesome! Why don't we give blackjack a try? I promise I don't have any tricks for that game," I

9

assured her as I finished my drink.

"Okay, but I warn you, I can't even do basic math," Annabelle said, and we walked over to the table. The rest of the night went on without incident. Annabelle turned out to be really lucky and did well in blackjack. It helped that the dealer did the counting for her.

As the games were closing, we turned our chips in for raffle tickets. I didn't win anything, which didn't surprise me. I never won raffles. Annabelle, though, won a thirty-two-inch flat screen television. I helped her carry it to her room before we said good night.

I fell asleep thinking of Hercules. I could not believe I didn't even get his name. It just seemed out of place to ask for it. So I guessed I would keep calling him Hercules. Though I doubted we would see each other again. The school was small but it wasn't that small. He was older, so probably in the more advanced classes or he was part of one of the master's degree programs the school had. Even though I assured myself we would not meet again, I found myself dreaming of a different time where he and I could be together.

Chapter 2

The next morning was a late one for me. I woke up in a state of utter confusion around eleven. I had no idea where I was for a couple of seconds. It was the first time I'd woken up in a new place without my family in the next room. I lay there for a second and let it set in. I felt a little bit of panic start to surge up inside me but then pushed it back down. I was ready for this.

I helped myself to my cereal stash and had some breakfast. While eating, I sat on my bed and looked out the window. It was sunny without a cloud in the sky. I never really was one for taking walks or being outside for long periods of time, but I had the urge. I threw on some jean shorts and a white cotton shirt. I found a pair of blue flip-flops and grabbed my wristlet. I figured I needed to get my books for class so I might as well walk over there and pick them up. With this thought, I went back to my room and grabbed my hot pink backpack.

***

It was a beautiful campus. There were all sorts of benches and tables scattered around the field to allow students a place to study outside. Next to the benches were flower beds with pink, white, purple, and yellow flowers bursting about. But it was the castle that really took my breath away. It was the first time I would walk through those doors since I visited the college last year for orientation.

I took a deep breath and opened the doors of the castle. The inside had been modernized, much to my dismay. There were phone charging stations in each hall and vending machines that accepted credit cards. That was until I reached the basement. The integrity of the castle had been kept down here. The stone walls were gray and felt smooth and cool to the touch. It would probably be freezing down here in winter but I almost didn't care. It would be worth it just to walk under the massive arches and sit on the stone bench in the corner by the window overlooking the garden. Apparently, the school had a degree program in horticulture and they worked down there. It was a quiet safe haven and I had a feeling I would spend a lot of time there.

I continued down the hall and eventually made it to the school store. Once inside, I went to talk to one of the clerks. There were two books that I couldn't buy online so I had to come to the store. One was for my computer class and the other for my intro to literature class. Apparently, the literature professor had written a textbook and wanted us to buy that. Frankly, I thought this was a little ridiculous. It was like he was using the class to increase his book sales.

"I really need the book that he wrote?" I asked the clerk as she went to a shelf in the back to get it.

"Yep. He made it very clear to us that it would be a big part of the class. He is some new professor visiting for a year from England while finishing his second textbook," the clerk said as she handed me a hard cover book with about three hundred pages. It was small but I had a feeling that smaller definitely meant we would have to know more of it.

The clerk disappeared to get my second book and came back holding what could only be described as bookzilla. It looked like it ate ten of my literature text books for lunch and then had another five for an early dinner. It also cost three hundred and forty-five dollars. I could tell that my computer class was going to be my least favorite class. But it was a requirement for all freshmen so I had no choice but to suffer. However, I would not do it quietly.

I paid and put bookzilla and the literature book inside my backpack and went to sit on one of the stone benches overlooking the garden. For a while, I was the only one there and it was nice to sit and relax. Then a man in a police uniform walked into the garden. He was built solid, like a football player, and he turned to smile at me. I waved politely back. The officer walked around the corner and handed me a daisy he had just picked.

"Thank you." I smiled and sniffed the flower politely.

"Don't mention it. I'm always around to offer

nice things to a pretty girl." He puffed out his chest a little and leaned a muscled arm against the wall.

I was about to respond when my phone went off. It was a text from Annabelle. I was going to be late meeting her. "Sorry, I need to go, but thanks again for the flower."

"Wait," the officer shouted at me as I was about to round the corner.

I stopped and turn back to look at him.

"Not a fan of daisies?" He flashed me a bright smile.

"Uh, the flower is fine. I'm just meeting a friend." I forced a smile and headed back to my dorm to meet up with Annabelle.

***

As it turned out, she wasn't ready yet so I took my make-up bag out and headed to the bathroom. After some time, the make-up started to have the desired effect. I put one more layer of mascara on and packed the bag up. I had just put the bag back in my room when there was a knock on my door. I grabbed my wristlet and opened the door to see Annabelle standing in front of me.

"Ready for the meeting?" she asked with her tote on her shoulder.

"Yep, let's go." I locked my door and we left.

We headed to the castle. Apparently, EET held their meetings in one of the large classrooms on the second floor. If I had known that, I would have met her there, but a little exercise was always a good thing.

I had never been on the second floor so I was hoping we didn't get too lost. I was not exactly known for my directional abilities back home. In fact, my parents had even bought me a portable GPS for my birthday one year. Luckily, Annabelle and I saw two girls with EET staff t-shirts on. We figured it was a safe bet to follow them.

They entered a classroom that could easily seat fifty. The desks were in a large semi-circle around the room, kind of like an amphitheater. It was welcoming and a little intimidating at the same time. There was nowhere to hide.

The girls we followed walked over to the blackboard, which was the focus of the semi-circle. We took two seats on the left and looked around. There were around thirty other students sitting in desks, chatting with each other, and a couple other ones sitting on the outside who, like us, were clearly new to the party. I turned to Annabelle to comment on the crowd but was cut short. Someone else had just walked into the room and he had a British accent.

"Oh shit, it's Hercules," I whispered as he turned around and his green eyes focused on me.

"What did you just say?" Annabelle asked. Apparently, that last comment was not in my head.

Hercules looked away and walked over to the girls at the blackboard. He appeared to be introducing himself to them. Unhappy with my lack of response, Annabelle slapped me on the forearm.

"His name is Hercules?" she asked, trying to figure out what I was talking about.

"No, well, maybe. I don't actually know his

name. Remember the guy from poker last night?" I said in more of a hushed tone, hoping she would follow suit.

"Oh, right. But why do you call him Hercules?" Annabelle responded in a quieter tone this time.

"Stop staring at him," I chastised, hoping he didn't already know we were talking about him. However, he took that moment to glance over at me. He quickly looked away, but not before he gave me a mischievous smirk.

"I think he recognizes you too," Annabelle said as she started to giggle. "Did something happen while I went to get drinks? Maybe a hand of strip poker or something?" She stole another glance at him while he was looking in the other direction.

"Yes, I stripped in a room full of horny guys and no one noticed." I rolled my eyes and tried not to smile. "We flirted a little and I kicked his ass in poker. I assumed he was a grad student or something and didn't think I'd see him again." I felt a blush begin to creep up my neck and settle in my cheeks.

"So did he introduce himself as Hercules?" Annabelle asked. I had a feeling she would not let the nickname go.

"Okay, don't laugh at me. He never mentioned his name so I just kind of referred to him in my head as Hercules. You know, he looks like a god but is still human. I'm a giant nerd." I dropped my head into my hands out of embarrassment. Once I heard the explanation out loud, I had to laugh at how ridiculous I was. Luckily, Annabelle seemed to be laughing with me and not at me.

"That's amazing. He really is good looking," Annabelle added as she glanced over at him again.

"I know! And he has a British accent. I'm such a sucker for that accent."

"Really? I am more of a southern twang kind of girl."

I was about to inform her that there was no way southern beat British, but one of the girls by the chalkboard cut me off to call the meeting to order.

"Hi, everyone! My name is Natalie, or Nat, and I am president of Elton Entertainment Team. This is Clarissa, our treasurer, Trent, our late night entertainment director, and this is Professor David Berneli, our new faculty adviser." Hercules was a professor. My mouth dropped. Well, so much for that idea.

"Did you know he was a professor?" Annabelle leaned over and asked me.

"No! I told you, I thought he was a graduate student," I whispered back.

"Well, this makes everything more interesting." Annabelle giggled softly and looked at me. I rolled my eyes and tried to focus on what Nat was saying.

"Professor, do you want to tell us about yourself?" Nat asked as she sat down on a stool in the front of the room next to Clarissa.

"As Nat said, I am Professor Berneli. I'm visiting from Lockland University, which is located just outside of London. I will be teaching here for about a year while I finish up a project. EET's faculty advisor retired last year and they asked me to replace her for the duration of my visit. I worked my way through university as a club promoter and talent manager so I have some experience booking and then handling the talent when they arrive. I'm available if you have any questions about what your role may be here. Clarissa, I believe you wanted to say some things now." Professor Berneli then took his seat on his own stool next to Nat. She turned to him and gave him a giant smile before leaning in to whisper something in his ear.

I tried not to be jealous and turned my attention to Clarissa, but I was having a hard time focusing on what she was saying. I was too busy replaying what Professor Berneli had said. Listening to him speak gave me a thrill. The way his tongue wrapped around some of the words excited me. It made me wonder what else his tongue could do.

Annabelle slid a piece of paper in front of me, completely ending my fantasy. It was a sign-in sheet. I wrote my name on the paper and slid it to the guy sitting next to me.

It was a little warm in the room, or maybe it was just my fantasy getting me all sorts of hot and bothered, so I slid my hair off my shoulders and pulled it up into a ponytail with a pen. I did that a lot but frequently forgot the pen was there. I looked back up toward the front of the room where he was sitting on his stool. As it turned out, he was looking at me too. I forced myself to look away and focus again on what Clarissa was saying.

"So our meetings are on Tuesdays at four. If you have class, then just come afterward or maybe drop in before your class. We set up a big concert for the school in April but we have not started to work on that yet. The first thing we have to do is pick a comedian for our show in October. We have some ideas but we are open to suggestions." Clarissa went to the blackboard and picked up a piece of chalk. Nat stood up and began talking again.

"If you have an idea, just shout it out. We aren't in class so you don't need to raise your hand."

A couple students began saying names. I, unfortunately, didn't recognize any of them. Apparently, I was not up to date with my comedians.

"Do you have any idea who these people are?" I asked Annabelle, who also seemed to be mighty quiet.

"No. I like comedians, but I can't really name anybody. I'd still like to help though."

"Do you think we would get to meet the comedians too?" I asked, getting a little excited. "I've never actually met anyone famous."

"I don't know, but I bet we could at least get in for free!" Annabelle said, and took a notebook out of her tote. She began writing a list.

"What are you writing? I am sure that they have a secretary."

"I want to look them up later so we can have some idea who they are," Annabelle told me as she copied down the names quickly.

"That's a good idea. You're a thinker, my friend!"

"I try."

The meeting continued with some more brainstorming and ended about twenty minutes later. Annabelle grabbed her bag and we started to get up when I heard my name. It nearly stopped my heart.

I turned around and saw Hercules staring at me. When I met his gaze, his strong hand beckoned me forward. I reminded myself to breathe and walked over to him. When we were playing poker, I didn't realize how tall he was. Standing next to him now, he must have been at least six feet tall. This did not help to calm me down, but rather accelerated my heart rate even more. I was determined to keep cool though. He could not know the effect he was having on me.

"What can I do for you, Professor?" I asked as I put extra emphasis on *professor*. He smiled and I fought the urge to look away. Instead, I held his gaze.

"So all those chips last night and you didn't win the tablet?" Hercules asked as he continued to stare.

"Yeah, I never win raffles. I don't have that kind of luck." I shifted my gaze down for a second. I looked back up at him slowly through my lashes. "Wait, how did you know I didn't win?" I asked.

"I notice things." He paused for what seemed like forever but then eventually looked down at his clipboard. "Like I noticed you did not put your student ID number on the form. We need full information for our records." He handed me the clipboard and his hand slightly grazed mine. I felt a shot of electricity flow through me. It was only there for a second but I could have sworn he felt it too.

"Do you have a pen?" I asked, trying to keep my voice calm.

He reached behind me and pulled the pen out of

my ponytail. My hair fell out of the knot and slid down my back.

"Oh," I laughed, "I forgot it was there." I looked down immediately, embarrassed at how ridiculous I was. How could I have forgotten I left the pen in my hair? I wrote down my student ID number. "Is there anything else you need from me?" I asked as I handed him the form. I was careful this time not to touch him. I wasn't sure what would happen if I did.

"That's it for now. I guess I'll see you on Tuesday, Violet."

One side of his mouth slid up in a smile and then he walked over to Nat and Clarissa. I was right about his tongue. His lips caressed my name like a man did his lover on a cold winter night. And I was left standing there trying to remember how to walk. Luckily, Annabelle took it upon herself to show up at that moment.

"So you are never going to guess what just happened," Annabelle shouted. She was practically bouncing with excitement.

"Nope. You're probably right." I turned to face her and shook my head to clear the dirty thoughts regarding his tongue.

"Clarissa noticed me taking notes in the meeting and said that their secretary quit last minute because she had a hard semester coming up and needed to focus on classes. So now they have a position open. Since the secretary ran unopposed, there was no one else to promote. They asked me if I had any experience in the position. I let her know I was secretary in student government for my senior year. That seemed to impress them and they offered me the position!" Annabelle looked as if she was trying hard not to squeal.

"That was lucky! It is a good thing we know nothing about comedians." I was truly happy to see her so thrilled and animated.

"I know, right!" Annabelle cheered as we headed out the door. "Clarissa said the executive board meets a half hour before the meeting to prepare. Since on Tuesdays my last class ends at two thirty, I'm completely free."

"Aww, I'm happy for you! I guess we are joining EET," I responded as we made our way through the castle.

"You do want to join the club too, right?" Annabelle asked me.

"Yeah, it sounds fun." I tried to match her enthusiasm. I really did think the club would be a good time, but I was just a little concerned about having to see Hercules weekly. I wasn't sure if my sanity or my libido could take it.

"Oh, and Clarissa said we do get into the shows for free and we also get to meet the stars," Annabelle informed me as we crossed the field.

"That's awesome." I just hoped we could get to see some really famous performers. "Did you eat lunch?" I asked her as we were walking.

"No, and I'm pretty hungry."

We headed to the cafeteria to get some food. It was after two in the afternoon so the cafeteria was pretty empty. We got our food and drinks and sat down at the table near the window. I was about to dig in to my salad when Annabelle spoke up.

"So what did Hercules want?"

I almost choked on a green pepper. I knew what I wanted from Hercules but I wasn't sure if he wanted the same thing.

"I forgot to put my student ID on the sign-in form and he asked me to fill it in." I hoped I sounded nonchalant. From the look on Annabelle's face, I got the distinct feeling that she did not believe me.

"I saw the hair thing. I am pretty sure he wants a little more than your student ID," Annabelle teased, waving her fork in the air as she spoke.

"I just needed a pen to write the number is all. I should have grabbed it myself. I was just being dumb," I said as I shifted my attention to my ham sandwich.

"Yeah, okay! You just keep telling yourself that."

"He's a teacher, nothing can happen with him anyway." I shrugged my shoulders and changed the subject. "Do you want to head back to my room and look up those comedians, Madam Secretary?"

"Yeah, that sounds like a plan. I just want to drop my bag off in my room first and change into sweatpants." We finished our lunches and speculated about what the comedy show would be like.

***

I told Annabelle to come over in ten minutes so I could pick up a few things in my room. I took my key out of my wristlet and opened the door but I was not prepared for what I saw.

Lying on a pink and lace bedspread was a shirtless guy reading a book. I closed the door instantly. I must have gone to the wrong room. Why would there be a guy lying on the bedspread, and who let him in? I looked at the number on the door—room two. Nope, this was my room. Was this my new roommate? I did not think the school had co-ed dorms. I shook my head and opened the door again. The guy had put his shirt on and was sitting on the chair in front of the desk now.

"I'm not your roommate. My girlfriend is in the shower," he said really quickly.

I laughed and put my wristlet down. "Sorry, I was so confused for a minute. I thought maybe they had co-ed dorms and you had an affinity for pink."

"No, my name is Tyler. Lola, my girlfriend, needed a different room so they offered her this one."

"Gotcha. I'm Violet." I walked over to him and shook his hand. Then I dropped my bag on the floor and texted Annabelle.

Can we meet in your room in fifteen mins? I'll explain later.

I sat on my bed and waited for her response.

Yeah. See you in a few.

I pretended to be engrossed in my phone while I waited. I wanted to meet my new roommate but I didn't want to sit around forever. Even though Tyler introduced himself, it was still a little weird.

I was just about to head over to Annabelle's room when my door, well, our door, opened. In walked a girl wrapped in a robe with her hair in a towel. She looked toward me and smiled.

"Hi, I'm Lauren, but everyone calls me Lola," she said as she crossed the room to my bed and we shook hands.

"I'm Violet, nice to meet you," I replied, and quickly looked away. She was in a robe after all. "I'll let you get dressed." I was about to get up but she stopped me.

"Oh, I have no shame. I am sure within the next year we are going to see a whole lot of each other." She laughed as she grabbed some clothes out of her closet. I was glad I convinced my mother not to hang clothes in her closet the other day. "We're headed out to get some dinner but we're going to a party tonight over in another dorm. You should come. We can get to know each other a little," Lola offered.

"Yeah, that sounds fun. I am about to run across the hall to see my friend, but we could meet up with you later." As soon as it came out of my mouth, I realized that I just invited Annabelle to Lola's party. "Do you mind if I bring my friend?" I added.

"Of course not, it's a party," Lola said as she slipped her clothes on. We exchanged phone numbers and agreed she would give me the details for the party later. She and Tyler went to the cafeteria and I headed to Annabelle's room.

***

"Want to go to a party tonight?" I asked as Annabelle opened the door. She looked at me a little funny and then moved aside. The last time I saw Annabelle's room it was covered in storage containers. Now there appeared to be a method to her madness. Most of the storage bins had been placed under the bed. The remaining were next to the head and foot of the bed and served as nightstands. It was organizational furniture.

She had wire rim baskets hanging on the walls and they were all packed with school supplies and other random things. In between the baskets were pictures from home and beach scenes. Annabelle patted a spot on her bed, indicating I could sit on the paisley bedspread. I told her about Lola and Tyler and she just laughed.

"Wow. I am pretty impressed that you didn't scream. I would have freaked out!"

"I know. I wasn't really sure how to react! But she seems nice. I think we should go to that party. It could be fun," I said, hoping that she would want to go.

"We can give it a try. I mean, it's in a dorm, right, so we could just head back here if we wanted." The idea that it was only a few buildings away relaxed me too. Obviously, I had never been to a college party. I was excited but still a little nervous.

In the meantime, we looked up some of the comedians on the computer and eventually ordered a pizza for dinner. We had gotten through three of them on the list and I had a definite favorite. Her name was Carmen Holly and her father was in the

Army. As a result, she told jokes based on all the different places she lived. She played up stereotypes but totally attacked New Jersey. That irritated Annabelle, a true Jersey girl, which, of course, made it funnier.

***

Around eight, Lola texted me the details of the party. It was now going to be in a few of the apartments on the other side of campus. I wasn't so sure about this anymore. Neither of us had ever been to the apartments and we wouldn't know anyone but Lola and Tyler.

Annabelle flat out said she wasn't going until she got a text from Clarissa. Apparently, she and Nat were hosting a party in the apartments and they wanted her to come. They told her she could bring a friend if she wanted. It was also an open party.

"Do you think they're the same party?" I wondered as Annabelle read me the message.

"Probably not. I mean, the college is not that small," Annabelle said. "We could go to that one and then head over to Lola's party after if we still want to."

"Yeah, we could do that. Now we just have to figure out what we're going to wear. You first since you take longer," I insisted as I asked Lola for the address of the party.

"Rude! But you make a valid point." Annabelle texted Clarissa back and after four outfit changes, she finally picked something. She was wearing a blue tank top with large white flowers and blue jeans. She put a white cardigan on top and believe it or not, she also had a matching blue and white Mary Poppins size tote. She came into my room and smiled when she looked at the pink bedspread.

"I cannot handle how you just walked in and he was lying shirtless on the bed. Did it cross your mind that he could have been a stripper or a hooker?"

"No," I stammered, and started laughing. "If he was a stripper or a hooker, then I would hope he'd be lying in my bed. That would be a pretty high maintenance hooker for him to bring his own sheets." I was going through my closet to figure out what I wanted to wear. I had been a big fan of purple for a couple of years now and my closet completely reflected that.

It only took me two outfit changes before I decided to slip on a purple sun dress. It had cap sleeves, an empire waist, and it fell at mid-thigh. It also showed off the girls. Annabelle and I bonded in the bathroom while we did our make-up and I straightened my hair. Looking in the mirror, we determined that we looked good enough to go out in public.

***

The apartments on the other side of campus were where the upper classmen lived. There was a path through the campus that led there from the dorms. The castle was on our right, and even in moonlight it was stunning.

Most of the lights were off but there were a

couple of windows lit up. I wondered if one of those lights belonged to Hercules. I could picture him going over lesson plans late at night with his brow furrowed in concentration. He would be murmuring to himself as he wrote down brilliant lectures and prepared for the next EET meeting. I wondered what would happen when I saw him again on Tuesday.

It was about a ten-minute walk to the apartments and we were by no means alone. All sorts of students were walking to and from the apartments. Apparently, this was a pretty well-traveled path. There were street lights but they were pretty far apart from each other. It seemed they were just close enough to keep you out of total darkness but not close enough to completely illuminate your way. Annabelle and I took out our cellphones and used them as makeshift flashlights.

We got to the cluster of apartments and began trying to find Clarissa and Nat's place. The setup seemed to be idiot proof. The buildings were in alphabetical order from left to right and then had numbers for each apartment. The even numbers were upstairs and the odd numbers were downstairs. This I could manage. Clarissa and Nat's place was apartment C10. Annabelle texted Clarissa and told her that we were outside.

I was not prepared for what I saw when Clarissa invited us in. An apartment where four people lived now managed to hold around twenty-five. I recognized a lot of them from the meeting earlier but there were still several strangers. Clarissa walked over and greeted Annabelle. The way her eyes were lit up and her movements slightly uncoordinated led me to believe she was already slightly drunk.

"Annabelle! I'm glad you could make it. We have to get to know each other since we're going to be spending so much time together." Clarissa put her drink down and grabbed Annabelle's hands.

"Thanks. It looks like you guys are already having a lot of fun," Annabelle commented, looking around the room. "Oh, and this is Violet. She is also going to join EET," she said as she nodded toward me.

Clarissa turned to me and then took my hands. "Oh, I remember you! I'm sure we'll spend a lot of time together too." Clarissa then let go of me and brought us to the kitchen. Nat was in there with a few other people, including Trent from the EET meeting. When I saw him my mouth went dry. He was even better looking up close. How had I not noticed during the meeting? I turned to Annabelle and the look on her face told me that she thought the same thing. Clarissa brought us over to Nat and introduced me.

"Can I get either of you a drink?" Nat asked us.

"What do you have?" I asked. I had never really had alcohol before but I kind of wanted to try it.

"We have Jell-O shots, some beer, and vodka," Nat responded as she opened the fridge.

"I've never had a Jell-O shot before." I smiled, a little embarrassed, and looked at Nat.

"Well, then let's take one. I'll show you how. Annabelle, what about you?" Nat said as she grabbed two Jell-O shots out of the refrigerator.

"No, I think I am okay for now. Maybe just a soda, if you have any." She looked a little nervous. I had a feeling she didn't drink either.

"I have some in the mini fridge in my room. Follow me," Clarissa told Annabelle, and she grabbed her drink on the way out. Annabelle looked at me as if to say, "Have fun," and followed Clarissa.

"Okay, so basically you run your finger around the outer rim of the plastic cup to loosen the Jell-O. Then you kind of suck it out." She handed me the shot and took one herself. "Ready?" she asked as we both took a big breath.

"Yes," I said, and did as I was told. I took the shot down and tried not to gag. It tasted pretty good at first and then I felt the alcohol hit my system. It was almost like an electric shock and I started to cough a bit. Nat patted me on the back.

"Good job for your first one. You downed that whole thing," Nat praised as she pulled out a beer from the refrigerator. "Here, try this as a chaser. It will help the alcohol go down easier." She handed me the beer and we took another shot.

As soon as I swallowed the shot, I took a big swig of beer. She was right, it helped, and I actually kind of liked the beer.

"Better?" she asked once she finished her shot, and I nodded. "Here, let me introduce you to a few people." She told me the name of everyone in the kitchen. As she started talking about some crazy professor she had to take again, Clarissa and Annabelle came in. I was going to walk over to see them when I noticed I was standing next to Trent. I looked up at him and he smiled down at me.

"So you're a freshman? How did you get here?" he asked before taking a sip of some dark brown drink that smelled like cleaning solution. I assumed it was vodka mixed with something.

"I met Nat earlier today at the EET meeting," I said, trying to keep from swooning. His blue eyes were crystal clear and he was looking straight at me. I had no choice but to return his gaze.

"Are you going to join? It'd be nice to see some fresh faces."

"Yeah, it sounds like fun. It's really cool that you get to meet the comedians and the musicians." I took another sip of the beer, finally breaking eye contact. His gaze was a little strong and I had to look away.

"Of course. We have this big signing and photograph session usually before the show. That is the part I set up. I am in charge of helping the talent and making sure they get everything they need. It's very cool," Trent assured me as he leaned a little closer. He smelled amazing. I was not sure what kind of cologne he used but it had its desired effect. I was interested and I wanted to breathe it in a little more.

"Aww, I am jealous. That sounds like the best job. Have you met anyone interesting?" I asked as true excitement began to flow through my body. I had a bit of a fascination with famous people and was subscribed to two different tabloids. Trent listed a couple of comedians I obviously didn't know and then he said it.

"I also met Denny Lopez last year." Lopez was a

huge pop artist with several number one hits. He was also one of my favorite singers.

"Shut up," I shouted as I pushed his arm. "I absolutely love him!"

"Yeah, I like him a lot too. He was really nice. I have a couple of extra signed CDs in the EET office. If you are interested, I'll give you one." He winked at me and inched even closer.

"Really? That would be amazing. I'd be so grateful," I gushed as I looked up into his eyes. I was inches away from his face. Now that I was a little closer, the alcohol was all I could smell. It was definitely not a turn-on, but his light eyes distracted me so I almost didn't even care.

"Oh really? How grateful?" he asked as he brought his face even closer to mine.

I looked down for a split second and noticed his lips. They were full and smooth. I was dying to know what they tasted like. My head was spinning and I could not figure out if it was because of the alcohol or my attraction to Trent. It might have been a little bit of both.

I was going to respond with a good old-fashion sexual innuendo when there was a heavy knock on the door. It seemed to bring us out of our trance and we both jumped a little and looked at the door.

There was a short guy there and I had a feeling he was not there for the party. He had dark tanned skin and was wearing and Elton Hall shirt with tan slacks. Clarissa and Nat ran over to the door. I started to inch over to see what was going on but Trent pulled me back. He wrapped his arm around my waist and moved me out of the sightline of the door.

"That's Randy. He's their RA and is trying to crash the party. If he sees you and realizes you're a freshman, then you may get written up for drinking. Stay back here." Trent rushed over to Randy. A cold sensation went through my body after he let me go. I silently cursed Randy for ruining my fun.

"What's going on? Is it getting a little loud? I told them charades were a bad idea," Trent teased as he clapped hands with Randy and they gave each other the bro hug.

"Yeah, charades. Okay, Trent," Randy chastised as he turned to Nat and Clarissa. "Ladies, I need you to shut the party down. I know there is drinking and it's getting really loud. I know everyone just moved back so I will just give you a warning this time. I'm going to leave, and as long as everyone clears out within five minutes, I'll let you all slide," he decided, and then turned back to Trent. "I'll see you tomorrow at Greek Council." Then Randy headed out the door.

I remembered how to breathe and started to walk out of the kitchen.

"So, I guess if you want to see that CD, you'll have to see me again," Trent said as he leaned against the kitchen wall.

"I guess Denny's signature is worth it," I teased as I ran my fingers through my hair. I had great hair and I liked to use it when I flirted. It must have worked because Trent followed my hair as it flowed back down my shoulders and over my chest. He reached over and tucked a couple of strands behind my ear.

"Violet!" I jumped again and looked over to see Annabelle. "We gotta go," Annabelle ordered as she grabbed my hand and pulled me to the door.

I looked back at Trent and he smiled as we headed out.

***

"Nice timing," I told Annabelle as we were headed back down the path to our dorm.

"I know! I'm sorry but you two were taking too long. We needed to leave before we ended up with underage drinking citations," Annabelle said as she hiked her tote bag up onto her shoulder.

"I just met him! What did you want me to do? Jump his bones right there in the kitchen? We could have gone at it on the counter. I'm sure no one would have minded." Actually, I probably would not have minded, but I wasn't one for big public displays of affection.

"No, I just mean Clarissa and I were trying to figure out when you were going to kiss. I lost a dollar betting on you!"

"Big spender! We were not that bad." I said as I tried to keep from smiling.

"Oh, okay! Whatever you say," Annabelle said as she heard her phone go off. "Oh my god! You have to see what Clarissa said."

Annabelle showed me her phone and I got really excited.

Clarissa: So, Trent wants Violet's number. Can you ask her for it and then text it to me?

"What do you want me to say?" Annabelle asked. We had both stopped walking and were currently standing in the middle of the path.

"Give her my number. You probably dragged me away before he could ask for it." She sent her my number and we headed back to the dorm. We had decided there was no point going to Lola's party since the one we went to was busted.

We had just gotten back to our dorm building when my phone went off. I pulled it out of my wristlet and sure enough it was from an unknown number.

Hey, Violet. It's Trent.

My heart stopped. That was pretty fast. I had hoped he was going to text me but I really didn't think it was going to be tonight. I showed the phone to Annabelle and we headed upstairs to my room. Lola wasn't there yet so we had it to ourselves.

"What are you going to say?" Annabelle asked as we both sat down on the bed.

"I think I'm going to go with *Hi* or something like that," I suggested as I laughed.

Hi. What's up?

I figured I would keep it simple but my heart was racing a mile a minute. I got up to get a bottle of water so I had something to do besides wait for my phone to go off. I grabbed Annabelle one also and returned to the bed.

"So, do you like him?" Annabelle asked after

taking a big swig of water.

"I don't know. I just met him, but I think I could like him." I started thinking about our conversation. "He told me that he has an extra signed CD from Denny Lopez he could give me. I about fell over. He is one of my favorite singers. Basically, I would worship the ground he walked on for that CD."

"I was never a big fan but I know he was pretty popular."

My phone went off again and we both stared at it sitting on the bed between us. After his last text, I turned the phone on full sound. Ironically enough, the ringtone was one of Denny's latest hits. Annabelle looked sideways at me.

"Really? He is your ringtone?"

"Yes! What part of I would worship the ground Trent walked on for one of the signed CDs did you misunderstand?" I said as I picked up the phone and opened Trent's next text.

Did you make it back to your room okay?

"Aww, look, that's cute. He cares." I showed Annabelle the text. "When the RA came, he hid me in the kitchen so I wouldn't get caught for underage drinking. Where did you go?" I asked, realizing she hadn't been hiding with me.

"Oh, Clarissa told me to go into the bathroom. She and Nat are both twenty-one so they were fine."

"That was lucky." I sent a reply to Trent.

I did. Thanks to you. My hero ;p

"Did he mention if he was single?" Annabelle asked me.

"Uh, I hope so. We didn't really get that far." I was starting to feel a little guilty about the flirting. I didn't know if he had a girlfriend.

"Let me see your computer." Annabelle put the water bottle on my desk as I got up and handed the laptop to her. She pulled up his social media page and started to creep.

"Well, his profile says that he is single. He has been for a while," Annabelle said as she continued to look through his page. "Trent should probably make his page a little more private. Looks like he was in a relationship with a girl named Brittany until last January. I am gonna guess that she dumped him."

"How do you know that?" I looked over her shoulder but didn't see anything that indicated she dumped him.

"Well, I pulled her social media page up too and she posted that she was in a new relationship, like, two days after posting that she was single. And if you look at the guy she is with now, he talks about meeting his girl and having fun with her before she and Trent broke up. So at the very least, Trent dumped her for cheating," Annabelle explained as she continued to look through the social media pages.

"You're a little scary," I exclaimed, and made a mental note to increase the security on my social media page just in case I ever made an enemy of Annabelle.

"Eh, it's not that hard. Okay, so it looks like a lot

of girls have pictures with him, but there are very few regulars besides Clarissa and Nat from EET. Probably means he has either been staying single or playing the field. I would watch out for that," Annabelle warned as my phone went off again.

Trent: Don't heroes get some kind of prize when they rescue the damsel in distress?

I laughed. Nice. Maybe I should keep these texts to myself.

Me: I wouldn't say rescue. But maybe you do deserve a small prize. Any ideas?

Annabelle and I continued looking at his social media page for another ten minutes and determined that we couldn't find anything else out. We said good night and she headed to her room. I was going to get ready to shower when the sweet sounds of Denny Lopez hit my ears. It was another text from Trent.

Meet me for lunch tomorrow in the cafeteria at one. I'll even come all the way to your side of the path.

I smiled. My heart started racing again. I had to get that impulse under control before it got me in trouble.

Since you're going through so much trouble, I guess I could be there.

He responded almost instantly.

Can't wait.

I grabbed the rest of my things and headed to the shower, but not before texting him again.

Don't forget my CD ;)

Chapter 3

When I woke up the next morning, Lola's bed was empty and looked like it hadn't been slept in. She must have had a long night. It was around ten in the morning so I had plenty of time before my lunch date. I decided to spend a little time on the computer looking at my schedule. I put my classes and their locations in my planner and then I added the name of my professors next to the classes just in case I forgot.

What frustrated me, though, was that my Literature 101 class had not been assigned a professor yet. Or at least the class website had not been updated with a teacher's name. Looked like I was just going to have to wing it.

Once that was out of the way, I had some cereal to hold me until lunch. I was really bad about breakfast. I needed to have a bowl of cereal in the morning or I was grumpy for the rest of the day. So I finished my breakfast and went over to Annabelle's room. I needed to tell her about the date.

41

"Hey, you are still in pajamas," Annabelle pointed out as she opened the door.

"Yes, I need some help getting dressed. I have a date," I said, and then turned around quickly and headed to my room so I could hide the blush on my face.

"Wait, what?" Annabelle grabbed her keys and followed me into my room.

"After you left last night, Trent asked me to meet him in the cafeteria today for lunch." I walked over to the closet and began pulling things out.

"Yeah? Are you excited?" Annabelle asked as she joined me in front of the closet.

"I think so. I'm just not really sure what to expect. Like, it's the cafeteria, so clearly if he pays, it's part of his meal plan, so I am not sure if that counts as a date. I mean, I have been calling it one in my head, but he never actually used the word date. But we were flirting, so I think it may be one." I was rambling. It tended to be a nervous habit. Some people couldn't talk at all when they got nervous, but I had this uncanny ability to continue to talk until either someone interrupted me or I passed out.

"Okay, relax. Just breathe. Go there and see what happens. We will find you something awesome to wear, and even if it's not a date, it will become one," Annabelle assured me as she pulled a light pink blouse out of the closet. It was one sleeve and a little tight. I usually didn't feel that comfortable in it but what the hell. There was no way I was going to be comfortable today anyway so I might as well have something else to focus on than just Trent. I paired the top with a pair of white jeans and pink wedge heels.

Annabelle straightened my hair for me as we talked about EET and upcoming ideas she wanted to implement. Once my hair was perfect, we headed to the bathroom so I could do my make-up. Annabelle sat on the counter as I tried to keep it basic. This, of course, was not possible. I liked make-up, I liked the way I looked in make-up, and I liked what I could hide with make-up. I did the whole contouring thing, winged eyeliner thing, and bright lipstick thing. It was a process but it made me feel good. I blotted my lipstick and realized Trent was in for it. I looked good. It was twelve forty-five and I needed to head over.

"Come over and tell me everything afterward," Annabelle called over her shoulder as she left the bathroom.

I went back to my room and grabbed my wristlet. Still no sign of Lola, so I locked the door and headed to the cafeteria. As I got outside, I saw that it looked like it was going to rain. Of course it was, because I had straightened my hair. I ran back up to my room to grab my umbrella. I was probably going to be a little late, but fashionably late was still a thing, right?

I quickened my step a little and checked my phone. It was twelve fifty and I could see the cafeteria. I took a deep breath and slowed down. I wanted to look casual and cool in case he was looking for me. As I got to the door, I reminded myself to keep breathing and walked in.

***

Trent was sitting on a couch in the TV lounge right outside the cafeteria. I took a second to really look at him. Trent had his cell phone out and was playing some game. He was wearing a short-sleeved green polo and his tan muscles were practically busting out of the sleeves. Trent clearly worked out a lot. He also must have spent a lot of time outside because he while he was tan, there was no orange tinge. This was the kind of sun-kissed skin that only came from outdoor activities.

His blond curls were falling into his eyes so he reached up and ran his fingers through them. The curls were adorable. He seemed to try to tame them with gel but I had a feeling they really had a mind of their own. I smiled and decided it was time to stop staring before someone questioned my state of mind. I walked over and sat down next to him. This may have been a little forward because he jumped about three feet in the air.

"Woah! You scared me," he said as he closed out of the game and slipped his phone into his pocket. He looked straight into my eyes and my heart stopped for a second. There was something about his stare that caught me off guard. Maybe it was the small hint of lust and desire, or maybe it was that his chiseled features screamed sex. Whatever it was, it was a little intimidating and very intoxicating.

"Sorry!" Maybe I should have just said hi instead of sitting down with him. I was beginning to feel a little embarrassed.

He stood up and reached for my hand. "Don't

worry about it. Ready for lunch?" he asked, pulling me up from the couch. He had the cafeteria attendant swipe his card twice. It was cute that he paid with his meal plan, but I still was not sure if this qualified as a date. I shook my head and decided to forget trying to label it and enjoy the day.

Trent headed straight for the pizza. I laughed under my breath. It didn't matter how much a guy worked out; if there was pizza available, then he was interested. I headed over to the grill to have a panini made. He got his food way before my sandwich was ready, so after grabbing a drink, Trent walked over to me with his food tray.

"Do you want me to get you a drink while you wait for that?" he asked as he placed his tray next to mine.

"Sure. I'll take a Coke."

"Great. I'll be right back." Trent winked and then turned around.

The small butterflies I had been trying to control seemed to be growing by the minute. He ignited my body with the smallest things. I watched him walk away and had a perfect view of his glorious rear end. He was wearing khaki cargo shorts and I could not help but notice that his ass looked perfect. I had just started to wonder if his tan went all the way up his legs when the cook interrupted my thoughts.

"Ham panini?" he called, and placed the sandwich plate on the counter.

I thanked him, grabbed the plate, and put it on my tray. I turned around to meet up with Trent but he was already walking back over to me. "Good timing."

"I try. Let me grab that for you," Trent offered as he grabbed my tray and walked away, carrying both his and my lunch. My eyes widened. I had been known to trip over thin air so carrying one tray always made me a little nervous. Here he was walking the maze that was the cafeteria tables like it was an open field. He picked a table next to the window with a perfect view of the castle. We sat down across from each other and he slid my tray over to me.

"I'm impressed. I can barely carry one tray without tripping or spilling something."

"It is one of my many talents. Tray balancing is a real art and I have spent many years practicing just for this moment." Trent looked at me and laughed.

"Nice," I said as I rolled my eyes and tried not to smile at his lame joke. We started eating and there was a small moment of silence. I began to panic a little. I did not plan any points of conversation or what I would say to him. My mind raced, but luckily, Trent piped up before my mental breakdown had a chance to take over.

"So, what did you think of Casino Night?" Trent asked. I was grateful he had said something and relaxed a little.

"It was a lot of fun. My dad taught me to play poker when I was younger and he was always super competitive so we used to get really into it."

"That sounds awesome. It's kind of like my family. I've been playing lacrosse for, like, twelve years now but my favorite times were the family games. I have two brothers, and the three of us plus my dad would play two on two lacrosse a lot. My mom had to ref because she swears we all play dirty," Trent explained as he finished one slice of pizza.

"Do you play dirty?" I asked, and looked into Trent's eyes. I loved innuendos. A smile spread across Trent's face. It was a different smile from earlier. The corners of his mouth turned up in a bit of a smirk and he looked deliciously mischievous.

"When I have a willing partner I do," Trent responded, barely moving. He met my stare and seemed to challenge me.

"I will keep that in mind for later," I promised as I refused to look away. The sexual tension between us could have set the cafeteria on fire.

"Oh, there is going to be a later?" Trent asked as he leaned forward across the table. That mischievous look grew into what could only be described as a smolder. I decided to push him and see what he would do. I liked playing with fire.

"Down, boy. You couldn't handle me if you tried." I slid my foot up his toned calf and then right back down. Trent looked down in the general direction of where his leg was under the table.

"Maybe not, but I sure as hell would like to try," he said as he looked down toward my chest. As he returned his eyes to mine, he winked.

I was about to respond with another sexually fueled retort when someone called Trent's name. He held my glance for a second longer and turned around. I followed his eyes.

Two guys were headed over to our table. One of the guys was tall and thin with black hair. He had deep tan skin and was of Asian descent. He was not as muscular as Trent but he could hold his own. The other guy was about average height with blond hair. He was pale with lots of freckles.

"Trent, what's up?" the blond asked as he fist bumped with Trent.

"Not much, guys," Trent said as he nodded toward the black-haired guy in greeting. Both guys looked at me. "This is Violet. Violet, this is Mark and Shane," he said, first pointing toward the blond and then the black-haired guy.

"Hi," I said as Shane extended his hand to me. When I offered my hand to Mark, he took my hand and kissed the top of it. Trent rolled his eyes and shoved Mark away from me.

"What?" Mark asked, putting on an innocent front.

"Yeah, Trent, don't punish the guy for being chivalrous," I chastised with a mocking smile on my face.

"He can't even spell chivalrous," Trent teased as Mark and Shane walked away to get their food. Before turning around, Mark blew me a kiss.

"Maybe not, but I think I've found a Prince Charming," I continued to tease him.

"Prince Charming is overrated. He isn't even named in the movie," Trent exclaimed as he finished eating his second slice of pizza.

"Look at the Disney fan." I was genuinely shocked. Cinderella had always been my favorite fairy tale.

"My ex-girlfriend was obsessed with Disney so she used to make me watch the movies over and over again."

"Yeah, okay. I bet you watch them at night to help you go to sleep." I tried to steer the conversation away from his ex. Not exactly good first date talk. How did he not know that?

"You caught me. I can't fall asleep unless I hear Disney music. Luckily, I have every soundtrack on my phone." He picked up my tray and took it to the trash. Trent returned and leaned on the table. I could feel those butterflies again. "How about some ice cream?" Trent asked.

"I could use something sweet," I teased as Trent led me over to the ice cream bar and we each grabbed a bowl.

"Okay, so this is how it goes. I'm going to make you a sundae and you're going to make mine. You can't say what you like or don't like, and you have to eat the sundae the other one makes," Trent instructed as he looked around at the ice cream.

"I could give that a try. But I'm allergic to peanut butter so that could be bad." I had a small reaction to peanut butter as a kid. My mom freaked out and banned peanut butter from the house. Since then, I hadn't had so much as a spoon of peanut butter. We didn't know what would happen if I tried it now, but it was better to be safe and breathing than sorry and choking.

"Got it. Okay, turn around and I'll make yours. You can't watch." Trent started to scoop some vanilla ice cream into my bowl.

I turned around and leaned against the wall. "This game has a lot of rules," I complained as I tried to sneak a peek at what he was doing.

"No peeking. You're breaking the rules," he reprimanded.

"Rules were meant to be broken."

"You really are trouble, aren't you?" Trent asked as he handed me the bowl of vanilla ice cream with M&M's and sprinkles.

"That depends on how you define trouble," I said as I went to take a bite of the ice cream. I tried to be sexy as I slowly brought the spoon to my mouth and overemphasized licking the ice cream off of it.

"How do you define it?" Trent asked as he leaned in so that he was inches from my face.

"I guess you're going to have to stick around to find out." I turned around and started making him a bowl.

We headed back to my dorm with the bowls of ice cream as we talked about classes tomorrow and EET. We finished the ice cream and tossed the bowls in the trash can. Trent walked me to the door but stopped me before I could open it.

"I am going to stop you there. We went to the cafeteria so this is like half a date. I want to kiss you, but not like this. How about you let me take you to dinner off campus Tuesday after EET's meeting? We can have a real date and maybe discuss this kiss a little further," Trent suggested as he leaned against my doorframe.

"Sounds like a plan."

"Great. I'll see you Tuesday." But before he left, he reached into his pocket and pulled out my CD.

"Oh my gawd. Thank you!" I threw my arms around his neck and gave him a big hug. We stood like that for a moment and I had the distinct impression he was going to kiss me but he just turned around and left. I watched him go and admired the view from behind.

I opened the door and tossed my wristlet onto my desk. It was a date. Kind of. We were going on a real date Tuesday. I smiled and waited a couple minutes to take it all in. Then I headed to Annabelle's room so we could overanalyze the half date.

***

The rest of the day was pretty uneventful. Annabelle and I hung out and watched some TV before ordering Chinese for dinner. Turned out we were both crime show junkies. At around 10 p.m. I headed back to my room so that I could take a shower and get ready for the first day of class tomorrow.

My first class was literature at 9:15 in the morning. I had checked to see if the teacher had been assigned to the class yet but the school website still didn't have one listed. The book for the class said W. Johnson was the author. As this was pretty vague, I didn't think I could figure out who this was. I was just going to have to wait and see when I got to class.

***

I got up at 7:45 so I could get ready for my first day. I was having a bowl of cereal when the sounds of Denny Lopez erupted from my phone.

Good luck on your first day of school, baby!

My mom had sent me the text. I knew she was excited so I responded and told her I missed her. I wanted to call and talk to her because this was the longest we had gone without seeing each other. But I didn't want to be late for class. I made a mental note to call her later and tossed the phone onto my bed.

I put on a green tank top with a black sleeveless cardigan on top. I then slipped my jean shorts on and finished the look off with a pair of black wedge heels. Before I went to sleep last night, I had packed my backpack so I wouldn't forget anything. All I needed to do was put some make-up on and do my hair. As I was not exactly sure where I was going for my class, I wanted to leave a little early.

I brushed my hair and put some gel in it. With a little gel, my hair had beach waves, and I had always liked that look. After pulling some of the strands out of my face with a couple pins, I put my make-up on and then headed back to my room to grab my bag. Annabelle and I had exchanged schedules last night and figured out we didn't have any classes together. I wouldn't see her until one when we'd meet up in the cafeteria for lunch.

My literature class was in the castle on the second floor so I headed in that direction, thankful it was near the EET meeting. I had some idea where I was going but they were in different wings so I didn't want to be too presumptuous. I wanted to admire the castle again, but in reality, I needed to walk with a little haste. I had a feeling that being a freshman was not an excuse to be late on your first day. Luckily, the room was in the wing next to the EET classroom so I had an idea where I was going.

Turned out that it was not that hard to find the class. I ended up getting there ten minutes early so I walked in and picked a seat in the middle of the second row.

***

Generally, Elton didn't have more than twenty-five students in a class. However, there were some classes freshmen were all required to take, like freshmen literature, and they tended to have somewhere between thirty and forty students. I looked around the classroom and there were about fifteen students already seated. A couple of them were talking to each other, but for the most part, everyone was keeping to themselves. I was going to take my phone out and text Annabelle when he walked in.

Hercules walked to the front of the class and began writing his name on the board. Crap. He was going to be my professor. For some reason that I couldn't explain at the moment, this just made him seem even sexier. Maybe it had something to do with the authority he held, or maybe it was the way his green tie brought out his eyes, or maybe it was because student-teacher relationships were strictly forbidden. I wasn't always good at following rules.

As he turned around, I got a perfect view of his

chiseled ass in his black dress slacks. His clothes could not hide the muscles underneath. Once he finished writing his name, he turned around and surveyed the class. I took a deep breath and tried to look casual. His eyes fell on me almost instantly. A smile broke out on his face and he walked up to me.

"Miss Carrington, it is nice to see you again. Will I see you there tomorrow at the EET meeting?"

"My friend seems really into it so I will probably tag along," I said as I tried to focus on my breathing. He had glasses on today. They were thick, dark frames and they really just made him more attractive. Hercules was not only sexy when he was in casual clothes, but he could also pull off the fresh academic look.

"Great. Then I look forward to seeing you there." He didn't walk away at first. Rather, he stood in front of me as if he were assessing me. Maybe he was amused by how obvious it was that I was attracted to him, or maybe he was interested too and wanted to say more. Whatever it was kept his gaze fixed on me for longer than was appropriate.

After what seemed like an eternity, he turned and headed back to the front of the class. I imagined it. There was no sexual tension. He did not look at me as if he was undressing me with his eyes. He was just being friendly. I repeated this in my head. If I said it enough, then maybe I would believe it.

There was no way he found me attractive. Number one, it was not allowed, and number two, he was older. At least six or seven years older. Maybe even more. I shook my head and took out my notebook and a pen. This was going to be a long semester.

The class only made things worse. Hercules really knew what he was talking about and he was clearly passionate. All he did was go over the syllabus but his excitement was evident. He didn't have notes or a PowerPoint, but rather spoke from memory. As he went over the books that we would be studying, his eyes lit up and he began speaking even faster. It was as if his thoughts were coming so fast that his mouth couldn't keep up.

Apparently, at his position in England, he had written a textbook because he couldn't find one that he liked. This was the book we were using. I had originally thought it was extremely arrogant and self-serving that he required us to buy the book. At least I did until he said that all profits from this textbook went straight to a children's hospital near his childhood home. He never saw a singular royalty check and even wrote the book under a pen name. He really was perfect.

Hercules dismissed class and I packed up my belongings. But as I did this, I watched him from underneath my eyelashes. Several female students had walked up to him and began asking tons of questions. I felt a slight flash of jealousy, which was ridiculous.

I was sure they were just curious about the syllabus. And even if they weren't, what claim did I have over him? I shook the feeling off and headed out the door. Before leaving, I turned and took one last look. His eyes caught mine for a brief second. Then they were back on the tall blonde who was talking to him. As I walked out the door, I felt a smile spread on my face.

***

My second class, my freshman seminar, was pretty uneventful. I headed to the cafeteria to meet Annabelle for lunch. All she could do was talk about EET. Clarissa had invited her over tonight so they could go over her responsibilities and other parts of the job, and she was so excited. Her ideas were great and it would be nice to know someone on the executive board.

We headed back to our dorm so Annabelle could drop her school bag off, which, if you could believe, was bigger than her regular giant tote, and then head to Clarissa's. I went back to my room but was not prepared for what I walked in on.

Lola was sitting on the floor, crying her eyes out. I threw my bag on my desk and knelt beside her.

"Oh my god! What's wrong?" I asked as I got her some tissues.

"I don't even know where to start," she sobbed.

"Well, what is it about?" I asked as I stroked her hair, hoping that would help her calm down.

"He dumped me. Tyler has been seeing another girl for the last couple months behind my back. I just found out a few hours ago. I told him it was me or her and he picked her," Lola wailed, and began sobbing again.

"What an asshole! Can I get you anything?" I asked, hoping I could help her in some way. I had been cheated on so I could imagine how crushed she was.

"No, I just think I am going to go to one of my friend's. She is in the next building over." She tried to wipe her face and pull it together. "But thanks. It's nice to know that you are there."

"No problem! Text me if you need me." She left and I settled in for the afternoon. Back home, I wrote in a journal most nights. It was a good way for me to organize my thoughts and figure out the way I was feeling. Since coming to school, I hadn't had a spare second to express myself in writing. There was a lot I needed to catch up on.

***

I finished a couple of entries and decided to call it an early night. Too bad that would not last long. At around two in the morning there was a loud pounding on my door. Confused, I crawled out of bed and pulled my robe on. When I looked through the peephole, I saw Tyler. I opened the door and noticed he was not alone. There was a small redhead standing next to him and she did not look happy.

"Hey, Violet, is Lola there?" he asked me politely.

I blinked my eyes a couple of times, confused, and looked at the redhead. She sneered at me, cracked her knuckles, and then started ripping posters and signs off of the wall. I thought it was safe to say that she was in a bad mood or maybe she was trying to intimidate me. Whatever it was, she was acting really strange.

"Um, no. She went to see one of her friends

earlier today. I haven't seen her since," I told him as the redhead joined Tyler in front of the door.

"Okay, thanks," Tyler said as he turned to go.

"Are you sure that bitch isn't in there?" the redhead shouted at me with a whole lot of attitude. She pushed Tyler out of the way and stepped up to me.

"Yes. It's one room. I think I would notice if she was here," I assured her, getting defensive.

"I bet she is hiding. Let me in or I'll kick your ass," she threatened as she tried to get around me.

"Um, excuse you? You are not coming in here. As I said, she is not here and I don't know where she is. I also don't know who you are but I am definitely not letting you in here," I said as I grabbed my keys and closed the door. There was no way she was going to wreck my room or any of my stuff while "looking" for Lola.

"You know what, slut?" the redhead started, and got up in my face.

I interrupted her because, frankly, this was getting to be too much. "No! I don't know what is going on or why you are here, but you need to back up," I warned as I looked her dead in the eye. Luckily, Tyler stepped in.

"Katie, let's go. There is no way Lola would be hiding in the room." Tyler pulled her away and gave her a slight nudge toward the door of the dorm building.

"Violet, I'm sorry about that. It has been a pretty crazy day. Have a good night." Tyler and Katie headed out of the dorm and I closed the door.

I grabbed my phone and texted Lola. She needed

to know what happened. About five minutes after I sent the text, Lola called me.

"He did not go there with her!" Lola screamed when I answered the phone.

"Yep, they were here. She was tearing all the posters off the wall in the hallway. She tried to force her way into the room and got in my face. Tyler pulled her away before it could get bad because I was not dealing with her. Is that the girl Tyler cheated with?" I asked, even though I was pretty sure I knew the answer already.

"Yeah. She got my number and was texting and threatening me. So I told her to meet me here and we could settle this in the parking lot, but I guess she went to the wrong place. That dumb bitch."

"What do you mean settle this?" I asked, confused. Were they really going to get physical?

"She wanted to fight. I'm from North Jersey, we don't back down from a fight." Lola sounded serious and I had to take a moment to control myself. They were going to meet in the school parking lot after dark. It was like a bad chick flick.

"Well, they're gone. I just wanted to let you know." I really would prefer to stay out of this.

"Did she threaten you or break any of our stuff? Do you want to call the police on her?" Lola asked, showing some concern.

"No, she just got in my face when I wouldn't let her search the room for you. Everything is fine. We definitely don't need to call the police," I assured her.

"Okay. I'll talk to you tomorrow. Sorry you got dragged into this." With that, Lola hung up the phone.

I shook my head in disbelief. This was not happening. We were in college! I grabbed a water bottle and curled back up in bed. I was asleep after a couple of minutes. Again, it would not last long.

***

There was another loud knock on my door. I looked at the clock and I had only been asleep for forty-five minutes. Groaning, I threw the covers off again and looked through the peephole. Shocked, I grabbed my robe and threw it on. I was definitely not expecting him.

Standing on the other side of my door was the police officer from the garden. I opened the door and tried my best to smile at him.

"Miss Carrington?" The officer pulled out a notepad and a pen.

"Yes?" I asked tentatively. I had never even been pulled over by the cops while driving. This was my first real encounter with a police officer, and for the life of me, I could not figure out why he was there. The flower thing didn't count.

"My name is Officer Finn and I'm here regarding your roommate, Lauren Zimmerman. She called us saying there was a disturbance earlier and she was concerned for your safety."

I let out a huge breath of relief and rolled my eyes. "It was not really a disturbance. Her ex-boyfriend came by with his new girlfriend and just asked where Lola was. Ah, Lauren, she goes by Lola. I called Lauren and told her they were looking for her. It was not a big deal," I insisted, hoping he'd just go away.

"Did they threaten you at all?" the officer asked me with a grave face.

"Ah, there may have been words from the new girlfriend. But honestly, I didn't take her seriously. Tyler, the ex-boyfriend, grabbed her and they left. Really, I'm fine. Lola asked me if I wanted to call the police and I told her no." I tried to sound sure but the officer did not seem to agree.

"What were her words exactly when she threatened you?" Officer Finn had his pen poised above a notepad.

"She wanted to come into the room and I refused to let her. So she told me to let her in or she was going to kick my ass," I muttered, embarrassed that it had come to this.

"We are going to post an officer outside your door for the night to make sure that they do not come back. If you hear from them again, then let the officer know," Finn insisted with an air of both authority and arrogance. I had a feeling he was going to be the officer stuck babysitting the annoying freshman.

"I really do not think that is necessary. I'll be fine," I asserted as I tried to brush off the officer. This was going to be extremely embarrassing for me.

"Miss Carrington, this is not a request I am willing to ignore. There was an incident in the parking lot earlier. Miss Zimmerman does not want to press charges but we are still concerned for your safety. On top of that, we are actively looking for the young lady so that we can ensure she has left the campus."

It took a second but my heart stopped. "What kind of incident?" I all but screamed at the officer, ignoring what he said about pressing charges.

"I am not at liberty to discuss all of the details." Finn closed his face off.

"Just tell me if Lola is okay or not," I begged. I knew we literally just met but I felt a need to make sure she was all right. It may have been the concerned look on my face or the slight shake in my voice but Finn finally decided to take pity on me. His face changed and became more relaxed. He leaned forward and whispered close to my ear.

"Off the record, she is in the hospital but is stable and should be coming home tomorrow." He then leaned back against the wall outside my room and turned his head to me. "I will be here until you go to class. Have a good night."

"Thanks. Uh, have a good night too. Let me know if you need anything. I mean, I have water and, like, five different kinds of cereal in case you get hungry," I offered, feeling pretty bad. I didn't have class until ten so he was going to be there for about seven hours before I headed to the classroom.

The officer smiled and looked back at me. "I will be fine. Remember, I'm always willing to do something nice for a pretty girl. If you need anything, I will be right here." I thought I saw him wink at me but I must have imagined it. After all, it was really late.

I closed the door and texted Lola to try to check in. I didn't think she would respond but I needed to at least try. She had sent the officer here to make sure I was okay after all.

***

After tossing and turning all night, I fell back asleep minutes before my alarm went off. I crawled out of bed and grabbed some clothes. I pulled on my jean shorts and a cream V-neck t-shirt. I was about to grab my make-up kit when I remembered there was a police officer outside my room. I grabbed a granola bar and opened my door. Officer Finn was still standing there. He had circles under his eyes but he was still awake.

"Good morning, Miss Carrington. Don't you look nice," he offered, and smiled. I could tell he was tired but his stance still provided the necessary amount of intimidation. However, his eyes showed stress and fatigue.

"I know last night you claimed that you were fine but I thought you might want a granola bar or something. I'm just going to head to the bathroom and get ready to go to class so I guess you're off the hook," I said.

"Well, last night you offered me cereal. If you'd said you had granola bars, that would have been different," he joked as he took the bar. "I'll be outside the bathroom door if you need anything."

"Oh, no, you really don't have to stand out there while I am in there. I mean…" My sentence faded off as I tried to think of a less humiliating moment in my life. So far, a young police officer standing outside of a bathroom while I went in to take care of my business seemed to top my list.

"Don't worry! The walls are thick and I won't hear you talk or whatever you need to do in there. I'm not willing to let you go in there and risk you getting hurt because of a little pride."

My cheeks burned bright red. I was flattered that he was going to look after me but still humiliated that this had to happen. At the same time, I still thought it was unnecessary.

"Um, I don't think Tyler and Katie are going to accost me in the bathroom."

"You never know what people will do. I like to be prepared."

Seeing as I was not getting anywhere with Finn, I headed into the bathroom. I handled my business, brushed my teeth, and put a light layer of make-up on. It was going to be a long day. I had two classes and the EET meeting later. I just really hoped an officer was not going to follow me around all day. That would definitely send the wrong message to my teachers, classmates, Trent, and Hercules.

I closed my eyes and took a deep breath. It was time to face the day. As I came out of the bathroom, I saw the officer on his walkie-talkie. He looked up at me and smiled.

"So I just got word that it would appear the threat to you has been resolved. But I would still like to walk you to class. Just in case," Finn stated as he walked me to my door.

"Oh, okay. Uh, let me just get my bag and I'll be ready to go." I went back to my room, dropped my make-up bag off, grabbed my backpack and a granola bar, then met Finn at the door. We walked to the end of the hall in silence. I felt a little awkward and kind of like a kindergartner.

"So, what class are we going to?" he asked as we headed to the stairs. I didn't really like taking the elevator and it looked like Finn felt the same way.

"I have my computer class." I tried to walk quickly. I was really embarrassed that I needed an escort, but he took my embarrassment for nervousness.

"Deep breath." He chuckled under his breath. "You had a police officer outside your door last night because someone threatened you and you weren't nervous. Now you're nervous about a class?" He laughed a little harder.

"I could have taken her," I insisted, and tried to look tough. It apparently didn't work because Finn started laughing again.

"Whatever you say, Miss Carrington." Finn tried to conceal the laughing.

"Hey," I said as I gave him a playful shove.

"Watch out! You are assaulting a police officer. I could bring you in to the station for that." Finn tried to give me a serious look but a smile was threatening to escape.

"I'm pretty sure that you are off duty since I'm no longer in imminent danger," I pointed out, laughing at him.

"Okay, this time I will let you off with a warning!" He winked at me. We continued a little further in silence. I snuck a look at him and realized it was a bad idea. He was looking at me too, but in a different way. I wasn't sure I could explain exactly why it made me feel uncomfortable, but I felt a drop in my stomach.

Upon further inspection, Finn looked to be in his early twenties with big brown eyes. When our eyes connected, I noticed that his eyelashes were long and curly. It seemed a bit unfair for a guy to have eyelashes that amazing but there they were. He was a little over average height, maybe five-foot-nine or ten with massive biceps. It looked as though they were going to bust through his uniform. I liked muscles, but his seemed to be a little scary instead of sexy. He clearly worked out a lot.

For some reason, I wasn't interested. Probably because there were two other men currently occupying my thoughts. I was sure it was not the unease I had being in his presence.

I looked up and met his stare. He was giving me a look that was clearly him attempting to smolder but it just looked like he had to go to the bathroom.

Then my name was called and I breathed a sigh of relief. I turned around and saw Annabelle. When I turned back, Finn was still gazing at me. There was no way he was developing feelings for me. This was his job. At the same time, I had a hard time ignoring the warning in my head.

"Is this your class?" Finn asked, pointing to the door where Annabelle was standing.

I looked over and then back at him and nodded.

"I guess this is where I leave you. Here is my card. Please don't hesitate to call me if you ever need me. My office is on campus; our city police believe it's the safest place for our headquarters." He handed me his card and his fingers slid past mine and he tried to stroke them. I pulled away as fast as I could and turned to head down the hall. I could feel him watching me as I made my way to the classroom. I shook my head and hoped we would not meet again.

Chapter 4

"Um, hi. Why are you walking with a police officer?" Annabelle asked as we were standing outside my classroom.

"You would not believe my night." I proceeded to tell the story of how I met Finn and why he felt the need to be my police escort. I was going to get into exactly why I thought he really walked me to class but we had to go our separate ways.

Both of our classes let us out early so we met in the hallway. Annabelle was begging to hear about Officer Finn. It was too early for lunch so we decided to sit out on the grass and continue to talk about my night.

"So Lola is in the hospital now. Is she okay? Do you know what happened to her?" Annabelle asked as we got to an empty gazebo and sat down. Annabelle did not sit on grass apparently.

"I have no idea. Officer Finn wouldn't tell me exactly what happened, and Lola hasn't texted me back yet." I took my phone out again to see if she responded.

"So if Lola was in trouble, then why was he walking you to class?"

"He claimed that the new girlfriend threatened me so he thought I was in danger too. I think he just wanted some female attention," I said, rolling my eyes, still frustrated by all of this.

"Did you like him?"

"No. I mean, he is good looking, but there was no connection. I kind of felt the whole thing was awkward. He just seemed to be trying so hard to impress me. I don't know. He just gave me a bad vibe. I can't really explain it."

"Fair enough!" She shrugged her shoulders and then changed the subject. "Well, what about Trent? Don't you have your date tonight?"

My heart dropped. "Oh my god!" I could not believe I had forgotten. I looked down at my outfit. It was just a plain t-shirt and shorts. I would not have time to change after my next class before the EET meeting. It was good that I had gotten out of class early. "I need to change." I grabbed my bag and rushed back over to my dorm.

"Did you seriously forget?" Annabelle asked as she caught up to me.

"I had a busy night! My body was threatened and I had a police officer sit outside my door for hours on end. It's been crazy," I insisted, but I did feel a little guilty about forgetting the date. I ran into the room hoping that maybe Lola was there, but she wasn't. I took out my phone and texted her again just to check in.

"Okay! You were busy. What are you going to wear?" Annabelle asked.

I opened the closet and flipped through all the clothes. After three outfit changes we settled on a white top that pushed my breasts up to practically my chin and a denim jean skirt that gave the illusion I had a voluptuous butt. I finished the look with white platform sandals. These were pretty high but I could still walk in them comfortably for a few hours.

We then headed to the bathroom and updated my make-up and hair. Once we finished, I looked in the mirror and determined that I looked good, and more importantly, I felt good. It was going to be a great time.

***

We both had a class at two so, luckily, we still had time for lunch. I was on my way to Statistics for Psychology and Annabelle was going to her freshmen seminar. My class didn't involve a textbook but math was a serious issue for me. I had problems with it in high school. My ex-boyfriend was amazing at geometry, and if it were not for him, I would probably still be in high school.

Both of our classes took up the allotted time, much to our dismay, and we met up in the hall outside of the EET office.

"Are you ready for your first meeting, Madam Secretary?" I asked Annabelle as we stopped to go our separate ways. The computer lab was in the same wing as the EET office and the classroom where they held their meetings.

"I'm as ready as I will ever be. See you at the

meeting after." She wished me good luck and waved goodbye.

I watched Annabelle head into the office and I went into the computer lab. I had a little bit of statistics homework so I thought I would look up some tutorials. After about ten minutes, I realized that this turned into a hopeless case and decided to just surf the internet randomly.

After another fifteen minutes, I headed out of the room to check on the meeting. I saw Annabelle talking with Nat and I waited off to the side. Then Hercules walked out of the office and met my eyes. He stared, like he usually did, a little too long. Then he beckoned me over. When I did not immediately head over, he called my name and beckoned me again.

So I walked over to see him. But before I reached him, I saw Trent. I watched him look me up and down and then wink at me. It gave me a tingling feeling in my stomach and I gave him a knowing smile. Then I turned to look at Hercules, who clearly did not miss the exchange.

"May I have a word with you in the office, please?" Hercules requested as I stood in front of him.

"Ah, sure. Is everything okay?" I followed him to the office and he opened the door to let me in first. It gave me a bit of a jump when he closed the door behind him. But I would not let him intimidate me. At least that was the plan.

"So, I saw you walking around with a police officer and I was concerned. Is everything all right?" He sat in one of the office chairs and motioned for me to join him. I didn't see him watching me earlier. I was a little preoccupied, but usually I was pretty aware of whenever Hercules was near. Right now, his green eyes were staring at me with a genuine look of concern. It was so endearing and comforting. I really could stare into those eyes forever, but I decided I should probably focus and answer his question before I made myself seem any more helpless.

"Yeah, there was a problem with my roommate between her ex-boyfriend and his new girlfriend. Apparently, there were couple of threats and a fight. Um, my roommate was sent to the hospital because of this new girlfriend and she may have threatened me too. So they sent a cop to watch me and make sure that I was okay."

"Wait, you were threatened?" His voice escalated with what appeared to be rage.

"Yeah, but it was not a big deal. I had it handled!" I was beginning to get irritated that everyone had such little faith in me. It really was not that big of a deal.

"How did you have it handled? What did you do to have it handled?" His voice was still rising. At first I thought it was endearing that he was all concerned, but now I was getting annoyed.

"The new girlfriend was just looking for my roommate and I refused to let her check in our dorm room. She said she'd kick my ass if I didn't let her in but I wouldn't let it happen. They left. There was no harm done," I insisted as my own voice rose.

"Well, what happened later? They would not send a police officer there if it was no big deal.

They are real police officers. Not rent-a-cops," he informed me, showing a bit more concern than frustration. His voice had dropped a little bit and he stared directly into my eyes, pleading for me to see his point of view.

"Okay, there may have been a little harm done. This new girlfriend put my roommate in the hospital. They were concerned that she may come after me next but she didn't," I admitted rather reluctantly. Apparently, Hercules did not take it so well.

"She is in the hospital and you think that it was no big deal?" he asked quite forcefully as he stood up.

"No, it was a big deal for her! She was in the hospital, not me! I'm fine. The police protection was unnecessary because the new girlfriend never came back." I stood up too. This may have been the wrong move because he leaned forward.

"Oh yeah? Can you tell the future? Did you know that she wasn't going to come after you too? You could really have been in danger! Don't you care?" He was now inches away from my face and radiating with intensity.

"Why do you even care? You just met me a couple days ago!" I moved in closer and added my own passion to the situation. I was so close that I could feel his breath on my face.

"I'm always concerned about my students," he whispered. I could just barely hear him over the sound of our breathing.

"But why me?" I whispered back. It took all of my self-control to keep looking into his green eyes.

He wasn't looking away either, and as long as he kept his eyes on me, then there was no way I was going to break away.

"I don't know. There's just something about you." He looked away, but that was only so that he could glance at my lips. My heart was pounding so hard that I was sure he could hear it. He reached up and touched my face ever so gently. It was happening. He was going to kiss me.

I tilted my head up and he returned his gaze to my eyes. They had want and a desperate need almost pouring out of them. I wanted this. I shouldn't want this, but that made me all the more motivated. Then it happened. Someone was knocking at the office door. We broke apart and Hercules turned to open the door. It was Trent.

"Hey, Professor. We are starting the meeting in a couple of minutes. Just wanted to let you know," Trent said, and then turned to go. He was on his phone so he didn't notice me. That was probably for the best. I wasn't sure how I would explain this to him in the first place.

"Cheers, I'm on my way now. Just give me a minute," he replied, and shut the door again. "Um, Miss Carrington. That was, I mean, it was out of line. I apologize." He was avoiding my eyes now but I was not going to let him get out of this situation that easily.

"Don't apologize unless you actually regret it. Sometimes it is fun to cross the line." I walked past him out the door and never looked back. I was a few feet away from the office when I heard the door close. I knew he was behind me but I kept looking straight. The room holding the meeting was about twenty feet away but it may as well have been twenty miles.

Every step I took, I could feel his gaze drilling into me. It was thrilling, a little scary, but still thrilling. I made sure to give my walk a little shake so he could have something fun to look at.

As I walked into the meeting room, I saw Annabelle sitting in the corner with a couple more people I didn't recognize. There was an empty seat next to her which I assumed was for me. I slid into the seat just as Nat was starting the meeting. I noticed Hercules stood just inside the door. He was avoiding looking at me. I smiled to myself. It seemed I had a little bit of an impact on him.

***

"What did Berneli want?" Annabelle whispered to me.

"He saw me with the cop and he was just concerned. No big deal."

"Oh, okay. That was nice of him," she said, giving me a knowing look. I rolled my eyes and shoved her shoulder lightly.

I looked toward the front of the class and Trent was standing next to Clarissa and Nat. He caught me staring and smirked. I guessed he was ready for our date. I smiled at him and then returned my attention back to Clarissa, who was giving everyone updates on the comedienne situation.

I tried to focus on what she was saying but it was near impossible. Hercules and I had a moment. A real moment. And now I was about to go on a date with Trent. My heart started to race. I wasn't sure how this happened. To my knowledge, I had never had two guys interested in me like this. It was a little intimidating but I kind of liked it.

After about ten minutes we split into groups to start organizing different parts of the comedy event. Trent motioned for me to join his group and Annabelle started a group with the people sitting beside her. I grabbed my bag and walked over to Trent. I allowed myself a glance at Hercules and, just like I thought, he was watching me. Our eyes met for a second and then I looked away. I was going to make him work for it.

"Hey, beautiful," Trent greeted me, and I blushed, trying not to roll my eyes. I wasn't that used to being called beautiful and I wasn't sure how to react to it. "Ready for our date later?" he asked as I sat down at a desk next to him.

"Yes. Should be fun."

His blue eyes were glistening with trouble. One thing was for sure, it was going to be a fun night. Some other people joined our group and we started discussing marketing techniques for the event. We needed to advertise the show so that students would buy tickets.

After about fifteen minutes we had some ideas, some of them were even good, and the meeting was coming to a close. I started to get nervous. If the meeting was ending, then that meant my date was starting. I took a deep breath and reminded myself that he was just a guy and he seemed to really like me. There was no reason to be nervous. When that didn't work, I took another deep breath and hoped that would do the trick. As everyone started leaving, I walked over to Annabelle.

"Are you ready for your date?" she asked under her breath while putting her notebook away.

"Yeah. It should be a good time, right?" I asked, and took another deep breath. And then another, but I was still not calming down.

"Why would it not be fun?" Annabelle looked confused.

"I'm just nervous, that's all." I slid my bag onto my shoulder and steadied my hand.

"You'll be fine," she assured me as she watched one of the guys from her group walk out the door. I followed her glance and saw him too. He waved at Annabelle before he walked out of the classroom.

"Um, hi! Who is that?" I asked when Annabelle waved back.

"Oh, that's Jason. He's a freshman too," she said as she tossed her hair over her shoulder and started walking out the door.

"And?"

"And nothing. He is a nice guy." She pulled her phone out and checked her messages.

"Nice guy or *nice guy*?" I asked, finally returning her knowing look.

"No, it isn't like that. I think it's more of a friend relationship. He has a girlfriend," she said with an exasperated sigh.

"Okay, I was just wondering." I suppressed a laugh. Annabelle rolled her eyes at me.

"Have fun on your date. Come see me when it's done." She waved and walked toward the door.

"But what if you're with Jason?" I asked under my breath but loud enough for her to hear me.

"*Bye*," she yelled, and headed to the cafeteria.

I went over to where Trent was standing just outside the classroom. He was talking with a couple of guys. I didn't want to interrupt so I leaned against the wall and took my phone out. I was checking my social media site when he came over to me. From the look on his face, I had a bad feeling.

"Violet! I am so sorry! I need to run to the Greek Council office and handle something. Do you mind waiting?" He looked genuinely torn.

"Yeah, no problem." I tried not to sound too disappointed.

"I parked in the lot right outside so why don't you wait here and I'll be right back." He pointed toward the classroom we just had the meeting in and indicated I should take a seat.

"Okay, I guess I'll see you in a few minutes."

"Thanks, you're the best." He leaned in and gave me a gentle peck on the cheek. I smiled as he walked away.

I sat in the same desk I was in for the meeting and took my notebook out. I wanted to look at my statistics notes again in the hope that I could attempt to figure out my homework.

***

"What are you still doing in here?" Hercules asked from the door of the classroom. He was leaning against the doorframe and watching me. I looked up at him and my breath caught in my throat. We were alone again.

"Oh, I am meeting up with Trent for dinner. He had to run to the Greek Council office so he asked me to wait," I said, trying to sound relaxed.

"A real man doesn't let a woman wait. Didn't you say you were looking for a real man?" He walked in and sat on the table in the front of the classroom. He was about ten feet from me now.

"A real man doesn't shirk his responsibilities!" I stated, and then looked down at my homework. I felt a little embarrassed all of a sudden. Like he was judging me for being interested in Trent. Then I realized that was ridiculous. I would not let him hold that kind of power over me. I met his gaze with a look of defiance. Trent was a nice guy. If I wanted to go on a date with him, then I would.

He got up from the table and walked over to my desk. "So after what almost happened in the EET office, you're going to go out with another bloke." He slid into the desk next to mine and leaned over onto my desk.

"I said yes to him before the office. Besides, you made it quite clear that what almost happened in the EET office should never have happened. So why not?" I took a chance and met his gaze. We sat like that for a second and just looked into each other's eyes. My pulse was racing. I knew something had to happen but I was not about to be the one to move. It had to be up to him. Or my phone. It buzzed and the moment was over. I looked down and saw a text from Trent.

I'm sorry! I need to reschedule dinner.

I picked the phone up and showed it to Hercules. "I guess the date isn't going to happen." He took it and I started to put my statistics notes away.

"His loss," Hercules said as he handed the phone back to me.

"It's fine. I'm sure whatever he was doing was important and he didn't want me to wait," I said, trying not to sound upset. Things happened and I needed to accept it. As I was grabbing my last page of notes, it slid off the desk. Hercules got up quickly and grabbed it.

"You were working on statistics?" he asked as he handed me the page.

"Yeah, math has always been my weak spot, and statistics doesn't even seem like it's math. I have some homework but I'm pretty sure my teacher is speaking a different language so I'm probably going to have to see her during office hours to figure this out," I grumbled as I grabbed my bag and stood up.

"Let me have a look. I had to deal with statistics for my PhD so I can probably give you a hand." He patted the desk next to him, suggesting that I should sit back down. He took his glasses out of his pocket and slid them on. I took a deep breath. I was already nervous sitting in this room with him alone. I probably should have caught up with Annabelle in the cafeteria but I really did need the help. I shrugged and sat back down. We would just focus on homework and not what almost happened earlier.

"So far, it seems pretty simple. You just need to determine which formula you need to use," he said as he looked over the homework questions.

"That would be the problem. I am not really sure which goes where." I was trying to focus on the statistics notes and not his eyes. Hercules had many qualities that made a girl do a double take, but his eyes were my favorite. It wasn't just the color that made them special or the small specks of gold here and there. It was the way they held your gaze and made you forget everything. You could look into his eyes and just for one second the outside world would disappear and it was just you and him. Problems like statistics just didn't exist in his world.

I shook my head and tried to focus on what he was explaining. I had a distinct feeling it was important but I was struggling.

"What?" Hercules asked when it became obvious I was not paying attention to what he was saying.

"Sorry, I just got distracted. I was thinking about something," I stammered as I quickly looked down at my notes. Luckily, my phone went off at that moment and I had an excuse to take a break from the most unsuccessful study session ever. I got a text message and it was from Lola!

Hey, sorry! I was out of it today. I'm fine. I had a concussion so they wanted me to stay in the hospital for observation. I'm staying at my mom's tonight and then back to campus. I'm glad you're okay. C ya!

"Well, that's good," I exclaimed, and I put my phone away.

"What's up? Trent finished?" he practically

growled, and I tried not to choke on the masculinity battle.

"No, ah, it was my roommate, Lola. She said she had a concussion last night but is being released and then going to her mom's for the night so she's doing well." I decided to ignore the comment about Trent instead of feeding this fight.

"I'm glad she's doing better," he said, and looked down at my notes again. There was an awkward silence. I had a feeling he was thinking about what almost happened earlier. It was on my mind too. How could it not be? Lola clearly was fine but a concussion was not a small injury. Maybe I underestimated this whole thing. I probably should be grateful nothing happened.

"You're right. I should have taken this whole thing more seriously," I admitted to him.

He didn't say anything but looked up at me. I wanted to say something to break this silence but I wasn't sure where to go from here. He was my professor, Professor Berneli. I should start calling him that and not Hercules. Maybe that would help me think of him as a professor and not the almost Greek god I'd like to have my way with. Yes, that would be the plan. I looked up from my notes and met his gaze. My insides quickly turned to goo and I realized the problem with that plan.

"Look, I know that what happened earlier was out of line. I could pretend that I'm not attracted to you but that would be a lie. I am your professor so this cannot happen. We just have to accept that and move on," Berneli confessed.

My mouth fell open. I knew he was attracted to

me, obviously, he nearly kissed me, but it was a completely different thing to hear with his delicious accent.

"I know. I didn't think anything was going to happen between us anyway. I mean, it can't, right? That's why I was going out with Trent today," I acknowledged as I grabbed my notes and put them away. I didn't want to be in this conversation anymore.

"Really? Trent? Talk about all brawn and no brains. It is painful to have meetings with him. You could do better," Berneli said as he ran his hand through his hair.

"You have no right to say that about him. You just met him! He is a really nice guy," I insisted as I stood up. Now he was just being mean. It wasn't right for him to say those things about Trent and I was not going to sit around and listen to it. I started to walk toward the door but Berneli quickly got up and blocked my path.

"Violet, I feel like I know you and I just met you," he professed as he took his glasses off and slid them back in his pocket.

"Oh really? What do you know about me?" I asked, challenging him. I was actually curious about what he had to say.

"You're good at poker, obviously, but it's more than that. You can read people. It's very intimidating. It's almost as if you can see into people's soul with just one glance. I'm captivated by you whenever you cast a glance my way. You're a good friend too. Not many people would show up to a meeting they weren't invited to just so they could support their friend. You're also dedicated. While waiting for your date, you start working on homework you don't understand. And you're passionate. I see it in your eyes. I saw it earlier today and it's intoxicating." As he said this, he inched closer to me until he was right in front of me again.

"Well, I may be able to read most people, but I think you are giving me some mixed signals," I said as I stepped forward and closed the distance. He was now inches from my face.

"Let's see if I can clear that up for you, then," he said as he grabbed my face and brought it to his. In an instant, his lips were on mine. There was an urgency to his kiss and I answered with my own need. His lips begged me to open to him and I did. I felt his tongue slide into my mouth and take over. He controlled this kiss and I was trying desperately to hold on.

His hands slid from my face to the back of my head and my neck. I slid my hands up his back and felt the strong muscles rippling with his movements. I could have lived in this moment forever. Then it was over. Berneli ripped his lips from mine and took a couple of steps back.

"How is that for crossing the line?" he exclaimed as he walked out of the classroom.

I stood there for a second, unsure how to respond. On the one hand, he told me that he could not have anything to do with me. On the other hand, he kissed me with enough passion to wake the dead. Then he left! He left with me standing there trying to figure this out on my own.

I slid my bag back up my shoulder and headed to the cafeteria to try to get some dinner.

***

At this point, I wasn't even hungry, but I needed something to do. This was probably not something I could discuss with Annabelle, or really anybody. It could mean his job if the wrong people found out, and it was possible that I could get kicked out of school. I trusted Annabelle but I decided to keep this to myself for now. What I needed now was a distraction that did not come in the form of a Y-chromosome.

I walked into the cafeteria and saw Annabelle sitting at our usual table by the window. I walked over to drop my bag off before I got food and noticed Jason was sitting across from her. I smiled. Good for her. I was going to let her be but she saw me and waved.

"Hey, what happened to your date?" she asked as I walked over.

I had to think for a second. Everything with Berneli seemed to take over my brain that I almost forgot about the date.

"Trent had a Greek emergency so he had to cancel," I said after a second. It was crazy that Trent canceling led to the incident with Berneli. Hell, I almost forgot we were even supposed to go out. Berneli completely distracted me.

"You had a date with Trent?" Jason probed as he took a sip of soda.

"Yeah, why?" I put my bag down on the empty

chair and sat down.

"I just heard him talking before the meeting that he and his ex may be getting back together," he said gently, trying to be honest. Jason actually sounded concerned for me.

"Well, if that's the case, then I'm happy for them. It was a first date so no real feelings had been developed yet. I'm going to get some dinner. Are you guys hanging out here for a while or heading out?" I was not a big fan of eating alone but I didn't want to impose.

"I'll wait for you," Annabelle promised, even though she looked about done with her food. Jason looked at her and then said he would wait for me too. I had a feeling, though, it was not me he was waiting on. I left the two of them and went to grab some food. It looked like pasta day and that was perfect. I always had it at home when something upset me so it would definitely help with the Berneli incident.

I filled my plate with too much food and then grabbed a drink. I looked over at the table and Annabelle and Jason were laughing hysterically at something. They looked nice together. Jason was at least six feet tall and lean with bright blue eyes. His brown hair was tousled and messy but not too long. He was wearing a superhero t-shirt and Chucks. He basically looked like a grown child but he had a bright and enchanting smile. It lit up his face and became contagious. I headed over to the table and put my tray down between Annabelle and Jason. He had a girlfriend so maybe some cockblocking was needed.

They talked a lot about EET and the upcoming comedienne. Both of them seemed really excited. I sat in silence and ate my food. It was comforting just to listen to them talk. They did not need me to do more than agree with what they were saying and I was able to go over the day in my mind.

I decided to start with Trent. If he really was getting back with his ex-girlfriend, then why not say that? Why not give me the heads-up? Then again, he didn't ask to reschedule or suggest another date, so maybe the rumor was true. On the other hand, it was not really fair of me to date him if I was feeling this way about Berneli. I knew the chance of anything happening again with Berneli were slim, but hope was a dangerous feeling, and right now I was filled with it.

***

The three of us tossed our trash and headed toward the dorms. Jason went with us most of the way until he turned toward his dorm. Annabelle and I walked in silence until we saw Jason open the door.

"So, he has a girlfriend, right?" I double checked with her.

"Yeah, her name is Janice or something like that," she recalled, seemingly oblivious to the effect she seemed to have on Jason.

"Jason and Janice? They sound like twins or siblings," I commented, giggling a little.

"I never thought of it like that. I haven't met her yet since she wasn't at EET. So, Trent?" She was clearly trying to change the subject.

"Yeah, I don't know. I mean, he didn't try to reschedule the date or anything and I haven't heard from him except for the cancelation text," I said as we both headed to my room. I had told her about Lola on the way to the dorm so she knew that my room would be empty.

"Do you think he is going to reschedule?" she asked, and sat down on my bed. I grabbed a water bottle and joined her.

"I don't know. It's possible he really was busy and couldn't plan a new date. Or, you know, it is possible that he and his ex-girlfriend are getting back together," I said, and took a big sip of water.

"I guess we will just have to wait and see."

We spent the night watching television and doing the little bit of homework we had. Annabelle headed back to her room around ten and I climbed in the shower. As the hot water beat down on me, I imagined the stress of today rolling off of my shoulders.

I stepped out of the shower feeling a bit lighter and went to brush my teeth. After that, I washed my face and headed to bed. The relaxed feeling stayed with me until I closed my eyes. The thought hit me like a brick and my eyes shot open. I had Berneli's class first thing in the morning.

Chapter 5

I tossed and turned most of the night. Every time I closed my eyes, I saw him grab my face and felt his lips on mine. I saw his eyes gazing at me and heard him calling my name. His accent wrapped around the letters and it was as if I was hearing my name for the first time. I felt his hand on the back of my head, intertwining his fingers with my hair. He gently tugged on it and a thrill started at my core and radiated through my body.

I was awake way before my alarm went off and I grabbed a bowl of cereal and ate on my bed. I had been debating dressing up a little for class because I wanted to look nice for Berneli, but I didn't want to look like I was trying. In the end, I decided to go big or go home.

I straightened my hair and it fell down to my elbows. It was probably time for a haircut but the only person I would let cut my hair was back home in Maryland. It was just going to have to wait. I headed to the bathroom with my make-up bag and did it up. I was just putting my mascara on when

Annabelle walked into the bathroom with her shower bag.

"Um, hi." She looked at me, confused, trying to suppress a yawn.

"Good morning," I replied, and kind of laughed. She clearly was not even close to awake yet.

"What are you doing up so early?" she asked.

"I had a rough time sleeping so I figured if my hair looked pretty, then people wouldn't notice the bags under my eyes," I joked. There was no way to tell her I wanted to look good for Berneli.

"You look fine," she insisted, and shook her hand at me.

"I would believe you but your eyes are barely open."

She stuck her tongue out at me and headed to the shower.

"I'll see you at lunch?" I asked before I headed out the door.

"Yeah, I'll let you know what time I get out of class," she responded as the water started to run.

I headed back to my room and got dressed. This took me a little bit of time so it was good I started so early. Eventually, I decided on a pair of dark blue skinny jeans that made my butt look good and a red lace shirt. It had cap sleeves and a low neck that played up my assets. I looked in the mirror and smiled. It was going to be a good day or I was going to make it one. After one more look, I grabbed my backpack and headed out the door.

***

Berneli's class started in fifteen minutes but I didn't want to be there too early. That would be desperate, so I went down to the basement of the castle, where the flower garden was. This time, no one was lurking around so I took my time admiring the beauty in silence.

After walking around for about ten minutes, I decided it was time to make my way to class. I got there five minutes early. I took a seat in the second row and looked around. Berneli was not in the class yet and I instantly panicked. What if he canceled class? What if someone found out about the kiss? What if I would never see him again? Sweat started to prickle on my forehead and my pulse raced. I pulled my cell phone out and checked my email. There was no message canceling class so I'd have to just wait and see. Panicking came naturally to me but I needed to pull myself together.

With a minute left until class started, Berneli walked in. He was carrying a black briefcase that he placed on the desk behind him. He hopped onto the desk and pulled a sheet of paper out. I watched as he walked toward me but then stopped before the girl sitting in the desk in front of me. He handed it to her and then he walked in front of me and started speaking to the class.

"I have handed out an attendance sheet. It is set up to look like this classroom. Please put your name on the desk you are sitting at. This will be your permanent seat. I like to do this so that I can learn who all of you are and to eliminate any time picking seats. I do take attendance every class. It is vital to this class that you do not miss any lectures, but it will be your responsibility to contact me in advance if you need to miss a class." Berneli looked around at everyone to try to sink this point in. Then he continued.

"I accept doctor's notes and proof of funerals. That is how an absence is excused. Any more than two unexcused absences will automatically fail you. I know this sounds harsh but I'm not here to waste your time, so I hope you will offer me the same respect. Let's begin. I want to talk about books that interest you." Berneli said all of this while standing next to my desk.

He never met my glance but he kept hitting his knuckle on my desk to emphasize his points. He knew I was there and it brought a blush to my face. I took a few deep breaths to keep from fainting. Definitely not the impression I wanted to make today.

"Literature is meant to cause discussions. It is meant to make you think and question things. There are so many different interpretations of scenes and character motivations that we could spend an entire class talking about one scene from one chapter of one book. So that is my intention. Starting next week, each of you will decide on a scene from the ones listed on the syllabus. All of the scenes are in the textbook and some background has been provided. But I encourage and expect you to do some of your own research." He held up his textbook and then continued with his lecture.

"I will come up with a schedule as to when each of you will need to share your scene. I want you to talk about the scene and why it caused controversy.

While it will be up to each student to lead the discussion, it will be up to the rest of you to supply intelligent commentary. A large portion of your grade will come from your participation in these discussions." Berneli had begun pacing up and down the classroom. However, he did manage to stop directly in front of my desk...again.

Before heading back to the front of the class, he knocked his knuckle on my desk one final time. It grabbed my attention and I looked up at him. He was staring down at me and our eyes met. It seemed like forever but it was probably only half a second. I hoped no one else noticed.

My heart was beating so hard I could hear it in my ears, but he was my professor and should definitely not be causing these feelings. Yet, when I snuck a look at him again, I could feel the butterflies swarming in my stomach. He turned around to write something on the board and through his fitted button-down shirt I could see the slightest outline of muscle. I remembered how firm those muscles felt and a jolt of electricity surged through my body. It seemed to congregate toward my core and left me feeling stimulated.

Still, it made me think. I had seen good-looking men with their shirts off and it did nothing to me. I mean, I enjoyed the view, but it didn't leave me with a desperate feeling. But just the illusion of his solid, chiseled back left me aching. Maybe it was his position of authority, maybe it was the professional button-down, maybe it was the fact that he was unavailable, or maybe it was all of it. Whatever it was, I found myself licking my lips and visualizing how he would feel if I slid my hands down his shoulders to the middle of his back, and then down to his lower back, right above his gorgeous chiseled ass.

As if he could sense that I was admiring what was clearly the model for the David statue, he turned around and smiled. This seemed to take me out of my haze. I shook my head and tried to pay attention to what he was saying instead of what I'd like to do to him.

The rest of the class seemed to go by without any more crazy fantasies that would make my grandmother roll over in her grave, or at least I tried to keep them at bay. Berneli dismissed the class and I gathered up my things to leave.

The same thing that happened last class did this time. Most of the girls swarmed him, asking what all seemed to be deep and important questions. It was funny that these questions all involved the girl twirling her hair and sticking out her chest. I chuckled to myself and headed toward the door. Then it happened.

"Miss Carrington, will you wait a moment?" Berneli called as he headed in my direction. I turned around and closed the distance between us. "I have a question for you," he said as he quickly tried to usher his admirers out the door.

I put my bag down on one of the desks and took my phone out to distract myself as my nerves took over. Plus, I was meeting Annabelle after class so I figured I should shoot her a text that I may be running a couple of minutes late. Judging from the persistence of a few of my fellow classmates, it was going to take all day.

"Sorry about that!" He leaned against the desk next to me, flustered. "I don't get it! They ask a million questions about the assignment after the class but none during the class," he mused, bewildered. He slid his hands through his wavy hair, leaving it a little mussed. It was nice to see him looking a little rattled.

"They just want to have some one-on-one attention," I said, trying not to laugh. He really didn't realize that they all were trying to hit on the new hot professor.

"I guess I will need to get some office hours," he continued, still oblivious to his effect on the class. This seemed to make him even more attractive. He then shook his head and looked at me. "So, I asked you to stay behind a minute because I was wondering if you would be first to start the book discussion on Monday of next week. I realize it is a little nerve-racking leading something like this first and that some of the other students may be a little hesitant to respond. I just think you would be the best person to start. Of course, I will be a bit more lenient with your grade," he assured with a smug look on his face.

"Oh, you will go easy on me," I said, trying to hide my frustration. "I am up for the challenge," I insisted, sitting up a little taller, annoyed.

"I know you are. That is why I asked you," he told me, and leaned across the desk, entering my personal bubble.

"Really, I thought it was to watch me squirm," I countered as I leaned forward, closing most of the distance between us. I could feel his breath on my face. Unfortunately, this was becoming a normal feeling. Probably not something I should get used to.

"There is always that. You are quite gorgeous when you get flustered. Your cheeks turn a flattering pink and your eyes get a fire in them that makes it hard for me to look away." He swiped his knuckle gently down the side of my cheek.

"We cannot keep doing this," I insisted as I broke the overwhelming eye contact. I looked down at my desk and tried to keep calm. I really should have gotten up to leave but there was something that was keeping me anchored in place.

"Then walk away. If you really don't feel this spark between us, then walk out the door," he whispered softly in a tone that reached an unknown part of me. No other man had even come close to finding this part. I wanted him to fulfill my every carnal need. I looked up at him and saw the same raw desire in his eyes.

But he had given me an out. I should stand up right now and head out the door. Having an affair with a professor was a terrible idea. Having an affair with a professor who was only visiting for a year was probably an even worse idea. Yet here I was. Still glued to my seat and staring into the most enchanting eyes I had ever lost myself in.

"I don't see you moving."

"I am currently talking myself into getting up and walking out the door," I said, though it seemed to lack the confidence I was trying to convey.

"Maybe that is enough talking," he suggested,

and wrapped his hand around the back of my neck, pulling me into a kiss. It was light at first, with our lips barely touching. But then the kiss changed almost instantly to one filled with passion and wanton desire. His fingers weaved through my hair at the nape of my neck and he pulled ever so slightly. This seemed to ignite the animal within me and a moan escaped.

Even though this was only our second kiss, it was as if he belonged with me. I couldn't decide what made his kiss so different than the ones I'd had before. It could have been the power behind those soft and supple lips or the way he took control of the kiss. I didn't have to think, rather I just needed to follow his lead. It was relaxing not to have to think so much for once.

I tried to lean into him and realized there was a desk between us. We broke the kiss for a second and looked down at the desk. It appeared that he noticed the problem too and he decided to do something. He pulled me up out of my desk and around his so I was standing between his legs with his arms around my waist and mine around his neck.

This time I made a move. I leaned in and kissed him hard, hoping to get lost in the sensation of his lips again. I could feel his hands traveling down from my waist to my hips and resting there. Heat began to radiate from where his hands were and it filled me up. I slid my hand up the back of his neck and my hands skimmed into his silky, wavy hair. It was quite possibly the softest hair I had ever felt.

His hands had now moved to my ass and he

grabbed a hold of it, squeezing hard. My breathing turned ragged and I moaned again in pleasure. He chuckled and began to place a trail of kisses down the side of my neck. He got to the spot between my shoulder and my collarbone and he began to gently suck. My knees kind of buckled under me and I felt heat shoot between my legs. I wasn't sure if I could recover from the effect this man was having on me.

Then he broke away. Berneli pushed my hips away from him and slid off the desk.

"We, ah, we need to slow down." He took a couple deep breaths and then looked back up at me, the fire in his eyes still glowing. "I want nothing more than to take you here and now. But this is probably not the place for it. Someone could just walk in, and we definitely don't want that."

As desperately as I wanted him to bend me over the desk, I knew he was right. This was not the time or the place.

"Yeah. You're probably right," I admitted, but I still couldn't move. Apparently, neither could he. We stood there for what seemed like forever just looking at each other. I didn't want to let go until he did. It was so important that I stay connected with him. I couldn't explain why, but it seemed vital at that moment.

Who knew how long we would have stayed there just looking at each other if we had not been interrupted. Another professor walked into the room and placed his briefcase on the desk in the front. We quickly broke apart before the professor glanced over in our direction.

"Oh, was I interrupting something?" he asked,

looking a little bewildered.

"No. It is my mistake. I need to set up office hours so my students don't talk my ear off after classes. We were just about done here so we will get out of your way," Berneli covered as he headed to the desk and grabbed his own briefcase.

"Thank you for answering my questions, Professor Berneli," I managed to say, even though it sounded unbelievably cheesy.

"See you next class, Miss Carrington," Berneli said with a wink. I watched him leave the classroom and quickly grabbed my bag. My mind was racing. There was no way that this should have happened. I really needed to learn some restraint, but more than that, I wished I was still in contact with my friends from home. I just met Annabelle and I wasn't sure I felt comfortable talking to her about this.

I had friends back home but no real best friend I felt I could confide in with something this delicate. After I broke up with my ex-boyfriend for cheating, a lot of them deserted me in favor of the sob story he told them. It didn't just leave me disappointed in them, but also a little wounded. I wasn't exactly sure who I could trust.

It was just a physical thing. There was no way I was going to let something like that screw with either of our futures. No, I was going to need to put my foot down. This could not keep happening. Yes, Berneli was gorgeous and an amazing kisser, but there were plenty of other good-looking guys on campus. I was sure I could find one who would make me forget all about Berneli. I just needed to focus on not being alone with him. Public spaces were going to be my best friend.

***

I was heading to the cafeteria to see Annabelle when I heard my name called from behind me. I turned around and there was Trent. He had a big smile on his face and was heading my way. This was the perfect distraction.

"Hey, sorry about our date. My life gets a little crazy at the beginning of the year with Greek life," Trent said as he fell in line with my stride.

"I understand. Life happens, right?" I was trying not to sound too disappointed. I could like Trent. I wanted to like him, but then I remembered what Jason had said.

"Can I make it up to you?" he asked as we entered the cafeteria.

"I heard you were getting back together with your ex." I hoped I didn't come off as bitter, but even to my own ears I had failed.

"Nah, we're over. How about that date, then?"

"Depends on what you have in mind," I said, trying to contain my excitement. The very real excitement that was flowing through me.

"Do you have plans for Saturday? My frat is having a party and I'd love it if you were there." He looked me in the eye and I could feel his intensity. He did seem really sorry.

"Sure. Sounds like fun," I managed, biting my lip. My first frat party. This made me quite anxious, but I had a feeling it would be worth it. Or it would be a good story to tell one day.

"Great, I'll text you the details." We said bye and he headed back out the cafeteria door.

So within twenty minutes I was hooking up with my professor and setting up a date with a frat guy. I wasn't sure when my life got this exciting, or if I could even handle it. I shook my head and decided to worry about all of this later. I needed to get to my journal and write it out and analyze what I was feeling.

I looked around the cafeteria and saw Annabelle and Jason sitting near the windows again. His head was thrown back as he laughed at something she said. Her face lit up as he said something to her. For a minute, I didn't want to go over and break up their moment, but then Annabelle turned and waved at me. I headed over there and sat down.

"Sorry! My professor needed to talk with me after class about an assignment," I said, trying to sound innocent.

"What assignment? Classes just started," Annabelle asked, confused.

"We have one coming up in my literature class and the professor wants me to start this book discussion on Monday," I informed them, looking around the cafeteria. There was no way I could make eye contact and continue this conversation. Clearly it was not a lie, but it also was not the whole truth.

"Isn't Berneli the new literature professor?" Jason asked while he shoveled pizza into his mouth.

"Yes, he is," Annabelle responded before I had the chance. She looked at me and smiled, appearing way sneakier than I could have thought.

I tried to take some deep breaths to keep my face from turning bright red. She already suspected, I didn't need to confirm her theory.

"Man, I wish I was in one of his classes," she continued. "He is gorgeous and I could just listen to that accent for hours. I wouldn't mind being held after class to talk to him. What do you think, Violet?"

Luckily, Jason started talking so I did not have to reply.

"I think you're drooling, Annabelle," Jason teased as he handed her a napkin. She shoved his hand away and slapped him on the arm.

"Oh, did you just walk in with Trent?" Annabelle asked, changing the subject. I was thankful to have something else to talk about. I relaxed and told them about the party.

"So, are you guys coming with me? I don't want to go by myself," I pleaded.

"Yeah. Someone needs to keep you out of trouble," Annabelle said.

"Mind if I bring my girlfriend?" Jason asked.

"Who is your girlfriend?" I asked. Since they met, Annabelle and Jason had been pretty inseparable. I wasn't sure how his girlfriend felt about that, or even if she existed at this point.

"Her name is Janice. She is studying environmental science here. It takes up a lot of her time so I bet she will want to take a night to blow off some steam," he said, grabbing his phone and showing us a picture. Janice had brown hair that went down to her shoulders and those blue eyes that made men drool. It was a picture from the shoulders up so that was really all we were able to see of her but she seemed pretty.

"Yeah, bring her along. It will be nice to meet her," I told him, eyeing Annabelle's reaction. She started to grab her bag and was digging around for something. I had a feeling she was not as okay with meeting Janice as she was pretending.

"Great, I'll send her a text."

I went to get food and the rest of lunch went by without incident. We said goodbye to Jason, then Annabelle and I headed to our next class since they were both in the same wing of the castle. When Jason had turned the corner, I figured it was a good time to talk about Janice.

"She looked nice," I said, trying to gauge her response.

"I guess so, but I don't know why she has, like, no interest in hanging out. I spend so much time with Jason and I've never even glimpsed her. We are probably just going to have to wait and see on Saturday." It seemed to me she was being just a little bitter. I smiled. I had a hunch that she may like Jason more than she was letting on.

"I guess so," I said, deciding not to push her buttons too much yet. But Saturday was definitely going to be an interesting day for all of us.

We parted ways and headed to our classes.

***

After class ended, I headed back to my dorm room. Annabelle texted that she was going to the EET office to get some work done while she had some spare time. I wasn't hungry for dinner yet so I figured it would be a good time to work on my homework. I was still struggling with statistics so I probably needed to give it one more try.

I had been at my homework for about forty-five minutes when the door opened. Lola walked in with a bandage above her eye.

"Hey! Are you okay?" I rushed over to grab her bag and bring it in the room.

"Yeah, I'm fine. No need to fuss," she insisted, and then went to sit on her bed.

"So what happened? I only got bits and pieces out of the cop you sent over here."

"Well, Tyler's new girlfriend apparently was really upset because Tyler told her that he broke up with me for her but that I wouldn't leave him alone." She rolled her eyes and then continued.

"As if. So she was furious with me and wanted to fight. I wasn't actually going to fight until she swung at me. She missed because I dodged it and that's when I gave her a black eye." Lola gave me a smug smile and held up her fists like a boxer. "You don't mess with North Jersey."

I giggled because she was all of one hundred pounds soaking wet, so it was amusing to think of her actually hurting someone. Especially since Katie looked like she worked out. But then again, I also got the impression that she could probably kill me with two fingers or something like that.

"Anyway, something happened that I can't really remember and Tyler pushed me. I fell and hit my head on the curb. One of my friends, Lisa, called the police because I was still bleeding. I just have this cut now. Everything else is generally fine. They said I might feel a little dizzy for a couple of days but no real harm done. What happened here?"

It took me a second to process what she said. Tyler had pushed her and caused a concussion. I never pegged him for the violent type. He always seemed so nice and he was pretty calm when Katie was losing her mind.

I figured she'd been through enough lately and that we could talk about him a bit more later. I told Lola how the cop waited outside the door all night and that nothing else really happened. We talked some more about the whole thing, and Lola's mafia family was not happy. So she was going to let them handle the situation. I had never met anyone with family in the mob and I was not sure how to respond to this. After all, other than in gangster movies, who actually talked about the mob or even used them to settle a score?

We hung out for the rest of the night and ordered a pizza for dinner. Aside from her mafia ties, I really liked Lola. She loved old-school television shows, fashion, and had an even bigger tabloid subscription list than me. Also, she had an amazing junk food stash. I told her about the party on Saturday but she was not ready to go out just yet. She insisted that she was waiting for her bruise to heal but I thought she was still a little shaken up after the fight.

***

The rest of the week went by with little

excitement. Annabelle, Jason, and I had become a trio and rarely went anywhere without each other. I was really starting to like him. Janice still never made an appearance. Every time she was invited to hang out with us, she declined. It was starting to bother me.

Luckily, I didn't have another class with Berneli. He did send an email to the class about my assignment. I decided that *Pride and Prejudice* was my best bet. I planned to go into the Elizabeth and Darcy marriage with more detail. I was going to claim that they were perfect for each other and would maintain a happy marriage while other people claimed they were too different and had not actually gotten over their pride or their prejudice. It was ridiculous, and clearly those people hadn't read the book. Maybe the old English was throwing them off.

Berneli asked the class to look into these arguments and to be ready to comment on my discussion. Other than that, I had not heard from him. I kept telling myself this was for the best. The two of us being together would only cause a lot of trouble, and statistics was all the trouble I could handle right now. Especially if I upset the mafia princess sleeping in the bed next to mine.

Chapter 6

I slept in Saturday morning and then stayed in bed for a few more hours writing in my journal. I needed to talk to someone about the Berneli incident, well, incidents, and the journal was the closest thing I could get. After baring my soul for several pages, I was starting to feel a little better. I still had no answers, but I felt as if a weight had been released from my shoulders. This party and Trent were coming at the perfect time. I had a bowl of cereal and then headed to the shower.

I ran into Annabelle, who was brushing her teeth. We decided to meet up around two for a late lunch and then we would probably hang out until the party. After the shower, I still had a couple of hours to kill so I blow-dried my hair and started working on my presentation for Berneli. At 1:45 I had just about finished but decided I could wrap the project up tomorrow and headed over to Annabelle's room. We went to the cafeteria and met up with Jason, and I couldn't help but notice the way his face lit up when he saw us walk in. I had a feeling his joy had nothing to do with my good looks and glowing personality.

"Janice said she doesn't really want to go to the party tonight. She doesn't think a frat party is really her thing. Plus, she doesn't really like staying out past eleven," Jason said when Annabelle asked about the party

"Does that mean you aren't coming?" Annabelle asked with a look of disappointment on her face.

"No, I still want to go. Besides, someone has to be there to make sure the two of you behave," he badgered us, giving her a playful shove.

"What do you think we're going to do? Bang the whole frat in their clubhouse? Disappear for a few hours with the president and get a look at his paddle?" I asked, amused.

"Well, Vi, with you we never know."

I tossed a piece of my roll at him and rolled my eyes.

"I guess we are going to see tonight, right?" Annabelle said, smiling at me.

We finished lunch and headed back to Jason's dorm. He had a huge flat screen TV and we were right in the middle of a marathon for my new favorite crime show when Jason's roommate, Kyle, came in. He was also an environmental major but not as busy as Janice. Jason said it was because Janice was a perfectionist and Kyle spent a lot of time getting high.

We found out that Kyle was going to the party too. He had made friends with a couple of the frat boys and was intending to pledge. Kyle had short black hair and dark eyes. He was a little bit taller than Annabelle with dark olive skin. He also had a ring through his nostrils that reminded me of a bull, and when he took his shirt off to change, he showed off two giant pentagram tattoos on his back. He looked tough but his sweet smile told a different story.

***

Around eight, Annabelle and I grabbed our leftover Chinese food and headed back to our dorm so we could get ready. The guys said they would pick us up around ten and take us to the party. Apparently, Jason didn't drink and so he said he would drive.

Annabelle and I went to my room first to figure out what I was going to wear. Lola was there but still didn't want to go to the party. She was, however, more than willing to help us get ready. I borrowed a little, emphasis on *little*, black dress with a halter top that went a little too high on my thighs. Nothing was hanging out in the dress but there was not a whole lot left to the imagination.

"You can't underestimate the effect of a little black dress on a man," she asserted.

Both Lola and Annabelle insisted it would look better with heels but I decided to wear flats. Since my dress was going to be that short, I needed to have full balance. If I fell over, something would totally pop out.

Annabelle wasn't comfortable wearing a dress and settled for some dark skinny jeans and one of Lola's sequined yellow tops. She also wore flats but that was because she claimed her dancing was bad enough barefoot that she didn't need to complicate the matter.

Lola gave the ends of my hair a little curl while I straightened Annabelle's hair. We had a nice little hair train going on. After that, we headed to the bathroom and started the make-up game. I liked my make-up a little, okay a lot, darker than Annabelle so she would not let me touch her face. But in reality, I was jealous how well the natural look worked for her.

I was lining my eyes when Annabelle got a text. The guys were going to be heading over in a couple of minutes so we needed to hurry up. After some more swipes of mascara, we were ready to go. Annabelle and I thanked Lola and grabbed our wristlets. The guys were just pulling up in front of our dorm as we were heading out.

"What's up, girls? How much for the night?" Jason asked as we walked over to the car.

"Ha-ha, very funny," I said, and rolled my eyes. Kyle, on the other hand, was laughing hysterically. We climbed into the car and talked about the crime show almost the whole way to the house. The guys swore they stopped watching it after we left but we were getting the impression that they might have broken that deal.

We pulled up to what looked like a makeshift road in the woods.

"Violet, are you sure this is the address? It kind of looks like where you take people to die," Annabelle whined while looking out the window.

I double checked the text Trent sent me with the

address and confirmed that this was correct. "If you're this paranoid, we're definitely going to have to cut you off from the serial killer shows," I told her, pretending it didn't freak me out a little.

We continued down the dirt path and after a couple more minutes we came upon a house in the middle of the woods. There was dance music coming from it and we could see college kids all over the deck. I had a feeling we were in the right place or it was the beginning of a horror story.

Jason parked along the driveway but the car was really crooked.

"Do you know how to park, Jason?" I asked him as we got out.

"Yes! But now if someone blocks us in, I can get out easier," he claimed as if he were the party expert. Though I had to agree he had a point.

We headed into the house and instantly felt a little awkward. None of us recognized anyone yet but there were only ten people in the living room. We headed to the kitchen and I started to smile as I saw him.

"Violet!" Trent called my name and headed over to me. He gave me a hug and then waved at my friends. "I am glad you made it. Can I get you a drink?" he asked as he placed an arm around my waist.

"Sure, what do you have?" I asked, a little nervous.

Judging from his breath, Trent definitely started way before we showed up. He brought me over to this giant tub of purple-blue liquid, waving his arm in front of it as if to say it was a fountain of champagne. It looked disgusting and there was no way I was drinking it.

"Do you want some jungle juice?" he asked, indicating the purple-blue goo.

"No, ah, what else do you have?" It looked like they liquefied the Purple People Eater.

"Do you want a beer?" He pointed to the keg where Kyle, Annabelle, and Jason were all standing. Kyle had a cup in his hand but Annabelle and Jason didn't.

"Yes, that sounds good," I said, and we headed that way. As he was getting me a drink, some of his friends rushed over.

"Trent, there is this guy running the pong table. You have to come and teach him a lesson," one of them said, and dragged him to the other side of the room. He smiled at me and waved me over.

I put one finger up, indicating that I would be there in a second. I went to see my friends.

"Hey, guys! Kyle, what are you drinking?" I looked into his cup and saw the purple-blue goo.

"Jungle juice. Why, do you want some?" He offered me his cup.

"Nope, it smells like grape medicine," I said, and laughed. "Did you want anything, Annabelle?"

"No, it all kinda looks dirty. I am not a fan," she told us with a scrunched up face. I'd noticed that Annabelle was a serious germaphobe.

"*Violet, come here!*" Trent screamed over the crowd. I was pretty sure he was already drunk but at least he seemed like a fun drunk.

I said bye to my friends, who decided that they were going to check out the music downstairs. I headed over to Trent, who looked very unhappy.

"Help me out! I am usually good at this but I am struggling tonight." He handed me a slick ping-pong ball. It was really gross but throwing it meant that I got to let it go. So I took a giant gulp of beer and sent the ball flying. Surprisingly enough, it went into one of the cups. Everyone, including Trent, started cheering. I threw the second ball but that one missed. The game went on until both sides of the table were down to one cup each. Trent was trying hard but kept missing. His drinking had slowed down a little bit so maybe he was trying to focus.

"Babe, it's up to you," he said to me, and handed me the ball as if he were handing me a sword for battle.

I gave him a look to indicate I thought he was being weird but took the ball anyway. I took another sip of what was my second beer and threw the ball. By some miracle it went in. Trent picked me up and spun me around, kissing me hard and sloppily.

"We need to play again," he insisted, and started setting up the cups. We played another game and it was going pretty well. Trent was getting really touchy as the night went on and I liked it. When he was not throwing the ball, he had an arm around my waist or draped across my shoulders. This was the kind of relationship I needed.

After about ten more minutes we lost the game and were kicked off the table. He brought me to the keg and we each got another beer. Trent took a big sip and then we headed down to the basement.

The music was loud. Yelling in each other's ears loud. It suddenly made sense why the house was situated in the middle of the woods. No neighbors meant no one to mess up the party.

The basement had brown paneled walls with writing all over them. I looked closer at it and it appeared like people were writing their names everywhere. Trent noticed my interest.

"A lot of sorority girls like to write on the walls when they come over. It's like staking their claim or something. It's kind of a tradition," he said in my ear. We turned the corner and headed to the main room in the basement. There were speakers everywhere and a stage with a stripper pole.

"Really? You have a stripper pole?" I got on my tiptoes and shouted in his ear.

Trent laughed and leaned into me. His hand slid down my back and onto my hip. "This is a frat house. What do you expect? Want to give it a try?" he asked with a wink.

"Not even a little bit," I said, laughing. It would take a whole lot more than beer to get me up on a stripper pole.

I looked around the room and noticed Annabelle and Jason were standing in the corner. They weren't necessarily dancing together, more like dancing near the other since they weren't touching or facing each other. I did notice, though, that Jason could not keep his eyes off her. Annabelle didn't seem to be aware of it and just got herself lost in the music. Even I could see that she looked radiant.

Trent asked me to dance and then led me out on the floor. I wasn't really the best dancer. I could find the beat and sort of move to it but I was definitely not going to join any reality type TV show. Trent didn't seem to care, though, and after a few minutes, I didn't either.

It was exhilarating to feel his hands on me. He was holding my hips while I danced in front of him. Every once in a while his hands would slide down and rest on my pelvis. Then he spun me around and slid his hands right above my butt. He looked down at me and I could see that he was feeling just as exhilarated as I was.

He leaned into me so that there was no longer any space between us and kissed me. It was not like the kiss with Berneli. This kiss was demanding and wet. It was as if Trent needed the kiss now or he may explode. He controlled the kiss and I could barely keep up with the speed and intensity. Trent broke away and sauntered back a few feet to lean against the wall behind us. I bit my lip, trying to hold in the arousal that was pouring out of me.

The kiss continued and his hands roamed back down to my butt. He broke the kiss again and began trailing kisses down my neck and along my collar bone. These collarbone kisses were my kryptonite. They made my mind go empty and shudder uncontrollably. I pressed my body into him, encouraging Trent to go further.

He slid one of his hands up my stomach and stopped on the side of my breast. Everywhere Trent touched radiated with heat and I needed his hands on me at that moment. I needed his kiss and I pulled on his shirt, bringing his muscular chest even closer to me.

But then I opened my eyes for a second, I wasn't sure why, and saw the names of the sorority girls on the wall behind Trent and remembered where I was. I grabbed his hand and put it back on my waist, breaking the kiss.

"Not here," I said, and moved his other hand from my butt. "We can't do this here." I shook my head and backed up a little bit. His hands gave me a bit of room but they stayed on my waist.

"It's okay. I just got carried away," he groaned, looking a little disappointed. "You just look so hot tonight." He ran two fingers down my cheek. I started to blush and kissed him lightly.

"Thanks," I said, and made a mental note to thank Lola later. We went back out onto the floor and danced for a little bit longer but I needed a pee break. I went over and grabbed Annabelle because it was a rule that a girl could not go to the bathroom by herself.

"Oh my god! Did you see what just happened?" I asked her as we headed upstairs.

"You mean when you two were hooking up in the middle of a grungy basement? Yep, I saw it, Jason saw it, everyone saw it. How do you feel about it?" Annabelle asked as we tried to find the bathroom.

"I don't know. I mean, I wanted it at the time. It was great and he was a good kisser," I said, and stopped for a moment. Berneli was actually a better kisser but I was trying not to think about him. I internally chastised myself and focused on Trent

116

again.

"I just didn't feel comfortable doing that in a public room. I mean, there were names of sorority girls written all over the wall behind him. Talk about taking all of the romance out of a situation," I complained while we were waiting in line to get to the bathroom.

"Yeah, I can see why that would be a problem. What did he say?"

"He said it was fine and that he just got carried away 'cause, you know, I look amazing tonight," I teased, and flipped my hair over my shoulder.

"Oh, well, of course. It's the black dress," Annabelle said, and shoved my shoulder a little.

"What about you and Jason?" I asked with a smirk spreading on my face.

"What about us? We weren't the ones having sex with our clothes on in the basement, were we?" She gave me a judgmental look.

"No, but he was the one looking at you like a love struck puppy," I retaliated, and mimicked his look of desire.

"Shut up! He was not," she groaned.

"Oh, he was! I know he has a girlfriend but he is clearly catching feelings for you," I exclaimed as we walked into the bathroom.

"Exactly, he has a girlfriend! I am not a mistress so nothing is gonna happen even if he does catch feelings. What does that even mean, 'catch feelings'? It is such an awkward phrase," she stated, trying to change the subject.

"I don't know. Maybe you let feelings go when you flirt with someone and if they like you, then they catch them," I offered, trying to figure out where that phrase even came from.

"That makes no sense. I think you've had too many beers," she claimed as she was washing her hands.

"Well, I tried. You know what I mean. Let's head back downstairs," I said, and we went back to the basement. We found Kyle and Jason hanging out on the outskirts of the dance floor and headed over to join them. I saw Trent drinking with a couple of his frat brothers and decided not to bother him. If he was interested, then he could come over here. I was also slightly concerned with my self-control.

***

We hung out with the guys for a while. The four of us danced together and we were really getting into it. Kyle was pretty drunk but he was such an animated drunk. He took my hand and spun me around, then dipped me. He was adorable. We were having a lot of fun together but I knew Kyle and I would end up as nothing more than friends.

About an hour later, we decided to call it a night. I looked at Trent and we made eye contact. I tipped my head up, indicating we were heading upstairs. He nodded and shook hands with one of his friends then followed us upstairs. He said bye to Kyle, Jason, and Annabelle, then took my hand. He walked us outside and pulled me behind a tree. We were generally out of sight.

"I'm glad you came tonight," he whispered as he

wrapped his arms around my waist again.

"I am too. It was fun," I said as I stepped forward and leaned into him. I took a deep breath and inhaled his scent. It was like ocean air. It was amazing that he could still smell so good even after being in the equivalent of a men's locker room for hours.

"I think so too." He reached up and cupped my face, kissing me again. Unlike before, this was a softer kiss. It was more sweet and tender, with a touch of something else. Maybe those feelings were flying around here too. I pressed into him a little. The soft kiss was nice but it was not what I wanted. I kissed him with more intensity and he responded heavily.

His hands slid down to my butt and he gave it a little squeeze. I slipped my hand around his head and slid my fingers through his hair, then gave a little tug. A low growl escaped his mouth and he picked me up and pushed me against the tree.

I wrapped my legs around his waist and held on tight. His hand found my breast again and he squeezed, feeling around for my nipple. Once his fingers found it, he began to lightly twist it through my dress. I moaned in return.

I leaned my head back against the tree and squeezed my legs tighter around his middle as I was beginning to fall apart. My thoughts had all disappeared and were replaced by a carnal need. It was lucky that Jason honked the horn of his car when he did or I didn't know how far this would have gone, especially since I was wearing a dress.

The horn brought us back to reality and Trent

looked at me and smiled. He kissed my neck again and then placed me on the ground. Even though my friends could not see us, I was sure they had a pretty good idea what was keeping us and I quickly yanked my skirt down. I said goodbye to Trent and ran off to the car.

***

I listened to relentless teasing for the fifteen-minute drive home before the boys dropped us off in front of the dorm. When I got back to my room, Lola was sleeping. I hopped in the shower to wash off the grime of the frat house and then climbed into bed. I went to set an alarm on my phone since I had to get up tomorrow and finish some homework and noticed that Trent texted me.

Trent: Hope you made it back safe :)

I smiled and responded.

Me: I did. U?

Trent: I'm staying the night at the house but u'll b in my dreams tonight.

I giggled, loving the ridiculously cheesy lines he used.

Me: Wat kind of dreams?

Trent: The kind that make me wish I wasn't

alone.

Me: Maybe next time you won't be.

Trent: Don't tease me.

Me: ;) Good night.

I fell asleep with a smile on my face and blood rushing to my core. If I was lucky, I'd have some good dreams tonight too.

Chapter 7

Sunday was a pretty productive day. I finished my project for Berneli and worked on the rest of my homework. I went over to Annabelle's room and we attempted to get some math done. I struggled with statistics and she basically ignored her calculus homework.

We both decided there was no hope and headed over to Kyle and Jason's to watch more of our show. The four of us hung out for the rest of the night and then we all headed to bed. I was returning from my shower when Lola climbed into her bed. It had been a little while since we hung out, so we decided we would catch up over lunch tomorrow.

***

I woke up early Monday because I wanted to go over my presentation for Berneli. I changed a few things and practiced the speech in the bathroom mirror twice. Then I threw some gel in my hair to

122

accentuate my curls and pulled the front into a little bump on the top of my head. I was in the middle of my make-up when Annabelle walked in.

"Ready for your presentation?" she asked as she started to brush her teeth.

"As ready as I can be. I went over it a couple of times and switched some things around. I feel like if I go over it again, I'll probably second guess myself and freak out. It just needs to be left alone."

"What about Berneli?" she asked, and I dropped my mascara brush into the sink.

"What about him?" I hadn't told her anything about what had happened between us, but could she know? Did other people know? No, there was no way for them to know. I was just being paranoid. I took a breath and tried to stay calm.

"Is he a hard professor? I mean, it's kind of early for you to have a presentation already," she commented innocently enough. In the mirror, I saw her watching me. She knew. I didn't know to what extent she knew, but she definitely knew something.

"I don't know. He just gets passionate when it comes to books. I guess we are gonna have to wait and see," I said, and realized passionate was the wrong word to use. The image of his lips on mine flashed through my mind and I watched a blush creep up my face.

I added a little extra foundation in case I blushed in class. There was no way I could think of him like that while going over *Pride and Prejudice*. It would completely distract me, and I needed to prove that he would not phase me.

Furthermore, we couldn't have a relationship

anyway. I needed to just get over it and focus on Trent. He was real, sexy, and available. Plus, he had already proven that he could be just as passionate. Trent was just as good as Berneli, right? I repeated that a couple of times hoping that one day I would believe it.

Annabelle and I decided we would meet up in about ten minutes and head to class together. I spent a little extra time getting dressed. I put a light green blouse on with a tan skirt that went about three quarters of the way down my thigh. I also added tan wedges. I didn't want to look like I was going to a job interview but I wanted to look nice.

Annabelle had an issue with being late. She wanted to sit in the back of the class where she could avoid being called on. As a result of this, Annabelle liked to get to class fifteen to twenty minutes early. This was good the first week of class since I didn't really know where I was going, but now that I did, I was the first person there.

I put my bag down next to my desk and got my notes out. I had just started going over them when I noticed Berneli walk in. Honestly, it was more like I felt him since I kept my eyes focused on my notes and pretended not to notice him. But he sure did notice me. He walked up to my desk and stood there.

"Last minute preparations? I would have thought that you would be ready. Did you party too much over the weekend?" he asked, and my heart stopped. Did he know about Trent? I looked up at him and noticed his eyes revealed he was joking.

"I did go out actually, but don't worry, I was just

rereading my notes. I am prepared," I insisted with some initiative.

I watched the struggle in his eyes as he seemed desperate to know what I did over the weekend, and dealing with time and place.

"I guess we will see. I'm prepared to give you a good run for your money today," he said, and winked at me. Then Berneli turned around and walked toward the lecture stand.

"What do you mean run for my money?" I demanded as I got up and followed him. With my wedges, my head only reached his chin so I had to look up to give him the evil eye. This man liked to play with me and I was beginning to lose my patience.

"You're pretty easy to read, remember? I already know what points you are going to make and I intend to counter them," he informed me, and then leaned in close. "Mostly, I just want to see you squirm. Maybe I need to remind you the difference between a boy and a man."

My heart began to race. "I think I have it figured out. Thanks for the offer though," I said sweetly, and walked back to my desk. If he wanted to play with me, I wasn't going to sit by and give up.

Berneli went in front of the room and brought the class to order.

"So, we are going to start with Violet Carrington's discussion on *Pride and Prejudice*. Violet, if you could please come to the front of the room." Berneli looked at me and gestured for me to come stand next to him.

I took a deep breath and grabbed my notes.

When I got to Berneli's side, he smiled and then went to sit at my desk. I began to recite my notes, which discussed the great love Darcy and Elizabeth shared, when I looked at Berneli. He was smiling back at me but it was not an innocent smile. It was devious and sexy as hell. I knew he was going to tear apart everything I had to say. I continued with my notes and prepared for the worst.

Once I finished my presentation, Berneli asked the class for comments or discussions. As in any good college class, no one wanted to be the first to comment so there were no hands in the air.

I swallowed harshly. This was kind of embarrassing. I was just standing in front of the class with everyone staring at me and it was dead silent. Then my eyes fell on Berneli. He was wearing that devious smile again and I just had to smile back. He set me up knowing this was probably going to happen.

"So, Miss Carrington, what would you say to people who claimed Darcy was just looking for a trophy wife and Elizabeth happened to fit the bill?" Berneli finally asked.

"I would say that he would have married Jane. Elizabeth wasn't known for her beauty like Jane was and she wasn't as easy as Lydia. Darcy was worth a lot more than Bingley, and if he wanted a trophy wife, it would have been a lot easier to get one. But he didn't. In fact, I don't believe he was even looking for a bride. The only woman he danced with, other than Bingley's sister, was Elizabeth. Why would he choose someone who was that difficult if he was just looking for a pretty girl?" I asked in retaliation. I looked around and someone in the second row raised her hand.

"Do you think he was just interested in the chase?" she asked.

"I think at first, part of what intrigued him about Elizabeth was the chase. Then she shut down his first proposal. This would have crushed his pride. Then he protected her sister's reputation and went out of his way to help Jane and Bingley. There was no promise of a relationship or a marriage if he helped her. He did it because he wanted to see her happy. This is the important key in their relationship. The chase was over and he still wanted to be there for her." I felt some relief that someone was interested in what I was saying, or at least was pretending to be.

A few other students asked some questions and the discussion continued for another ten minutes, but Berneli was not done. I started to relax a little as we fell into a smooth debate.

"I happen to think Elizabeth was a gold digger," Berneli countered as he crossed his arms in front of him. My mouth fell open. He was bad mouthing my girl Lizzie and I was not going to tolerate it.

"Then she would have accepted his first proposal," I said, mentioning this scene again.

"How do you know she wasn't playing hard to get?"

"A woman who knows what she wants doesn't need to play hard to get. That is a game for a confused little girl. Any man who thinks a woman is playing hard to get is simply trying to ignore the fact that she is, as the movie says, just not that into him," I said, smiling pleasantly back at him.

"I will keep that in mind," he said after a few seconds. Berneli stared at me for a second longer and I felt a chill creep up my spine. It was almost as if I could see the wheels in his head turning. I was going to pay for that last comment. I returned to my seat and Berneli started his discussion for the day.

***

I tried to take notes but really I was just relieved that it was over.

Berneli wrapped the class up and another student was picked to do the discussion on Wednesday. I was packing my books up to leave when Berneli asked me to stay so that he could give me some feedback on the project. We waited for everyone to file out of the class.

"We have got to stop meeting like this. People will start to talk," I said, trying to lighten the mood.

"And what would they say?"

"That I'm banging the professor for an A."

"After that presentation, no one would question that." Berneli walked over to my desk and handed me a sheet of paper. It was my rubric for the assignment. I got a perfect score.

"Did you go easy on me? I really wanted to earn this grade," I said, looking at him disappointedly.

He sat down on the special desk next to me and smiled. "No, you had a well thought out project. There were questions that you answered with proof from the text and you lasted the appropriate amount of time," he said, pointing to the rubric. "I didn't need to go easy on you."

"Really?" I asked, and I couldn't keep the smile off my face. I was proud of the grade.

"Of course. I am grateful you were willing to go first. I don't know any other student who would have done as well. I didn't want the whole class to be afraid of the project," he said, and then looked deep into my eyes. I could feel my defenses slipping and quickly put them back up. I was done with this game.

"No! I am walking out the door now. We are not going to keep doing this," I insisted as I grabbed my bag and headed to the door. I was not going to be the student he fooled around with after class. He just gave me a perfect score. It was quite clear he wanted a thank you.

"What? I just looked at you," he insisted as he quickly got up and blocked my path.

"It was the way you looked at me. You looked at me that way last week and we almost got caught making out by that teacher. Look, we both know this is a bad idea, so why are you pushing it?" I asked as I looked up at him. I wanted him to see my frustration.

He ran his fingers through his luscious hair and looked down at me. "I can't help it but you're right. This is probably a terrible idea. But aren't the worst ideas the most fun?" That dangerous smirk was back and it almost worked.

I closed my eyes and took a deep breath. "Nope, I can't do this," I said, and rushed to the door.

"You aren't playing hard to get, are you?"

I was about to turn the handle. I whipped back

around and looked at him. "Honey, if I wanted you, it would only be too easy to take you," I said before raising my eyebrows at him in an *I told you* manner. I ran out the door before he could respond and call my bluff. Who was I kidding? I was just a confused little girl.

I needed to focus on making it work with Trent. There was the possibility of a future with him. Besides, Berneli was leaving at the end of the year. I headed to the cafeteria to meet up with Lola, mind set on Trent.

***

I told her all about the party and my time with Trent. She was glad the dress worked and claimed responsibility for my success. I asked her how she was doing since the accident and the incident with Tyler.

"I took him back," she confessed, trying not to look guilty.

"What?"

"Well, after the fight, he realized Katie was crazy and he wanted me back. The two of us have so much history that I couldn't say no."

"Aren't you concerned? Wasn't he a little rough with you?" I was still trying to control the shock. But it was a mess. How could you take a guy back after he hit you?

"Well, kind of. He was the one who pushed me. But he was just trying to protect me from Katie. I had hit her and he didn't want her to retaliate so he pushed me out of the way. He promised that he hadn't meant to do it that hard and the whole thing just kind of spiraled out of control," she said, defending him.

"Wasn't the push the reason you ended up in the hospital?"

"Yes, but he didn't mean it," Lola insisted.

"But, Lola…" I tried to argue but she quickly cut me off.

"I don't want to argue about it. I am choosing to be happy," she said sternly.

"Well, it's your choice. Just please be careful," I urged.

"He won't hurt me again," Lola said, but she seemed to be trying to convince herself more than me. We spent the rest of lunch talking about superficial things. It seemed to me that she had shut me out since I had not agreed with her. I hoped this wouldn't be the end to what could have been a real friendship.

***

I had my second class of the day later and that was pretty uneventful. Annabelle, Jason, Kyle, and I were heading to the cafeteria when I heard my name. I turned around and smiled. It was Trent. He walked over to me and told my friends I would meet them inside. I was beginning to wonder why he always found me at the cafeteria. Maybe it had something to do with how much twenty-year-old guys ate.

"Hey, babe, what's up?" Trent asked as he leaned in for a kiss. It was a light peck on the lips, but considering we were in the school hallway, I was not going to push it further.

"Not much. How are you?" I asked as we walked over to one of the sofas in the lobby.

"Better now that you're here," he cooed.

I blushed and rolled my eyes. "Is that the line you use on all the girls?" I asked, giving him a sassy look.

"Hey! I like that line. It's a good one," he said, pretending to look innocent and wounded. "Are you going to the EET meeting tomorrow?" He took my hand and kissed the knuckles lightly.

"Yeah, I think so, why?" I looked down at his hands. I remembered he played lacrosse, which probably explained why they were a little rough, but this seemed to make him even sexier. They were a mark of his manliness or something like that. I thought it was a feeling left over from our more primal times.

"I'm going to miss it. I have some Greek stuff to do since it is rush week and I didn't want you to think I was avoiding you or anything."

"Aww, thanks for the update," I said, trying not to sound disappointed. I had been looking forward to seeing him at the meeting.

"This is going to be a crazy week for me. We are going to have another party this weekend to celebrate rush week being over so you should come to that," he said, and leaned into my personal space.

"I wouldn't miss it," I said as I almost closed the gap.

He looked deep into my eyes and then kissed me again. It was still a light kiss but it meant something

132

different. It was a kiss you gave someone you cared about, or at least someone you were beginning to care about. The kiss was not filled with lust or desire, but pure joy. I kept my eyes closed for a second after we broke apart and when I opened them, I noticed that he was studying me.

"What? Do I have something on my face?" I quickly tried to wipe whatever it could be.

"No, you are just beautiful." He kissed me and then headed out of the cafeteria. I sat frozen in my seat for a minute. He really did always say the right thing. I had a nagging feeling in the back of my head that maybe it was an act but I quickly pushed that away. I was not going to overanalyze this. For once I was just going to take it one step at a time and see how it went. I stood up and went to meet my friends for dinner.

***

There was another guy at the table when I headed over there. I didn't know who he was but I thought I recognized him from the party. I sat down with my tray of food and nodded at everyone.

Kyle introduced their new friend. "This is Kenny, he lives on our floor and is probably going to rush with me so we've been hanging out. This is Violet."

"Weren't you the girl hookin' up with Trent at the party?" he asked, and my face turned bright red. Annabelle and Jason busted out laughing. Kyle, on the other hand, tried to hide his laughter but he was starting to snort a little. Kenny was a little bit taller than Kyle but not much, and he was pretty pale. He had light brown hair and small blue eyes. He was kind of attractive but I had seen better.

"I prefer Violet, but yeah. Trent and I have been seeing each other for the past week," I said, trying to maintain a little dignity. "He said they are having another party this weekend if you guys want to go again." I avoided looking at Kenny. I didn't want to invite him but I was not going to be blatantly rude.

"I'm down. Jason, do you mind driving again?" Kyle asked, getting excited.

"I can drive this time," Annabelle offered. I had a feeling she was looking for a reason not to drink.

"Cool. Sounds good to me," Jason said, and got up to throw his trash out.

"Do you think he is going to bring Janice?" I asked Kyle and Annabelle. I was going to continue to pretend Kenny was not there.

"Last time she said that parties are not her thing so I doubt she will come this time," Annabelle said, sounding a little too cheerful.

Jason sat back down and Kyle seemed to take it upon himself to ask.

"Are you going to bring Janice?" I got the distinct impression that Kyle was also not the biggest Janice fan. It just made me like Kyle more.

"I am going to ask her but I am pretty sure she won't come," he said, and got out his phone to text her.

"So what time should we meet up?" Kenny asked, inviting himself along. He was starting to get a little annoying. We made plans and then I headed out.

I had a little more homework to do so I headed back to my room, but Annabelle went over to Jason and Kyle's. I informed them that death would be imminent if they watched our show without me, but I had a feeling they did not find me as menacing as I would like to think. Kenny headed back to his dorm. As I was right outside my building, I ran into Lola.

"Hey, heading out?" I asked.

"Yeah, Tyler and I are going to go out for dinner," she said, looking a little smitten. I really hoped he was going to treat her right, but I had a really bad feeling.

"Well, have fun! Be careful," I warned, and waved goodbye.

She smiled and headed to her car. The bandage was off and she had covered the mark with make-up but it was still there. I hoped it would remind her to be a little wary of him.

***

It was nice to have the room to myself. I took my journal out and did some writing then started on my homework again. At around eleven, I was heading to bed when Lola came back. She looked really happy.

"Did you have fun?" I asked, trying to hold back a yawn.

"Yes! It was perfect and it actually isn't done yet. I'm going to go spend the night at his place. I just need to get a few things." She went to her dresser and grabbed something that looked a lot like a silky nightie.

"Go get him!"

She giggled and winked at me before heading back out.

I sighed and got up to turn the lights off. It had been a long time since I had gotten some. In high school, I had a boyfriend for two years and he was my first. I thought that I loved him and decided it was the right time. This was the boyfriend who cheated on me a couple of times, so it clearly was not.

I had learned to appreciate sex for what it was instead of what it should be. Just a good time between a guy and a girl. It was nice when there were feelings but they seemed to complicate everything. After Tommy, I had been with a few other guys from school but it was never poetic or like it was portrayed in the romance novels I devoured. I just felt even lonelier.

One day, I knew I would find a guy to make love to instead of one just for sex. Who knew, maybe I already had. This thought left me with some hope as I drifted off to sleep.

When I woke up the next day, Lola was still not there, so I supposed the night went pretty well. I was struggling getting ready for class today and I did not feel like dressing up or even attempting to put make-up on. Besides, Trent wasn't going to be at the EET meeting anyway.

I threw my hair up in a ponytail and slipped into a pair of jeans with a red tank top. I grabbed a cardigan to throw over it in case it got cold and headed out the door with my backpack. I knocked on Annabelle's door and heard a scream of frustration. I was going to knock again but decided to wait for her to open the door.

"I hate calculus," she whined as she greeted me at her door.

"Ah! Still couldn't figure out that homework?"

"Not even close. I'm going to fail this class and then get kicked out of school and end up a bum on the street."

"I think that may be a little dramatic. You won't end up on the street. You could always sleep on my floor." I offered, trying to make her laugh.

"Thank you. It relaxes me to have a Plan B."

***

We parted ways and headed to our separate classes. Luckily, I had sort of figured out my statistics homework so I was not as screwed as Annabelle. At least so I thought. The problem with math classes was once you figured out how to do one equation, the professor introduced another one. The new one was usually even more confusing than the first one. As a result, I was still confused.

I left this class and headed to the cafeteria for an early lunch with Jason and Annabelle. The two of them were walking into the cafeteria together just ahead of me. I caught up and we went to our table near the windows with our food.

The three of us were talking about classes when Kenny set his tray down next to us. Apparently, he was our new friend.

"Who is having trouble with math?" he asked

before starting to eat.

"Annabelle. Apparently, failing this class will lead to her being homeless," I said, mocking her.

"I just don't get it, and I'm too high maintenance to be homeless." She dropped her head in her hands and sighed.

"I'm actually great at math," Kenny informed us, beaming with a sense of pride.

"Maybe you can help Annabelle, then?" I asked, hoping he would say yes. Annabelle was beginning to really worry.

"Yeah, no problem. When do you want to meet up?" Kenny asked, fiddling with his phone. He wouldn't even look at her.

"I have to go to the EET meeting tonight, so maybe after. Around seven," she begged him.

"Sure." They exchanged numbers. "I'll head over to your dorm building around then."

"Great," she said, and smiled shyly at him.

He looked up at her from his phone, as if noticing her for the first time, and returned the smile, staring at her for just a few moments longer.

I couldn't help but notice the way they kept sneaking looks at each other while we finished eating. A little jitter went through my system and I hoped this could be the start of something amazing between the two of them. While Jason and Annabelle would have made a cute couple, she couldn't wait forever just in case he and Janice broke up.

***

After our second class, Annabelle and I met up to head to EET for her executive board meeting. As we turned down the hallway, I saw Trent. He was about to head out but stopped when he saw me.

"Hey, I thought you weren't able to make the meeting." I couldn't help but smile up at him as he greeted me with a sweet kiss on the cheek. It was nice that he was happy to see him.

"Yeah, I still can't, but I wanted to drop off my report so Clarissa could read it," he said as we walked around the corner toward the classroom. Annabelle went inside and left us in the hallway. Trent then pulled me in for a kiss. It was a long kiss, and this time I could feel his desire, and I was eager to match it. But it ended too soon.

"Sorry, I need to go. But I will see you this weekend, right?" He looked at me hopefully.

"I think I can squeeze you in my busy calendar."

"Oh, well, then let me give you some more motivation," he said, and kissed me again. I felt a zing from the tips of my toes all the way to my head as his strong hands pressed me against him. He broke away and walked off but I was left standing there with a goofy smile on my face.

"Really, so you'd rather play games with Trent?" Berneli asked, and I jumped about three feet in the air.

I turned around and he was leaning against the wall with his hair slightly tousled and eyes staring at me through his thick frames. He looked so sexy. What I had been feeling earlier for Trent seemed to trickle out of me. I shook my head and refused to think about him like that. Kissing Trent had felt good and I wanted to remember that.

"I'm not playing games. I'm actually interested in him, and in case you missed it, he is interested in me too." I gave him a combative look with my eyebrows raised high and my lips pursed.

"Oh yeah? What's the difference between us? I fancy you and clearly you fancy me back."

"That's a little arrogant, isn't it? To assume that I fancy you," I said, and put air quotes around the word *fancy*.

"It's cute really. Watching you try to pretend that this kid can make you feel half as good as I can with one touch." Berneli smirked and started walking toward me.

"Honey, let's not forget. I was just in his arms and not yours. It looks to me like he is making me feel an awful lot better than you are," I said, and walked around him to the computer lab. I was proud of myself. He deserved to be put in his place every now and then. I sat down in front of a computer to try to convince myself that Berneli wasn't right.

***

It wasn't long before Annabelle came to get me.

"Hey, anything interesting going on today?" I asked her, referring to what they discussed as an executive board, as we walked into the large classroom for the regular meeting.

"Not much. We are assigning jobs for the comedy event and that's really it for the meeting. But on a side note, Nat has a huge crush on Berneli. She always sits next to him and agrees with everything he says. She even laughs at his horrible dry humor. It's getting pretty pathetic." As she said this, I looked over at Berneli, and Nat was right there talking to him.

She appeared to be hanging on his every word. Every few seconds, she would touch his shoulder or his forearm. I had no reason to be pissed but I felt rage begin to flow through my body when he looked down at her and smiled.

"I have a feeling he is not interested in her," I said, trying not to spit fire.

"Yeah, no kidding," Annabelle said, and looked at me, that knowing look back on her face.

We headed to our seats and I swallowed the anger that was trying to eat me up inside. I felt a sting of guilt since I was not being completely honest with her. However, I still felt it was best to keep this a secret. Besides, it was over, right?

"Are there any good jobs? Like, which one should I pick?" I needed to change the subject to calm down.

"Uh, there is a position where you get the rider ready for the bands and comedians. If you do that, then you are guaranteed to meet them." She was skimming her list of jobs.

"What is a rider? It sounds dirty." I giggled but it came out a little forced. I couldn't look away from Berneli and Nat.

"A rider is what the talent wants in their dressing room. Like ninety-nine green M&M's or thirty-one wash cloths made of Egyptian cotton. Stuff like that. Since you are getting what they need, you will have a lot of contact with them and their manager. It is a pretty cool job. Trent was supposed to do it alone but he said that he wants someone to help him in case he can't do it all by himself."

"Oh, pick me," I said pretty eagerly. It would be nice to work with Trent on this since, so far, we really only saw each other at the parties and in the hall.

"Yeah, I figured. Trent actually suggested you so your name is already on the list for that job. I just figured I would make sure you wanted to do this."

I started blushing. "Really? That's nice." Trent wanted to work with me. It boosted my ego just a little bit and I couldn't contain how giddy I was feeling. He really wanted to spend more time with me. This thing between us, it really was going to work.

Just then, Annabelle was called over by Nat. I got up and went to sit down near Jason. We started talking about our crime show until Annabelle came over to us and gave me a sad look.

"Don't get mad," she warned.

"Why?" My heart started to race and I could hear it thumping in my ears. Did Nat know about Berneli and me? Was she jealous? Was I getting kicked out of the club?

"Berneli decided that the rider was too important to leave to Trent since his availability is not always reliable. So…he will be taking over the job of sorting out the rider," she said, and then glanced at Berneli.

"That's fine. Trent and I can find another job. Let me see the list." I looked over at her desk for the list of jobs.

"No, Berneli still wants you on the rider with him. He said he has you in one of his classes so he kind of knows you."

"That asshole," I said. That was meant to be in my head but it just came out.

"Well, that escalated quickly," Annabelle said, giving me a confused look. "Really, he doesn't seem that bad during our meetings. Is something else going on?"

I looked at her and realized I really did need to tell her soon. "Oh, no, I just wanted to work with Trent," I murmured, avoiding eye contact with Annabelle. I gave Berneli an evil look. He smiled in that scheming way back at me and beckoned me to come over. Clarissa was calling the meeting to order and Annabelle made her way to the front of the class.

I took a deep breath and went to see Berneli.

"You play dirty," I growled to him under my breath.

"Oh, you have no idea how dirty I can be," he whispered so only I could hear.

"Don't try to flirt with me."

"It just comes naturally. Besides, you look sexy when you're mad." He gave me a dirty smolder, squinting his eyes at me slightly. I fought to keep my angry expression as my knees weakened a little. "Come on, we need to go over how to do a rider," he said, and walked out the door.

I followed close behind but then went back in the class—I'd left my bag on my desk. Jason was still sitting there and he looked at me, confused.

"Where are you going?" He furrowed his brow.

143

"Berneli wants to go over stuff for the rider. I'll catch up with you guys after the meeting for dinner," I said as I headed back out the door.

***

"Is that part of your game? Making me wait?"

He was beginning to really frustrate me. Everything he said couldn't be sexual. I liked innuendos but his were just constant. Damn, where was his off switch?

"You're going to be waiting a long time for me, buddy," I said as we entered the EET office. "I could be happy with Trent."

"Why be just happy?"

We looked at each other, seemingly trying to decide which way this interaction was going to go. I decided to stick to my guns.

"Oh, so we are actually going to work today?" I asked, and sat down in the chair next to him.

"I assumed so. Is there something you would prefer to do?" He gave me an innocent smile but his eyes gave him away. From behind his glasses, the look he was giving me was dangerous. It made my stomach turn and my toes curl in my shoes, and not necessarily in a bad way.

"Nope, work sounds good to me," I said, trying to ignore the flames he was igniting inside me.

Surprisingly enough, we did work for about half an hour. He went over example riders he had worked on in the past and how something like Diet Coke versus Diet Pepsi could really create problems.

"Celebrities have these riders for two reasons. The first one is because they can. They can ask for these ridiculous things because we will provide them. It makes them feel even more popular and loved. The second reason is superstition. There are a lot of celebrities who believe that if they don't have certain rituals before a show, it will be a disaster. So even though it sounds pathetic that they can only eat peanut M&M's in child size and not king size, maybe it has some significance to them that you don't know about," Berneli explained to me. He ran his fingers through his hair and took his glasses off. He was beginning to look tired.

"You okay?"

"Yeah, I have just had some long nights working on my second textbook," he said, and stretched.

"You could give us less homework. I'm sure that would give you plenty of time to work on it," I suggested, trying to make him laugh. It worked. His laugh was deep and shook his whole body. It was a pleasant sound. I was surprised, but the fact that I got him to laugh sent a surge of pride through me. It felt powerful.

"No, I think you all are getting off pretty easily. Besides, I think you kind of enjoyed the project. I could see you getting fired up and excited. Seeing the passion in your eyes is exhilarating. I forgot almost all of the arguments I had set up to put you in your place," he said as he inched the chair closer to me.

"I think you made up for it at the end." I couldn't move. My eyes were fixed on his and I was trapped. Trapped by my desire to feel his lips on mine, my need to feel his strong hands caressing my body, and my fear of what would happen if I acted upon any of these feelings.

"You mesmerized me," he whispered, and pulled my chair a little closer to him.

"We can't do this, Berneli," I begged softly.

"When it's just you and me, please call me David."

"David, we can't do this," I reiterated, trying hard to remember all the reasons why this was a bad idea.

"I've been waiting to hear my name on your lips." David leaned in and was now inches away from my face.

"You're my professor," I reminded him as my defenses were falling.

"You would get top marks in that class no matter who your professor was. I can put my personal life aside when I'm teaching. But once the clock says class is over, you are back at the forefront of my mind."

"You could get fired," I said as I closed my eyes. Looking at him was becoming a problem. He gazed at me as if I was the only thing holding him together. If it weren't for me, he'd fall apart.

"Let me worry about that," he said, and lifted my chin up toward his face.

I opened my eyes and inhaled deeply. "I could get kicked out of school."

"I would never let that happen. I can ensure we'll be careful," he promised.

I watched him, almost afraid to even breathe. Finally, he leaned in and kissed me.

Before I realized it, I was kissing him back. I was filled with a wanton need that I couldn't force down. I had been kidding myself when I said I felt something with Trent. It was nothing like the sensation that coursed through me when I was near David.

He pulled me up on my feet and wrapped his hands around the back of my neck and held me closer to him. I clung to his waist and felt the chiseled muscles of his back. They were even tauter than I remembered. David let go of the back of my neck and took my arms in his hands. He wrapped them around his neck and slipped his arms around my waist. All of this without breaking the kiss.

I was barely breathing just trying to keep up with the intensity and need in this kiss. Before I could suppress it, a moan escaped my lips and David took that as a green light to continue. He reached down and rested his hands on my butt. With both hands he squeezed and lifted me up in the air, placing me on the desk next to the computer. He leaned into me and moaned deeply. I wrapped my legs around his waist and gripped tightly. With one hand, he started at my knee and slid along my thigh up to my hip.

David then pushed me back a little bit on the desk so I was almost lying down. He was using the leverage to get a better grasp on my ass and I wasn't complaining.

I finally broke the kiss to get a deep breath. This didn't slow David down. He placed kisses down my neck and stopped at my collarbone. David started kissing around that spot he found in the classroom. The tension radiating from my core was becoming too much.

"David," I gasped, hoping he would get the hint that I had enough of this teasing game.

"Yes, Violet?"

He chuckled a little and with one hand he started to grope my breast. His other hand soon found the bottom of my tank top and he went up my belly slowly, finally settling over the top of my bra. Fortunately, the lace one I'd thrown on this morning had been the first one I grabbed. It could have been the sports bra if I had truly dressed the way I was feeling.

While his strong hand was massaging my breast, he was still kissing a circle around my collarbone. He reached up, leaving my breast for a moment, and pulled my ponytail holder out so my hair fell down my back.

"Your hair is so beautiful." David ran a hand through it and tugged a little. I gasped deeply and my head fell back.

Then it happened. He brought his hand back to my breast and took my nipple between two fingers, then tugged gently. David dipped his head and suckled at my collarbone and I completely fell apart. I let out a moan that was a lot louder than I meant it to be. He chuckled under his breath.

"Better keep it down, love. You don't want anyone to get jealous," he teased, and quickly kissed me again before I could give a smart-ass response. I reached up and pulled him by his tie so that he was pressed up against me as close as he could get. He growled and slid his other hand up my shirt and started to feel my other breast.

148

I broke the kiss and my head fell back again as I tried desperately to keep from moaning again. I bit my lip hard, trying to keep it inside, but I couldn't fight the sheer ecstasy that built up as he placed kisses down from my collarbone and then between my breasts. He let go of my breast and pulled my tank top down so that he had better access. He was kissing the side of one of my breasts and along the top of it while groping the other one. But it wasn't enough, I needed more.

David seemed to sense my distress and he reached up my arm and pulled the bra strap down. Again, I praised my luck that I was not wearing my sports bra because that would not have been possible, and damn, I needed it.

He cupped my bare breast with one hand and began placing light kisses all around it. David was not letting one inch of the breast go unkissed, except for, of course, my nipple.

He was doing everything he could to avoid it and I was going crazy. I arched my back to give him a better angle but he was still avoiding the one area I needed him to kiss most. Just as he inched closer to my nipple, he stopped and moved to the other side. He slid my other bra strap down and repeated the torture session.

It got to the point where I was going to explode with frustration. I grabbed him by the hair on the back of his neck and jerked his head up so that we were eye to eye.

"Teasing is not nice," I said through gritted teeth.

"You started this, teasing me about Trent and all that. I'm teaching you a lesson." He smiled and kissed the tip of my nose. I went to bite at him and he actually laughed. "I like it when you get feisty. It turns me on." He then kissed me hard on the lips.

I sat up so I was in a full sitting position. I reached down and started feeling around for his belt buckle. When I found it, I slowly, almost painfully slowly, began undoing it. I finally unhooked it and gradually began to slide the belt out of the loops. It fell on the floor and then I reached for the button on his slacks. I pretended to struggle with the button to create some drama for him. He needed to be punished for teasing me.

"Having some trouble down there, love?" he whispered breathlessly.

"No, just trying to prolong the tension," I teased in his ear, then nibbled a little. I heard a sharp intake of breath come from him and realized his ear must be his kryptonite. I began kissing around it, and nibbling every so often. I unbuttoned his slacks and went for the zipper. As I slid it down, I felt him. He was practically bursting and I needed to feel more of it. I skimmed my hand down his boxers and felt David shudder as I just grazed him.

We made eye contact and he glanced down with such longing that I was pushed to the edge. I reached down and clutched ahold of his shaft through the hole in his boxers. It was strong and very long. I was a little surprised at how big it was and the anticipation in my heart grew even more.

I slowly began to stroke him and his breathing picked up substantially. This didn't last long as he quickly pushed me down so that I was lying on the desk. I could no longer reach him and that was a little disappointing. At least it was until he wrapped his hands around my face and kissed me more passionately than anyone had ever done before. He let go and looked me dead in the eye.

"We cannot do this here," he said, but didn't move.

"You keep saying that and then continue to initiate this. Make up your mind, because I can't take it when you get me all worked up and then drop the ball," I complained, a little breathless. We stared at each other again, not moving. As we were inching closer to each other, my phone in the back pocket of my jeans went off.

"Divine intervention," he said, and climbed off of the desk.

I sat up and pulled it out of my pocket. Jason had texted asking when we were going to be done. I took a deep breath and then realized that my breasts were still hanging out of my tank top. I quickly shoved them back in and pulled my straps up. David smiled and looked down at my chest.

"Now that is a real shame," he said, and kind of licked his lips.

"Shut up," I said, blushing. "I have to go. I grabbed my bag and headed toward the door.

"I wish you didn't." David reached out and grabbed my hand. I looked back at him and took a deep breath.

"I know. I wish I didn't have to either," I said, and walked out the door. It was not easy but I was legitimately afraid of what would happen if I stayed in that office for a second more. I headed to the EET classroom to catch up with Jason and

Annabelle.

They were sitting on the table at the front of the class next to each other. I thought they were a little too close but hey, I clearly was not one to judge. When I entered the room, they both jumped up and looked at me.

"Hey, what took so long?" Annabelle asked me.

"Berneli is just really demanding," I said, trying to hide the blush creeping up my face.

"I bet," Annabelle said, but she gave me a suspicious look for what seemed like the hundredth time. "I have to get to dinner so that I can meet up with Kenny."

We all headed to the cafeteria.

***

After we finished eating, I was in my room writing in my journal, trying to figure out what my feelings were. When David held me and kissed me, my body felt alive. It felt right, and I knew he felt the same way. True, he hadn't said it, but somewhere deep inside of me, I was positive.

When I was with Trent, though, it was something real. He and I could walk down the hall together and gaze into each other's eyes in the lunch room. I got butterflies when I saw him and it felt amazing when I kissed him. Plus, he was available, and being with him was not against, like, fifty rules.

But the easy way wasn't always the best way. Then again, shouldn't it be easy when you're with the right person? Basically, I was really torn.

I was just finishing up my entry when there was

a pounding on my door. I got up and answered it. Annabelle was standing there and she looked panicked.

"Hi," I said when she didn't respond right away.

"Oh my gosh! You will not believe what just happened." She rushed into my room with her hands up in the air.

"You would be correct because I'm pretty sure you should be studying right now," I said as I climbed onto my bed and patted the spot next to me.

"I was studying with Kenny. He came to my room and we were studying and he explained it so well that I got it within, like, ten minutes. So we were just hanging out in my room and somehow started playing mercy."

"Wait, like, mercy the hand game where you try to hurt the other person?" I asked as I interrupted her. This was a weird story.

"Yeah, that game. And during the process of this game we somehow ended up on the bed and he was on top of me. Then he leaned in and kissed me."

My mouth fell open. "Shut up! He kissed you? Like French kiss, like a peck, like huge make-out session?"

"In between huge make-out session and French kiss. So, I pulled away 'cause I wasn't comfortable. I mean, this was my first kiss and he was pushing it real far. And when I stopped it, he asked what was wrong and I told him that it was my first kiss."

"Really, that was your first kiss?" I didn't know that about her.

"Yeah, but anyway, he looked deep into my eyes and asked, 'Why, you're so beautiful?' So I got really uncomfortable because no guy has said that to me before so I told him he had to go. He climbed off of me and went to leave. But then turned back around. You will never believe what he said. He asked me not to tell anyone. So, naturally, as soon as he left, I came over here to tell you."

"That's kind of an intense first kiss situation," I replied, still in shock.

"I know, right?"

"Wait, why were you in your room? I thought you would meet in the common area or somewhere public." I couldn't picture Annabelle inviting Kenny over to her room. Hell, she didn't want Jason or Kyle to hang out in there.

"I don't know. It just happened that way. It's not like I saw this going down."

"So why would he say not to tell anyone?" I asked, confused.

"I don't know. But, obviously, I was going to tell you," she said, and that made me feel like crap. She hooked up with Kenny, like, three minutes ago and here she was talking to me about it. Yet I had hooked up with David three times and she still had no idea. This was probably not the time to say something since it was her moment, but I decided then that I needed to find time to tell her.

"Well, did you like it?" I felt like this was an important question.

"I don't know. The whole thing took me by such surprise. I didn't know he found me attractive or anything. Did you pick up on anything?" she asked nervously.

"Um, after you guys exchanged numbers, I saw

him making eyes at you, but that's all," I said, feeling a little embarrassed. Maybe I missed something. I tried to think back to the couple of interactions the three of us had. I couldn't think of any other time, but we really didn't see him much. "I guess we'll see what happens this weekend at the party."

"Oh, I forgot he was going to that. I guess we will see." She looked hopeful and a little giddy. It was about time Jason got a little competition.

Chapter 8

When I woke up the next morning, Lola was still not there. I shot her a text just to make sure everything with her was going well and started to get dressed. I was halfway dressed when I realized I would be having class with Berneli this morning. I needed to look nice for him. I grabbed my black skinny jeans and put a purple off the shoulder blouse on. It accentuated the curves of my boobs perfectly, something I knew Berneli would appreciate.

I ran into the bathroom and started the make-up game. He had seen me yesterday with none on, but today, it would be on point. I didn't have time to straighten my hair so I used gel to make my waves behave. At the end of all that work, I looked pretty good. I grabbed my backpack and headed to class. I had tried to meet up with Annabelle but she had already left. Apparently, I was taking too long.

I walked into class about five minutes before it was supposed to start. David was there and so were a couple of other students. I didn't want to walk over to him since he was in deep conversation with one of my classmates. So I headed to my desk and sat down. I was getting my notebook out with my questions for today's discussion when I heard my name.

"Miss Carrington, can you come up here and pass these papers out regarding the first essay of the semester?" David, or rather Professor Berneli, asked me. I got up and headed to the front of the class. He handed me a stack of papers and then looked at me. "You look nice today. That color brings out your eyes," he whispered, and gave me a little wink.

I headed toward the other students to hand out the papers and attempted to calm the sexual need that was trying to pour out of me.

This class was helpful. For some reason, it gave me time to think about the two of us and what I wanted. I had no intention of almost hooking up with David in the middle of the classroom again. He kept starting something but never finishing it, and I was tired of that game.

If David wanted something to happen, then he was going to have to think of a new plan. As the class winded down, I packed up my books so that I could make a quick exit. I wasn't going to hang around after class. Besides, if we kept doing that, people were going to start asking questions.

***

I went to the snack shop to get a strudel and then headed to the library. I had a little extra time before my next class but I wasn't hungry enough for lunch. As I was looking into the book for the next discussion, I got a text from Trent.

Trent: Hey, I have some extra time. Wat are u up 2?

Me: Working on some homework in the library. U?

Trent: Hanging out in my Greek Council office. Wanna stop by?

Me: Sounds good.

He sent me the information for his office and I headed up. When I got there, he was engrossed in a phone call that did not appear to be going well. I decided it would be rude to stand there and listen but I didn't really want to interrupt him. So I went to the bathroom and checked on my hair and make-up.

As it was only about two hours since I originally did them, I still looked good. Nonetheless, I washed my hands and put a little extra water in my hair to reactivate the gel. Running out of things to do to kill time, I checked my phone, but had no new messages.

I remembered that I had texted Lola this morning and never heard back. I didn't want to sound like I was nagging her or anything but I made a note in my planner to make sure I checked in on her later tonight in case I didn't hear from her. I was sure she was fine, but after the incident with Tyler, I was a little jumpy.

Figuring I'd stalled enough, I went back to Trent's office and looked in the window. He was off the phone but still looking distraught. I knocked, and when he saw me in the window, any anguish he had initially shown on his face quickly dissipated and turned to pure joy.

I was sure something was still bothering him but it was nice to see that he was happy to see me. Trent stood up and let me in the office. When I walked in and placed my bag on the floor, he gave me a light kiss on the lips.

"Aww, I needed that," he assured me. I smiled and gave him a second kiss. It lingered a bit longer but the sweet sentiment was still there.

"What's going on?"

"Just Greek stuff. Rush week is always crazy and there is always somebody complaining about something. When you're president of Greek Council, you have to listen to the nonsense," he said, brushing off the incident. I didn't want to push if he was not willing to talk about it.

"Okay," I said, and lightly brushed the hair out of his eye. Except for the lunch, we hadn't really hung out without hooking up. I was a little nervous. There was an awkward pause where neither of us said anything. Luckily, Trent found something to say. Unfortunately, it was the wrong thing to say.

"So I heard Berneli stole my rider." He laughed and I tried to join him, but mine clearly sounded forced.

"Yeah, apparently he thinks it's a big deal and

you can't handle it. I just think he wants to meet with the comedienne." I was hoping to keep the conversation light.

"Makes sense. I mean, he has a point, things have become so crazy that I don't know if I would have had the time." He shook his head and looked a little disappointed for a second. Just as fast as it crossed his face, it was gone. "Are you excited about the show?" he asked, looking at me with his bright eyes.

"I actually have never heard of her. I looked up some of the other comedians but I didn't get to her."

"Oh, she's hysterical." He turned the computer on and we spent the next half hour watching some of her shows on the internet.

Turned out, she was pretty funny. But it was even better to just hang out with Trent. We had the same sense of humor and laughed at all of the same jokes. I was really starting to like him. Before I said goodbye and headed to my next class, Trent took my head in his hands and gave me a long and meaningful kiss. Once the kiss ended and I opened my eyes, the look on Trent's face was so beautiful and pure. It made me a little weak in the knees. I left the office on cloud nine, thoughts of Berneli long forgotten.

***

The rest of the week went by with little commotion. Trent was completely overwhelmed with Greek week so I was unable to see him. He did text me occasionally though. Some of the texts said how much he missed me or how excited he was to see me at the party. Then some text messages were a little on the dirtier side. They were intense enough to make my mother blush from head to toe and I liked them the most.

Things with Lola were going well. She and Tyler were still going strong and she spent most of her time at his dorm. Apparently, he had a single. We managed to catch up for lunch and dinner a couple of times.

Kenny seemed to be busy when we met up for meals or hung out so Annabelle didn't get to see him. This seemed weird to me because we couldn't get rid of him before. I had a bad feeling about him but Annabelle didn't want to listen.

But then again, I didn't have a lot of room to talk. I hadn't seen Berneli either. Well, I hadn't seen him outside of class. Even then, I walked into class and then walked out. There was no funny business. This was probably for the best since my feelings for Trent were growing and I needed to try to make that work.

Saturday finally came, so I slept in late and worked on a little homework. Eventually, I met up with Annabelle for dinner. Jason was going to spend a couple of hours with Janice before the party, so Annabelle decided to spend the night getting ready and watching reality TV.

I curled Annabelle's hair and she let me do her make-up. Of course, that lasted a matter of five minutes before she washed it off and did it again herself. Apparently, my toned down version of make-up was still too much for her. I shook my head and started my own make-up game. After that I straightened my hair while Annabelle changed her outfit five times.

She maintained that she hated her legs so she refused to wear a skirt or a dress. I insisted she looked great but I was overruled. Finally, she settled on a blue one-shouldered top with dark skinny jeans. She slipped on blue sandals and some layered costume jewelry. She topped the look off with a white sweater as she wouldn't leave the house without some kind of jacket.

"You look amazing! Kenny will be impressed."

"You don't think it's too much?" she asked for the fifth time.

"If you change again, I will lock you out of your room," I informed her, trying not to sound irritated.

"Okay! I'm done." She grabbed her keys and I followed her outside to the car. I was wearing a grey blouse with some amazing sequins and a tight black skirt. Annabelle suggested I wear heels or at least platform sandals but I decided to stick with the flats again. I planned on doing a lot of dancing.

Jason, Kyle, and Kenny were all hanging out near their dorm. Kyle and Kenny appeared to have prepared for the party a little differently than Annabelle and I. They climbed into the car laughing hysterically. They were a little tipsy, and Annabelle was pissed.

"If either of you throw up in my car, I will pull it over, drag you out into the street, and then murder you," Annabelle warned.

"Relax! We're not that drunk yet," Kyle said, laughing. The two of them continued to carry on and even though I found it quite funny, Annabelle didn't. By the time we got to the party, I was slightly concerned she was going to be homicidal. The boys barreled out of the back and headed into the party. Annabelle and I did a quick make-up check and then followed behind them.

"Well, at least it wasn't awkward with Kenny," I offered, trying not to laugh.

Annabelle gave me a dirty look as we headed into the living room where the guys were. Kenny and Kyle already had more drinks in their hands.

I looked a bit closer at Kenny and noticed he was watching Annabelle. She had gone over to talk to Jason near the couch. Kenny was talking with a couple other guys but he was completely focused on her. I smiled. It was nice to see that he seemed to still be interested. Kyle realized I was looking in that direction and called me over. I smiled and walked over to him.

"Violet, beer or jungle juice?" He pointed behind him to the keg or a dark blue liquid in what appeared to be a sports drink cooler. It looked even worse than the purple gunk from last week.

"Beer, please!"

"One beer coming up!" He pumped the keg for me and handed me the beer with an overdramatic flourish. Then he introduced me to the guys he was talking to. Apparently, these were the guys rushing Trent's fraternity. I hung out with them for another ten minutes or so until I saw Trent enter the room.

His eyes found mine almost instantly and a huge smile spread across his face. I felt myself start to blush and I headed over to where he was standing.

Trent leaned down and gave me a big kiss. He smelled of straight liquor and I backed away a little. I was beginning to realize that alcohol was one of his most popular colognes, and I was not a fan.

"When did you get here?" he asked, draping his arm around my shoulders.

"Like fifteen minutes ago. I met your new members." I tried to smile up at him but I noticed Trent was leaning on me a little more than normal. I got the slight impression he was having difficulty standing up on his own. He was clearly already drunk.

"Oh good. They're some good guys." He pointed at one of the guys and whispered in my ear, "That is Mat and he's going to be my little. But keep it a secret. He doesn't know it yet." He brought his finger to his lips and made a shushing sound.

"Your secret is safe with me," I said, and winked at him.

"That's my girl." Trent leaned down and kissed me hard. This kiss was wet and sloppy. I was not impressed with this version of Trent. But he'd had a crazy week so maybe things would be better if we hung out during the week or at least not at a party.

"So, I guess you started drinking early?" I asked, breaking the kiss.

"It's been a stressful week so some of the guys and I started pretty early."

We headed downstairs to start dancing but my Spidey Senses were tingling.

I looked over to the dance floor and couldn't believe what I saw. Annabelle and Kenny were kissing in the corner. I couldn't keep the smile off

164

my face. Good for Annabelle.

Trent finished his drink and we both headed onto the dance floor. I didn't want to crowd Annabelle so we went to the other side of the room. But when I passed her, I saw Kenny was whispering in her ear. She looked really happy. I smiled to myself and returned my attention to Trent.

***

After about half an hour of dancing, I was hot. I told Trent I needed to step outside for a few minutes. He offered to go with me, but then I saw Jason sitting on the deck by himself so I told him I was fine. I sat down on the step next to Jason and looked at him, shoulders slouched and an untouched drink next to him.

"You okay?" I gave his shoulder a slight shove and smiled when he looked up at me.

"Yeah, I'm just bored. Kyle is off with some of the brothers smoking pot, and that's not really my thing so I came out here for a little air."

"Yeah, and I guess Annabelle is a little busy," I said, smiling. Then I looked at his face. He looked devastated. Apparently, that was why he was upset. I instantly felt terrible. I remembered that Annabelle never told him about the kiss with Kenny. This probably completely blindsided him.

"I didn't see that one coming. I didn't even realize she liked him." He took a deep sip of water and I decided to break girl code. I told him about the little study/make-out session.

"What! Why did no one tell me?" He was

exasperated and rubbed his face.

"It was not my story to tell." I shrugged and hoped Annabelle wouldn't kill me when she found out that I told him. It was not my place to say anything and I felt guilty.

"I don't think he is a good fit for her." Jason crossed his arms and his leg started bouncing. I had a pretty good idea why he didn't think Kenny was a good fit for her but I wasn't going to bring it up just yet.

"Yeah, I'm not his biggest fan. I have a bad feeling about him too, but she seems to be happy." We sat there for a little bit longer in silence.

"Well, I guess we should probably head back into the party and watch out for her. Plus, I should probably check to make sure Kyle is still upright." We both laughed but it was definitely forced.

I let him lead the way and he opened the door for me. I smiled and walked in. We both headed downstairs to the dance floor. Trent was no longer there but Kyle was. He was playing beer pong with Mat while Annabelle and Kenny were watching nearby. Kenny had his arm wrapped around Annabelle's stomach and kept leaning in to whisper things in her ear.

Jason seemed to tense instantly but he didn't say anything. I asked him if he wanted a beer but he declined. I went over to the keg and convinced one of the new members to pump me a beer. The game lasted an unbearably long time. Both teams were pretty drunk so they were not even close to making the cups.

Annabelle and I decided we were ready to leave

after this game ended. I went over to talk to Kyle and let him know. That was when I saw it.

Trent was on the dance floor with another girl. He was kissing her neck and his hands were all over her. She had long black hair but even longer legs. They didn't look good together but I may have been a little biased. My face dropped when they turned slightly. I got a good look at her and saw that it was his ex-girlfriend. I remembered her from the social media stalking. Kyle noticed my face and followed my gaze.

He cursed and looked back at me. "You okay?"

"Yeah, I mean, we never said we were exclusive or anything." I was trying to ignore the knot in the pit of my stomach. After all, I had done far worse with David, so I really didn't have any right to be jealous. But I was not about to tell him that. Kyle leaned over to one of the brothers and started talking to him.

"So, that is actually his ex-girlfriend." Kyle gave them a disgusted look and tried to push me up the stairs, but I stood my ground. Then Trent grabbed the girl by the back of her head and kissed her deeply, pushing her against the wall like he had done with me the other night.

"Nice," I groaned, and looked at Kyle with hurt eyes.

"Right. Look, this game isn't going anywhere. Why don't we head out?" He ran over to Mat and told him we were leaving. Kyle motioned to Jason and Annabelle, then we headed upstairs.

As we were heading up the stairs, Trent looked over and made eye contact with me. He looked like a deer in headlights and rushed up the stairs after me. When we got outside, Trent led me back to the same tree where he had kissed me so passionately at the end of the last party.

"Violet, I thought you left," he said, running his fingers through his hair.

"No, I was just hanging out with my friends for a couple of minutes." I was trying to keep my voice even. I was upset with him but I knew I technically didn't have a leg to stand on.

"Brittney and I have history but we were just dancing." Trent tried to wrap his arms around my waist.

I pushed him away, frustrated. "Look, I know we never decided to be exclusive, so you can kiss whoever you want. Just don't lie to my face. You weren't just dancing and you clearly aren't done with her like you told me earlier." I spun around and walked toward the car. He followed and grabbed my wrist.

I looked down at his hand and then up at him. "Let go." He was squeezing my arm hard and panic began to build up in my stomach.

"Violet, don't walk away from me when I'm talking to you," he ordered, still holding my arm. I twisted to get out of his grasp but he tightened his grip.

"Trent, that hurts. Let me go," I begged. I was starting to get a little scared. He was still holding on to me but my knights in shining armor showed up.

"Let her go, asshole!" Kyle screamed as he and Jason rushed over.

"Hey, back off! This has nothing to do with

you." Trent pulled me a little closer to him and tightened his grip on me, twisting my arm. My breathing quickened and I tried to pull away but he was too strong.

"No, it does concern us. Let her go," Jason yelled.

Trent's grip was not loosening and I turned around to look at him. I didn't even recognize the man staring back at me. I took a deep breath and punched him in the nose.

Trent let go and grabbed his nose. There was blood rushing out of it and all over his hands. He looked down at the blood and took a step toward me. Kyle and Jason pulled me behind them and he backed off. The boys escorted me to the car and Trent went back inside.

***

"Are you okay?" Jason asked as he opened the front passenger door for me.

I slid into the seat and noticed my hand was throbbing. Punching hurt. "Yeah, but I think I need some ice for my hand." I could bend all of my fingers so I didn't think anything was broken but it still hurt like hell.

"I cannot believe you punched him! That was awesome," Kyle said from the backseat.

I tried not to think about what could have happened. I looked down at my arm and there was a slight bruise forming. "Thank you for coming to my rescue, guys," I said, turning around to look at them.

"Please, you didn't need us," Jason exclaimed.

I looked at him and then realized the car was missing a passenger. It was at that moment I realized Kenny was not with us.

"What happened to Kenny?" I asked, looking at Annabelle.

"He ran into some of his friends from home so he is hanging out with them. But he told me to tell you all bye," Annabelle mumbled, trying to contain her giant smile. Lucky for Jason, we pulled into the parking lot of a convenience store at that moment so the subject was quickly changed. I knew he didn't want to talk about Annabelle and Kenny.

"I'll run in and get you something to put on your hand. Anyone else want anything?" Jason asked as he opened the car door to head into the store. Kyle wanted something to snack on so he went in with Jason. I stayed in the car with Annabelle.

"I cannot believe Trent did that," she said, turning to look at me.

"I know." I filled her in on the rest of the conversation. "Yeah, I was upset that he was with his ex, but we weren't exclusive so, technically, he didn't do anything wrong. But then he lied to my face. That is what pissed me off. Oh, and the physical abuse. Yeah, that was bad."

"You think?"

"Well, I don't want to talk about it anymore. What was going on with you and Kenny? I saw you two kissing in the corner." I didn't want to keep talking about that so I changed the subject. I was still shaking a little with adrenaline but that was beginning to wear off. I was upset and kind of scared. No man had ever laid a hand on me like that and I hoped no other man would. I couldn't keep focusing on it.

"Really? I thought we were being a little sneaky!" Annabelle blushed bright red.

"Yeah, no! Everyone saw you, including Jason. He seemed really jealous." I had just started to tell her about what happened when I met him outside but Kyle and Jason were heading back to the car.

"Okay, so the cashier gave us this small bag and we got some ice from the soda machine." Jason handed me the clear baggie. "I also got you something for when the shock wears off," he said, and gave me a pint of ice cream and two spoons.

I smiled from ear to ear. "You are quite possibly one of my favorite people right now," I gushed, and rested the ice on my hand. I secured it to my wrist with a hair tie so that I could eat the ice cream. I removed the lid and Annabelle screamed.

"Don't you dare eat that in my car!" She sounded a bit more like a school bus monitor than she probably intended to.

"Seriously?" I asked, showing her my best pouting face.

"I don't want you to leave a stain in the car. We are, like, five minutes from the school. It won't melt," she insisted.

"Fine!" I slipped it back in the plastic bag. We dropped the boys off near their dorm and headed to the parking lot. My hand was really starting to sting. I guessed the adrenaline was officially gone. We parted ways after I assured her that I would be okay. When I entered my room, I sat on the floor and tore into the ice cream.

***

I really was not okay. For a few seconds there, I was really terrified. Trent's face was filled with rage and his eyes, the eyes that I loved to look into, had turned a dark, cloudy color. I looked down at my arm and saw the imprint of his hand. It was starting to form a black bruise. This was not something I was going to be able to easily forget.

I had a few extra scoops of ice cream and put it away in the fridge. It tasted good but I was not feeling better. I grabbed my towel and shower stuff and headed to the bathroom. Hot showers helped me to think and unwind. But this time it didn't work.

My hand was swollen and I had started to cry while in the shower. Unfortunately, I was not able to stop. I knew it was late but I knocked on Annabelle's door in my pajamas. She opened the door and took one look at my tear streaked face. She opened her door wider so I could walk in and then she pulled me into a big hug.

"I had a feeling you weren't okay." She held me tight and we stood like that for a minute and then she let go. "Okay, so we have two options here. We can talk about it or we can find some trash TV to watch to distract you for tonight and we can try to talk about it in the morning when it isn't so fresh. Personally, I am not the biggest fan of tears so I vote we find the last season of one of those dating shows." She walked me over to her bed and handed me some tissues.

"I love competition dating shows." I didn't want to talk about it right this second.

Annabelle found a full season online and hooked her computer up to the television so we could watch it on the big screen.

Chapter 9

Annabelle and I didn't make it past the second episode before we fell asleep. We both woke up around eight and uncurled ourselves from the pile of blankets all around us. Honestly, I was surprised we didn't die of heat stroke last night. Annabelle went to shower and I headed back to my room to change out of my pajamas. We met up and decided to go to the cafeteria for breakfast.

On the way, we didn't delve into any other topic besides the dating show. We had every intention of continuing the marathon after breakfast. Well, at least I did. It appeared Annabelle had a different plan as she forced me to go to the campus urgent care center after we finished eating. My hand was pretty swollen, and even though I wanted to pretend it was going to be fine, I probably needed to see a doctor.

She came with me and we decided what I was going to say.

"You should really just tell them what happened," Annabelle insisted.

"Oh yeah! That would go well! So last night I went to a fraternity party and there was a lot of underage drinking. While I was there, the guy I have sort of been seeing grabbed my arm and wouldn't let go so I punched him in the face. That's why my hand hurts." I pursed my lips and raised my eyebrows at her.

"Okay, so maybe you shouldn't go into exact detail like that."

"I'm just going to say that I hit the wall when I was sleeping last night. I don't want to make a big deal about this."

"What if he does this to another girl?" she asked, getting serious. "Reporting it may help other girls."

"I can't, okay? I'm just not ready for that. Besides, I was drinking and I hit him, so I could get in a lot of trouble too." We were standing outside the urgent care center and I was procrastinating going in.

"Okay. It's your choice." She opened the door and pushed me inside.

I blinked a couple of times and tried to keep the tears at bay. I didn't want to talk about this with police or the dean. Hell, I didn't even want to talk to Annabelle about it. The whole situation made me feel stupid and small. I should never have let it get that far.

As I signed my name on the check-in list, I heard my name called from the door. I turned around and the officer from the other night with Lola walked into the center.

"Officer Finn, what can I do for you?"

He looked down at my swollen hand and then up

at my face. "No, what can I do for you? Are you all right?" He rushed over to me.

"Yeah, I just had an accident last night so I figured I should probably see a doctor about it." I was hoping he'd drop this as I was already embarrassed.

"Let me deal with this," Finn insisted, walking up to the counter. "We need a doctor now." He was shouting at the poor secretary and I placed a hand on his forearm.

"It's all right. I don't mind waiting," I told him, hoping he'd calm down.

"Well, I mind. You're hurt and we need this dealt with." Then, without another word, he walked me into an exam room without permission and settled me in to wait for the doctor.

"Thanks for doing this."

"Of course. I'd do anything to help."

"I can take it from here though. You don't need to be around for this bit."

"Are you sure? I don't mind staying if you want me to." He reached out and placed his hand over mine. I tried not to rip my hand away from him since he was being nice.

"I'm sure, but I'll let you know if I need anything."

He winked at me and headed out the door.

Fortunately, the doctor believed that I was clumsy since I tripped over my own two feet when I walked into the exam room. He didn't ask any other questions about my injury. It helped that I had worn a sweater to cover the bruise on my other arm.

My hand wasn't broken but there was a sprain.

He wrapped it with a compression bandage and said I needed to wear it for at least the next week, longer if it still hurt. As we were leaving the urgent care center, we ran into Kyle and Jason.

"Did you really hit him that hard?" Kyle asked when they saw my hand in the wrap.

"I guess." We started walking together and ended up going to the boys' place. We spent the rest of the morning hanging out and watching our detective show. Turned out they did watch several episodes without Annabelle and me, but we played the pity card and they agreed to rewatch the ones we missed.

No one was really hungry for lunch so we just decided to have an early dinner. Afterward, Annabelle and I had homework we needed to finish so we headed back to our rooms to get that done. Lola was still not there but that was fine. I used the quiet time to work on math since I was still struggling.

***

I spent the next couple hours on the internet trying to research how other people solved these math problems. Several websites and videos later, I still was not getting the right answers. It was officially time to go see my professor. I sent him an email and asked if we could set up an appointment.

After putting my homework away, I got ready for bed and began writing in my journal. I started explaining the incident with Trent and tried to express my feelings. As I was writing, I noticed

177

there were tears running down my face, but I kept going. There was something therapeutic about writing my feelings. It was almost as if I was letting go of the sadness and the fear as the words hit the page. Soon the tears were mixing with the words, but I didn't care, and pushed on.

As I was trying to reread what I wrote, I realized it wasn't my fault. I had done nothing to deserve his actions. He was the one who had lied to me, and he was the one who lost his temper. It didn't matter that I was with Berneli and he was with Brittney. Trent never should have laid a hand on me, and he definitely should have let me go when I asked him to. This realization did seem to help calm my anxiety a little. But I was still nervous to see him.

Luckily, I had punched Trent with my non writing hand or this would have been a problem. I looked down at my injured hand and noticed that it did seem like the swelling had gone down. It still hurt but I didn't like pain pills. They tended to make me sick to my stomach.

I took a sip of water and then looked at my other arm. The bruise was darkening and still very visible. I was definitely going to have to wear something with long sleeves for a while to ensure no one would see it. I sighed and put the journal down. That was enough therapy for today. I turned the television on and fell asleep as a reality show droned on.

***

I woke up and checked my email. As it turned

out, Berneli emailed us and canceled class. He didn't say why and I was extremely excited to crawl back into bed. Also, I was a little worried about what he would say if he saw my hand. Obviously, I wasn't going to tell him what happened, but he seemed to know everything.

I spent the rest of the day meeting with my statistics professor and watching TV. I needed the mental health day and my nerves were still kind of shot.

The next day was the EET meeting. I was really nervous because I hadn't seen Trent yet.

Annabelle seemed to pick up on this fear as we were eating lunch. "Are you going to be all right seeing Trent?"

"Yeah. I mean, he won't be drinking. I think that was the reason he got physical in the first place. I'm not excusing it, but at least I don't think he would hurt me sober. Plus, what could he do in a large group?" I wasn't going to let him stop me from living my life. I wallowed enough yesterday and it was time to move on.

As if on cue, my hand started to hurt. I probably needed to ice it but I didn't really want to draw attention to it. I would just have to suck it up.

"Just don't go anywhere with him by yourself." Annabelle gave me a stern, motherly look.

"I definitely don't plan to." I headed to the computer lab and Annabelle went to the executive board meeting. I needed to stop procrastinating working on a paper that was due at the end of the week. I was opening the door to the lab when Berneli called my name. I looked at him and he called me over.

"What happened to your hand?" He looked concerned. His brow was furrowed and his big eyes looked scared. My heart started pounding as I tried to avoid his gaze. His glasses were in his front pocket so his eyes were on full view. They were powerful enough to make me forget my own name, let alone that I intended to lie to him about Trent.

I shook my head and looked down at my feet. "I punched a wall when I was sleeping. It's no big deal." I tried to head to the computer lab in the hope of making it clear that the conversation was over.

"If that's how you want to play it," he said to my back as I started to walk away.

I kept going. I didn't want to get into it again so I kept moving until I heard my name again. This time it was Trent.

I turned around and saw him walking toward me. He had sunglasses on but they didn't hide the bandage on his nose.

"Not now, Trent."

He ran in front of me and blocked my path. "I am so sorry about the other night. I texted you a couple of times trying to tell you that." His sunglasses fell a little and his black eyes were on full display.

"What the hell?" Berneli yelled from behind me. My heart sank. Berneli must have noticed Trent's face. "Why did she hit you?"

"I didn't. Stop," I begged, looking up at him. I did not want him involved in this. I shifted my gaze to Trent. He looked pale as a ghost, which only made his bruises all the more evident.

180

"Mr. Haven, I asked you a question," Berneli bellowed, ignoring me.

"There was a misunderstanding and I grabbed her arm. Nothing happened. Like she said, it is not a big deal," Trent said really quickly.

Berneli acted just as fast. He pushed Trent up against the closest wall and shoved his arm under Trent's neck while holding him against the wall with his other arm. "You never lay a hand on a woman. If I ever hear that you have touched another woman against her will, I will make it so you never play lacrosse again."

"Professor! Let him go!" My voice went up a couple of octaves as I tried to pry Berneli off of Trent. But with my hurt hand it wasn't possible.

As I was struggling to get Berneli away from Trent, my sleeve slid up my arm and my bruises were apparent. Trent noticed them first and his eyes grew wide. Berneli followed his glance and I would swear smoke came out of his ears.

"I thought you said it was nothing," he said with a snakelike accusation.

"It was a mistake, all right. I already told her I was sorry." Trent had a look of deep regret in his eyes. I almost believed him.

"If at any time you attempt to contact Violet, I will not only report this incident to campus police, but I will also kick you out of EET for good. Our comedian is a woman, and as you clearly do not know how to treat women, you will have no contact with her. Am I understood?" Berneli was inches from Trent's face but he was yelling as if Trent were down the hall.

"Yeah, I got it. Relax."

Berneli relented and finally released Trent. He ran off down the hall and I turned to Berneli.

"Really? Was that necessary?" I stood with my hands on my hips and gave him a stern look.

"What happened?" he asked, me ignoring my question entirely.

"It is not your business. I handled it."

"Oh, so you are proud that you had to hit him?" His hands flew up in the air in frustration.

"No, I'm proud that a man put his hand on me and I got out of it on my own. I didn't need you to fight my battle for me then and I don't need it now." My anger was close to exploding.

"That was not just your fight. You realize that if he was willing to do this to you, then he is willing to do it to another woman. It needs to be reported to campus security."

"I can't report it. I was drinking when I hit him."

"Violet! You hit him in self-defense. They're not going to care that you were drinking. What if he does this again? He needs to be taught that this is not the way to treat a woman." He leaned against the wall and looked at me.

"So you did that for womankind? Seriously, that seems a little ambitious."

"What do you want me to say, Violet? I saw red. No man should ever place his hands on a woman in anger. I don't like seeing any woman hurt, especially not you." He seemed to be a lot calmer and there was a sweet tone in his voice. Berneli looked down at his feet and then back up at my hand.

"More violence is not the answer." I was calming down too. It was hard not to. Berneli cared about me. He actually cared. It was touching and I was having a hard time staying mad at him.

"I know. I'm sorry I lost it like that." He reached out and slipped a few loose strands of my hair behind my ear. "Are you all right?"

"They said I sprained my hand when I punched him. Other than that I'm okay."

"Good." We looked at each other for a few more seconds as he seemed to be trying to assess if I was really doing all right.

"I promise, I'm going to be fine." I stroked his arm gently and smiled up at him.

Berneli returned the smile but then quickly looked down at his feet again. "We should probably head into the meeting before anyone wonders where we are." He then took my hurt hand and brought it to his lips. He placed a gentle kiss on top of the bandage and I almost swooned right then and there. Then we turned around and headed to EET.

To my surprise, Trent was nowhere to be seen. I guessed he wasn't really in the mood to see Berneli or me again. I walked straight toward Annabelle and Jason. I sat down between them and Jason rubbed my back gently.

"Glad you're doing better." He smiled up at me. I tried to return the smile but my heart was pounding and my hands were shaking a little bit.

Nat started the meeting and I tried to control my breathing. It took a couple of minutes but I realized my problem. I was really turned on. There was something about the raw masculinity of Berneli defending my honor that touched me in some very personal places. At the time, it seemed outrageous that he was pushing Trent around. But now I realized that part of the rage I felt may have been sexually charged.

I glanced over at Berneli and smiled to myself. He had slipped his glasses back on and his sleeves were rolled back down to his wrists. I remembered how amazing his hands felt on my body and my panties dampened. My hurt hand tingled from where he left the kiss and I bit my lip to try to control these feelings before I collapsed on the floor from desire.

This was not the time or place for those thoughts. I shook my head and tried to focus on what Nat was saying. The comedienne was coming in two weeks and this weekend was homecoming. EET was in charge of a lot of the events for homecoming so we had a lot that we needed to handle.

Everyone split off into groups again so they could organize the individual events. Berneli seemed to be overseeing all of it so this time I didn't have the option to be in his group, but with my new realization, this was probably for the best.

I stayed with Annabelle and Jason and we joined the decorations group. We were responsible for ensuring that all the decorations inside the auditorium and around the school were put up and perfect. I wasn't the most artistic person in the world but I figured we could make something work. When in doubt, just throw some glitter on it.

The meeting ran about twenty minutes over the normal time but we still had a lot of work to do. Our group decided to meet again tomorrow night to start working on the decorations. Berneli had to run and get ready for a class so I did not get to see him after the meeting. Tomorrow's class was going to be interesting. The group disbanded, and Annabelle, Jason, and I headed to dinner talking over each other with ideas for decorations.

All of us went back to our dorms with these plans in mind. Lola was not there when I got back so I decided it might be a good time for me to get some homework done. I had a paper due and I needed to prepare for Berneli's class. I worked for about two hours and decided to take a little break and shower. I still had two pages left in the paper but I needed to walk around. As soon as the hot water hit my skin, I felt myself instantly relax. Today really wore on me. With the stress from my classes, the stress from homecoming, and the stress from the men in my life, I was completely worn out.

***

I stayed in the shower longer than I intended but my muscles felt a little like Jell-O when I finally shut the water off. I slipped into my robe and headed back to my room. While I was walking there I saw Annabelle with her shower stuff.

"Hey! I guess we had the same idea." I looked closer and noticed her face was red and her eyes a little puffy. "What's wrong?"

"Nothing, I just think it's crazy that we're going to work so hard for this dance and I don't have a date."

To tell the truth, I'd kind of forgotten about getting a date for the dance. "I don't have a date either! Who cares?" I was trying to sound secure in this statement but the same realization was now crushing my soul.

"I thought maybe Kenny would ask me but I haven't even really seen him. Maybe he just can't find me," she said as she attempted to grasp at a straw. I did not have the heart to tell her that if he was interested, he would find a way to contact her. Annabelle had mentioned that she did not randomly hook up so I figured it was a big deal that she and Kenny had made out twice.

"It probably isn't his scene. We can go together with Jason and Kyle," I said hopefully.

"Jason is probably going with Janice," she said, and made a face. I hoped this was not the real reason she was upset. She and Jason seemed to have a bit of a connection, but so far he still had a girlfriend and they seemed to respect that. Or at least so far they did.

"Oh, I forgot about her since she is never around. That doesn't mean we can't hang out together. It will still be fun. Do you know what you are wearing?" I asked her, trying to change the subject.

"I have a couple of dresses that I brought from home but I am not sure. What about you?" she asked, and my heart stopped.

"I don't think I have anything to wear. None of my dresses are that nice." I really needed to go shopping.

"We can go shopping Friday afternoon. Your last class ends at four, right?"

"Yeah. Sounds good. We may not have dates but we are going to look good." I smiled, feeling a little better. I liked having a plan. We said goodbye and I headed back to my room. Lola was there watching television but it didn't bother me. We talked for a little bit before I fell asleep to an old family sitcom.

Chapter 10

The next morning, I had to get up bright and early for Berneli's class. My hand was really hurting so I didn't put in a whole lot of effort in my appearance. Lola was awake, getting ready for her class, and braided my hair so I wouldn't have to worry about it for the day. I threw on a t-shirt from my favorite football team with a pair of skinny jeans and then headed to class.

I knew I was going to see Berneli but I was not in the mood to look cute. He had seen me looking pretty multiple times, so seeing as a bum should not change his mind. If it did, then I didn't need him. In reality, I shouldn't be thinking like this since I couldn't have him anyway. But a girl could dream.

Even though I got up early I was still struggling this morning, and as a result, I was running a few minutes late. So, I grabbed a granola bar for my breakfast and ripped open the wrapper. I did attempt to rush to class and eat at the same time. This could have ended with me choking but I was lucky and finished the bar with only one close call.

I opened the door to the lecture room and everyone looked at me. I turned bright red and headed to my seat. I took my notebook out and tried not to look around. Out of the corner of my eye I noticed Berneli come to my desk.

"Miss Carrington, nice of you to join us."

I forced myself to bite my tongue.

"Sorry. It won't happen again," I managed under my breath, swallowing the response I really wanted to spout.

"I'd like to see you after class." Berneli knocked his knuckle on my desk and then continued his speech. Another student was going over her controversial scene and he was setting the stage for her presentation.

I tried to pay attention but decided not to participate this time. I was wondering why he wanted to meet with me. To be honest, part of me wanted to be alone with him, and this part scared me a little.

Time seemed to creep by and I was getting more and more nervous. Finally, the class ended. All the other students got up and headed to the door but I just sat in my seat and waited. As the last student exited, Berneli came over and sat in the desk next to mine.

"Is everything okay?" His brows furrowed and his eyes were dripping with concern.

"Yeah, everything is fine, why?" My hand was beginning to throb and I didn't think I'd have the strength or will power to resist him. I was practically desperate to find some kind of distraction. Feeling his hands on me certainly fit the bill.

"Really? It seems like something is bothering you." He looked deep into my eyes and any wall I had placed up crumbled.

I dropped my head into my good hand and rubbed at my eyes. "My hand hurts and I just took a little bit longer to get ready this morning, and things with school and homecoming are just starting to pile up."

"Do you have any pain killers?"

"Yeah, but I don't like to take them. They upset my stomach. I just need to get some ice but I don't want to make a big deal out of it."

I started to grab my bag but he stopped me.

"You don't have to be so tough all the time. It's okay to let someone take care of you every now and then." Berneli reached a hand out to stroke my cheek. I closed my eyes for a second and soaked it in.

"I'll keep that in mind." I wanted to kiss him. Scratch that, I needed to kiss him. There was a magnet between us, and fighting it was becoming even more difficult. I took a deep breath, reached up with my good hand, and pulled him close to me. In that moment, I desired nothing more than letting him take care of me, but I knew that wasn't an option. So I was going to take what I could get and I kissed him hard.

His kiss was something I could take and hold on to. My breathing became ragged as the kiss grew deeper and more intense. The desks were still between us and that kept me from climbing on top of him. I held on for a few more seconds and then broke the kiss. I looked deep into his eyes and panicked. I wasn't feeling lust anymore. It was replaced by a scarier feeling I was too terrified to label.

I grabbed my bag and ran out the door before he could say anything. I really didn't trust myself to stay in that room any longer. I sighed and headed to my next class.

***

The rest of the day went by in a blur. Before I knew it we were in the lounge outside the EET office making decorations. The theme was Can't Fight the Moonlight and we were working hard to keep the cheese on the pizza and not on the decorations.

I was doing the best I could with one hand but really my artistic abilities were questionable with two hands. As a result, I was on rhinestone duty.

Annabelle became the boss real quick. It turned out that she was crazy artistic and creative. With her help, our vision was quickly becoming a reality. Jason had joined us and there were four other members there as well. Plus, Kyle showed up. He hadn't asked anyone to homecoming either so he was going stag with us.

We finished some of the decorations and headed back to our dorms around ten. Unfortunately, we were only about halfway done so we decided to meet again tomorrow night.

Initially, the plan was to meet at eight, but only Jason, Kyle, Annabelle, myself, and one other

191

person showed up. There were not enough people to finish the decorations. Annabelle texted Clarissa and asked for help. She sent out an SOS text.

About twenty minutes later, Clarissa, Nat, and Trent showed up. Annabelle gave me a look of concern but I shook my head, indicating I was fine. The reality was I was going to see him around. I liked this club and I wasn't going to quit just to avoid him. I wasn't going to take any more violence though.

Jason ignored me and came over to "help me" anyway. He really was a good guy. Annabelle gave Trent a job that would keep him busy and away from me. I let go of the breath I'd been subconsciously holding and continued with the bling.

We finally finished the decorations around eleven. All of us were exhausted but we were satisfied, well, except Annabelle. She was a bit of a perfectionist and maintained that there were more things she could do but Jason and I dragged her away.

I got up a little early and started to get ready. I grabbed everything I needed for the day since we would be going shopping after my second class.

I was five minutes early for Berneli's class so I headed in and grabbed my seat. Berneli wasn't there yet so I pulled my notebook out and looked over my notes for today's speaker. He showed up a few minutes later and started class.

He was avoiding me. Probably because it was becoming harder to hide our feelings. It wasn't until the last five minutes of class that he glanced my way. I smiled at him and he held my gaze. The corner of his mouth turned up in a crooked smile. I knew he understood. Almost as soon as the smile had crept its way onto his face it was gone.

He dismissed class and I dragged my feet for a second. I didn't want to stay since I clearly could not be trusted in this room, but I did want to catch his glance again. I grabbed my bag and walked past his desk. He was talking to a couple of students but he looked at me for a second. For now, it was enough. I smiled and turned to walk out the door. I didn't need to turn around to know that he had seen it. I felt his gaze burning into me.

My next class, the seminar, let us out about a half hour early. My professor said that he was an Elton alumnus and had big homecoming plans. He was actually giving us extra credit if we showed up to some of the events. I smiled. I would be at most of them with EET so they were easy points for me.

I met up with Annabelle so that we could go to the mall and the hunt began. She ended up settling on a beautiful red dress with an A-line skirt and eyelet lace cutouts near the hem. It had thin straps and dipped low in the front. She looked amazing. I picked a pink halter dress with layers of frills on the skirt. The top had a bejeweled sweetheart neckline and it gave me more push than a normal bra. The girls looked good but were secure in place, which was a task that was somewhat difficult in a dress.

We bought some accessories and then headed back to school for the night.

***

193

I met up with Annabelle bright and early Saturday morning to help with the homecoming carnival. It was happening in the field outside of our dorm so we didn't have far to go. As we got to the field, we saw Nat and Clarissa. Nat looked stressed out and was yelling at some poor, defenseless workers so we had a distinct feeling we were about to walk into the lion's den.

"Hey, girls," Clarissa said as she headed over to us.

"Hey, Clarissa," Annabelle responded as I waved at her.

"So, we don't have a lot of volunteers, as I am sure you can see, and we need a lot of help," Clarissa admitted.

"Okay, what do you need us to do?" I scanned the crowd. I didn't see Trent, which helped me relax a little.

We were sent over to the alumni tent to set up some small carnival games, and Jason joined us a little later. Once that was finished, we stocked the prize table with tons of school memorabilia.

At that point, we had been working for three hours so I was getting hungry. Clarissa delivered us a big box of donuts and we had just started munching on them when I heard my name. I turned around and saw Trent standing there with puppy dog eyes. I almost dropped the donut as I realized he was asking me a question. I barely registered it so he repeated himself.

"Can I talk to you for a second, in private?"

"Sure." I walked over to him with my shoulders back and my head high. I glanced back and made eye contact with Annabelle and Jason. I knew they would be watching us so I had that small comfort. I followed him out of the welcome tent and off to the side.

I tried to control my breathing. We were in the middle of a crowded field. No one was right next to us, but surely he wouldn't try anything when so many people would witness it. That, and I didn't smell any liquor on his breath. Still, my hand started hurting again and I wished I had decided to wear the wrap.

"I just wanted to talk to you about the other night. I was way out of line to grab you like that. I was drunk, and I know that isn't an excuse but I wasn't thinking clearly." He looked down at his feet. "But I was hoping you could forget about it and come to the dance with me? I really think we have something special here."

"No. I mean, yes, I forgive you. But I can't trust you now," I said as I tried not to get hysterical. I showed him my arm with the bruise. "Look at this."

"Really, you caused that. Let's just move on. We both did things we shouldn't have that night."

"What? I don't regret hitting you. You wouldn't let me go and it scared me."

"You're really being a bitch right now," he stammered, and his voice rose. "You should never have made a big deal about Brittney. I wasn't your boyfriend." He stuck his finger in my face and I jerked back.

My heart was pounding but I refused to show my fear. "I made a big deal about you lying to me! I don't care what the hell you do with other girls. I never asked you to be my boyfriend. Don't you blame this on me! I didn't ask you to grab me so hard that my arm is still bruised," I responded, but I backed up a few steps. He was still too close.

"Oh, that's right. It is always the guy's fault. Well, not this time. You brought this on yourself. Then you went and cried to Berneli. Were you just trying to get a sympathy bang? Well, get in line, sweetheart. About every girl in school is trying to jump his bones. Don't think I haven't noticed you watching him." He grimaced as he said this and then stepped up into my face again, closing the distance between us.

"Berneli figured it out. I didn't whine to him." I couldn't breathe. I took two giant steps back and just glared at Trent. My head was reeling. Was Berneli seeing other students? Did other people notice my attraction to him? Could he be jealous of Berneli? But most importantly, why did he need to stand so close to me?

"You're just a dumb freshman. I can't believe I ever wasted my time on you." He leaned in even closer and was now inches from my face. All thoughts of Berneli quickly left and were replaced by true fear.

Trent's eyes were harsh and I saw raw emotion. Except this time, that emotion was anger, maybe even rage. He was too close. Too close. *Too close!* I had to get away. This conversation was only going to get worse.

I was in the middle of a giant field with no clear sanctuary in sight. So I did the only thing I could do. I ran back to my dorm, leaving my dignity at the carnival.

***

Apparently, Annabelle saw me and was at my door only minutes behind me.

"What the hell happened?" Jason followed her in and sat on my floor.

I explained how he had the nerve to ask me out and to brush the whole thing aside. Then how he blamed me for the fight and got in my face.

"I just panicked. He was too close to me and I got scared. I mean, I can't hit him again. And, guys, you didn't see the look in his eyes. I've never seen someone so upset in my life. I didn't know what he was going to do."

"What an ass," Jason declared, looking disgusted.

"It definitely is not your fault," Annabelle insisted as she sat down on the bed next to me.

I was trying to hold back the tears but it wasn't working. I knew tears made her feel uncomfortable so it was nice that she hadn't run away yet.

"I know it isn't my fault. It just made things worse when he was in my face and blaming me. I just freaked out for a moment."

"If it makes you feel better, Clarissa was telling me that Trent is going to be kicked off the executive board. He just isn't around enough to get the job done. So you probably won't have to see him as much," she offered, trying to sound helpful. "He will probably still show up at meetings but at least he won't have any authority."

197

"That's good since I find authority so sexy," I said, trying to lighten the mood.

Just then, Jason stood up and pulled me into a hug.

"Vi, you're too good for him and this is not your fault," he whispered, and slowly released me from the hug.

I smiled up at him and wiped my eyes. Jason was becoming one of the best friends I had ever had and I was so grateful for him.

"Thanks, sweetie pie," I teased him.

"Anything for you, babycakes." We all laughed for a minute and the tension seemed to diffuse. Annabelle and Jason headed back out to the carnival and I went to the bathroom to wipe my tears and splash some cold water on my face.

I left the Berneli part out of our talk. If my attraction to him was really that obvious, then I didn't need to confirm the rumor. It was bothering me that Trent said all the girls were trying to get with him. True, I'd noticed Nat all over him, but he didn't seem interested. Then again, he didn't make his interest in me well known. I was beginning to wonder if maybe I wasn't the only one he was secretly seeing.

Berneli never gave me a reason to think he was interested in anyone else. We weren't dating, so I technically had no claim on him at all, but it still didn't feel good. There were a lot of people who liked to operate in a world without labels, but that world was really beginning to annoy me.

***

After another half hour we had most of the carnival put together. Kyle joined us and we started going on all of the spinning rides. It was the perfect medicine to get my mind off of the incident with Trent.

We took a late lunch and then headed into the auditorium to help put up the decorations for the dance.

"This looks amazing." Clarissa beamed after we had been hanging decorations for about two hours. There were mirrors to make the stars sparkle and the giant moon looked incredible. Annabelle had really worked her magic. She did this crazy paint job that made it look remarkably realistic. She included craters that appeared to be three dimensional and the colors blended in perfect swirls. It was flawless.

Clarissa helped us put the rest of the decorations up and then surprised us with pizza for dinner. Clearly today was all about the healthy food. Once we finished the pizza, Annabelle and I headed back to our rooms to get ready for the dance.

Jason, who claimed he could get ready in ten minutes, stayed to lay out the refreshments table. He had not mentioned Janice but Kyle said he was bringing her. I was really curious to meet her but I could not say the same for Annabelle. She claimed to be excited to see Kenny but I noticed a couple long glances at Jason throughout the day. Funny enough, he was giving her the same looks. It was a real shame they never noticed each other at the same time.

Annabelle came over to my room and I curled

her hair. Her beautiful thick brown hair would make a model jealous. It was even more gorgeous when it was curled. I stood back to admire my handy work and got a little giddy. Annabelle was a natural beauty. She looked amazing getting up in the morning before even putting make-up on. I had to admit that I was envious. It took some effort for me to look as good as I tried to.

Then it was my turn. She curled my hair as we jabbered on about EET. Annabelle was trying really hard to put my name in the mix for Trent's position. She thought it would be a lot of fun for the two of us to be on the executive board together. But then the conversation shifted as we went to the bathroom to start our make-up.

"Do you think it's weird that I haven't heard from Kenny? I mean, I didn't hear from him the last time we hooked up until I saw him in person. Maybe I just need to see him again?"

"Maybe. But don't let it ruin your night if it doesn't happen." I was trying to sound hopeful but I was worried he was trying to use her.

"I won't," she insisted as she started her make-up. I desperately wanted to believe her but there was something in her eyes that told me this wouldn't be the case.

We finished with our make-up and then headed back to our rooms to get dressed. Lola was there and she looked amazing. She had straightened her tight curly strands and her hair was actually pretty long. Her make-up was done but she was walking around in sweats.

We both got dressed and when I turned around I

noticed she was wearing this gorgeous floor-length red dress. She looked amazing and was definitely a lot more dressed up than I was. Her dress hugged her slim frame and gave her curves that were not normally there. It had a sweetheart neckline and thick shoulder straps. She looked ready to step onto the red carpet.

"Wow, you look amazing!" I tried to keep my jaw from hitting the floor. This was possibly one of the most beautiful dresses I'd ever seen. If Jessica Rabbit and Marilyn Monroe had gotten together to design a dress, this was definitely what it would have looked like.

"Thanks. It was my prom dress. Tyler and I were going to go but we got in a fight the day before and he refused to take me. I never had a chance to wear it." She giggled as she fiddled with her hair.

"Well, it is way worth the wait." I couldn't help but smile at her. She looked really happy.

"Thanks. You look amazing too. I love that color!"

I knew bubble gum was the way to go.

I knocked on Annabelle's door and she agreed that we needed to head out. I had on four-inch black heels while Annabelle had cream wedges on. As a result, we were walking a little slower than normal.

By the time we got to the auditorium, EET had started to let people in. Turned out there really was nothing we needed to do. So we did what any girls in this position would do. We headed over to the moon backdrop and started to take pictures. Clarissa and her boyfriend, Patrick, soon joined our photofest. Once we ran out of silly faces, we decided to get some drinks and sit down.

"Do you guys want a little something in your drink?" Patrick asked as he slyly pulled out a flask.

"Patrick, they are babies. Put that away," Clarissa chastised.

"Let them be, Rissa. They worked hard all day." Patrick winked at her as he poured some into her drink.

"I'll take some," I said, handing him my drink. I wasn't wearing my brace and I was a little worried my hand would start hurting. The bruise on my arm had faded, and with a little help from Sephora, it was completely covered tonight. But it still hurt if it brushed against anything or someone touched it. Maybe a little numbing was a good idea.

A few minutes later, Nat joined us. We all sat and talked while the DJ started to play some dance music. The lights came down and he started this crazy laser show. It looked like what I always imagined a club would. The lights were all different bright colors and they bounced off the mirrors, sending them everywhere. We didn't anticipate this, but it looked amazing.

"Good thing we got pictures earlier. I don't think anything would come out now," Annabelle said as she finished her non-spiked drink.

I nodded and laughed a little. Annabelle was a shutterbug. She took pictures of everything— buildings, flowers, fields, people, lights, or animals. Her walls were now covered with landscapes from around the campus.

I took another sip of my drink and felt the alcohol slide down my throat. It occurred to me that

I had no idea what I was drinking but it tasted good. I looked around the room and noticed Jason walking in.

"Hey, look, there's Jason." I pointed near the door and Annabelle looked over there.

"Yeah, and I guess that's Janice," Annabelle said with a bit of resentment in her voice. Not enough that a stranger would notice but there was no way I could miss it.

At that point, I felt my phone vibrate. I checked it and noticed Jason had texted me.

Vi, I need to talk to you. Meet me outside without Annabelle.

I texted back,

Okay. Coming.

"Hey, my mom needs me to call her real quick. Can you watch my bag?" I asked, trying to sound subtle.

"Sure. Is everything okay?" She was giving me a look of concern, which twisted my gut and sent guilt flowing through me.

"Yeah, I'm sure everything is fine." I ran toward the hall before she could ask any other questions. I didn't like to lie.

As I turned the corner, I noticed Jason off by himself. "What is going on?"

"Look, I swear I just found this out. Kenny has a girlfriend and he is bringing her tonight," he stammered quickly.

"Oh my god! So he cheated on her with Annabelle?" My eyes grew wide and my mouth fell open again. "I guess that's why he asked her not to tell anyone."

"That makes sense. I met her in the hall of my dorm and I wanted to give you a heads-up so you can handle Annabelle. I know she was hoping to meet up with him tonight."

"Yeah, I know. Hey, you just wimped out! Why aren't you telling her?"

"Oh, I don't want to be the one who crushes her. It will sound better coming from you," he assured me.

"Fine!" I turned to head back to Annabelle but Jason stopped me.

"Vi, uh, before you ruin Annabelle's night, I want to introduce you to my girlfriend." He brought me over to where Janice was sitting by herself. She was a little shorter than me and skinny as a bean pole. But for some reason her boobs were huge and they looked totally natural. Good for Jason.

"This is Janice."

"Hi, Vi, I've heard so much about you."

I tried to ignore the fact that she just called me Vi and I had never met her before. But then again, that was what Jason usually called me so maybe that was why. Either way, I needed to let it go and smile.

"Hi, Janice, Jason has told us a lot about you," I shouted over the music.

The song had changed and it was really loud. Jason had told us earlier that he wasn't a big dancer but that Janice loved to dance. She pulled him onto the dance floor and I headed over to see Annabelle. She was by herself now because Nat and Clarissa were dancing.

"Hey, sorry! I was coming in and I ran into Jason and Janice. She seems nice," I told her, trying to sound positive.

"I wonder why he didn't introduce her to me." She looked at him with her brow creased.

"She wanted to dance so maybe he didn't get the chance."

I knew the real reason he didn't want to talk to Annabelle but I was not sure how to say it. I was formulating a plan when I heard her gasp. When I followed her glance, I saw Kenny with a girl with deep tan skin. She had curly black hair that was styled into an elaborate elegant bun. She was really pretty, like model pretty, and had her hands all over Kenny.

"Who the hell is she?" Annabelle asked, looking shocked.

I took a deep breath. "I heard that's his girlfriend."

"Where did you hear that?" she asked, shooting daggers at Kenny. Annabelle cut me off before I could say anything. "So he was cheating on her. I'm the other woman?"

"Technically you were. But you didn't know he had a girlfriend so it's not your fault." I was trying to make her feel better. But I didn't think it was helping.

"Why are all guys jerks?" She grimaced, slamming her purse on the table.

"I don't know. You promised not to let him ruin

your night. You made this entire room look amazing, and I won't let you sit here and sulk. Come on, let's go dance," I insisted as I grabbed her hand and pulled her onto the floor. I headed over to where Jason and Janice were and we started dancing. It wasn't long until Kyle joined us. He was a crazy dancer and had all of us laughing.

We listened to a couple of songs before I left the group to get some air and go to the bathroom. Annabelle and Kyle were dancing so she didn't come with me.

As I was walking, I felt that someone was behind me. I turned around slightly and noticed David was following me. I passed the bathroom and went around the corner to an empty classroom.

It was dark but I stopped at a desk with my back to the door. I couldn't turn around to face him just yet. There were no windows so I just stared straight ahead at the empty wall in front of me. Finally, I felt his hands wrap around my waist.

It felt like I was waiting hours to feel his touch but it was probably less than a minute. He slid one hand down my hip and with the other he brushed hair off my shoulder. I shivered as the hair slid down my back, leaving my shoulder naked.

He leaned forward and started to kiss my neck. His stubble pricked my skin as he placed a trail of kisses from my shoulder to the back of my ear. I leaned my head into him and tilted it to the side.

"You look amazing tonight," he whispered in my ear. "You feel even better." He slid his other hand down to my hip.

I shivered as I waited for his next move. My

hands were on the desk in front of me but I was too nervous to move them.

David spun me around to face him and dropped his hands to cup my ass. I felt a tiny squeeze as he pulled me even closer to him. David leaned down and kissed me.

It was gentle at first. A soft greeting between two people. Then any nerves I had left and my body responded instantly. His tongue entered my mouth and quickly took control of the kiss. Just like that, I was lost in him as my brain turned off and I allowed myself to just feel.

I slid my hands up his chiseled chest and wrapped them around his neck. As the kiss became more intense, I let out a sigh, which only seemed to encourage him. David picked me up and put me on the desk. I reached up and pulled his head down to continue the kiss. His hands slid around to my back as he pushed me against him. There was no space between us as I gasped for breath. We broke the kiss for a second and looked at each other in the dark classroom.

"If you tell me to stop, I'll walk out of this classroom now and make sure we're never in this position again. If you don't leave, I'm going to take you up to my office and give you such pleasure that I will ruin you for any man who dares to come after me," he asserted in a gruff, deep voice.

A chill spread through my body. I could tell it was killing him to wait on my answer and I knew what I should do. It would be smart for me to walk away. We had been really lucky so far that no one had caught us, but it was only a matter of time before that luck would run out.

I broke his gaze and took a deep breath. In that moment, I knew there was no way I could walk away. Even if it was just a one-time thing before he moved on, I needed this.

"Which way to your office?" I looked back into his eyes and smiled.

David picked me up off the desk and put me on the floor. He then grabbed my hand and pulled me out the door of the classroom and down the hall to a back stairwell.

"We need to take a detour." David pushed me against the wall and started kissing me again. He pulled my leg up and wrapped it around his back. Then he slid his hand from my knee straight up my skirt and began stroking my thigh. I practically melted in his arms. This was apparently his plan because he stopped kissing me at that moment and smiled his crooked smile.

"Just to keep you on your toes." He backed off me and pulled me up the stairs.

"I will remember this game later," I murmured to myself. If he heard me, he didn't make it known because he kept right on moving.

His excitement was obvious because he was practically running up the stairs. As he was in flats and I was in heels, this was a little more difficult for me. David pulled me through the halls but I was still not moving fast enough for him. He picked me up and threw me over his shoulder. I started laughing like a giddy school girl.

"Seriously? Barbarian style?" I was actually enjoying this.

David chuckled but didn't put me down.

We got to his door and David reached into his pocket to get the key. He opened the door and carried me over the threshold, then put me down on top of his desk. Unfortunately, there was nothing really on his desk so he didn't have to do that sexy thing where the man slid everything on his desk onto the floor. I let that fantasy go as David walked back to the door and locked it. After the lock fell into place, David stood there for a moment, as if weighing the pros and cons of this decision.

He finally turned around to meet my gaze. Those eyes screamed with want and desire. I could only imagine that my eyes mirrored his. He turned the lights off and walked over to me slowly. The anticipation between us grew and I felt goose bumps appear on my arms.

When he was standing in front of me, I slid my hands up his chest, feeling the muscles rippling underneath. He reached up and started to unbutton his shirt and his fingers never fumbled once. As his olive skin became visible, I couldn't help but gasp. He really was a Greek god. His abdominals appeared to have been carved out of stone.

I reached out to trace his muscles and felt a tingle at my core. He brushed my hair off my shoulder again and slipped his hands behind my neck. His fingers groped for the tie of my dress and he slowly pulled at the knot until the straps fell free. The dress slipped to my waist, leaving me in only my strapless bra. I inhaled deeply. The two of us had kissed before and there had been some groping, but this time was different and we both knew it.

David seemed to notice my unease and dropped his hands to either side of me. He kissed me lightly. Pecks at first. He seemed to be letting me set the pace to make sure I was comfortable. That only made me want him more.

The pecks weren't doing the job so I grabbed him by the back of the neck and kissed him hard. That was all the encouragement he needed as he matched my kiss and then surpassed it. I was short of breath from the shear intensity of it all. Slowly, he reached his hand up and cupped my breast over the bra. He gently squeezed and I felt a heat flow through me and settle in my core.

He slid his thumb across my nipple and a soft whimper escaped my lips. Suddenly, the bra between us was too much fabric. He began lightly rolling my nipple between his two fingers. I let out a frustrated gasp and reached behind me to unhook the bra. David waited until I had taken it off and then he grabbed it and threw it on the floor behind him.

It was still dark but I could make out the animal in his eyes. He pulled me to the edge of the desk and stood between my legs. He bent his head and began placing kisses in a circle around the outside of my breast like he had done before. I was waiting impatiently as his kisses slowly made it to my nipple. When he finally got there, he licked it gently and then blew on it. The cold air made me shiver but I was far from chilled. Then he took my nipple into his mouth and sucked. My head fell back and I moaned loudly. I couldn't contain myself.

David chuckled under his breath and turned his

head to the other breast. He repeated the circle process and sucked on my nipple again while rolling the other nipple around in his fingers.

I clinched my legs together in an attempt to calm the storm that was brewing inside me but I couldn't find any relief. If this continued, I was going to climax right here before he even reached below my skirt. That was not how I wanted my first time with him to be. I groaned a little in frustration.

"Easy, baby. This is only the beginning," he whispered in my ear. I didn't think he realized how sensitive my nipples were. There needed to be an even playing field, so I reached down and began undoing his belt and then his pants.

I reached into his boxers. He was even bigger than I remembered and he was definitely at attention. I slowly began to stroke him and it was David's turn to moan. His was a lot softer than mine but I could tell he was excited. I slid my hand up and down his shaft even faster. As he grew harder, I felt him beginning to pulsate.

I gave a slight squeeze and then ran my fingers gently over the tip. David started to shudder. I looked him in the eyes and gently pushed him back. David watched me as I got up off the desk and dropped to my knees.

He let out a soft hiss of excitement when I slid his pants all the way down and then dropped his boxers. My breath caught in my throat for a second when I saw just how big he really was. That was what a man should look like.

I licked my lips and slowly took him inside my mouth. I started with the tip and ran my tongue along it, circling it tenderly. David let out a louder and grittier moan so I took him deeper. He reached for the desk and braced himself as I started sucking.

My pulse raced as I felt my own excitement heighten. Pleasing him was thrilling and I felt my excitement begin to dampen my panties. Then I started to move from the end of his shaft to his tip quickly, and before long, I could feel a little liquid beginning to come out of him. I smiled to myself and took him as deep as I could manage.

Apparently, David had enough of this and reached down to pull me up off my knees. He placed me back on the desk again and laid me down across it. He started to kiss me, and they were not gentle kisses. They were rough and fast. I wrapped my arms around his neck and pulled him tight against me. He slid his hand up my skirt and reached my lace panties.

"These feel nice. Remind me later to appreciate how sexy you look in them," he murmured as he slid them down my legs. Now, I was lying on his desk with my dress around my waist. David slid it down off my hips and threw it and my panties behind him.

We were both naked and staring up at each other. He took a minute and looked me over in the dark room. I started to feel self-conscious but I didn't reach to cover myself. I sat there for a second just staring back at him, almost challenging him.

He ran the back of his hand from my collarbone, down my chest, along my thighs, and then finishing at my ankle. "You have the most beautiful body I have ever seen." Then he climbed on top of me and braced himself on the desk so there wasn't an excess amount of weight on me.

David slid his hand down my leg and began stroking my inner thigh. I started to squirm a little because it wasn't what I needed. He chuckled as he slipped his finger between my folds and inside me. I started to shiver again. He found my nub, the secret spot that most boys struggled to reach, and he rubbed it. I could feel my climax building up. Finally, I said his name.

"David. I need more. David." I continued to squirm, as if somehow this would end the agony I was feeling.

"Okay, love, I'll give you what you need, just say my name again."

"David," I uttered, almost giving in to the sensation that was promising to bring me over the edge.

But then David withdrew his finger and I instantly felt its absence. He walked over to his pants and returned with a condom from his wallet. I watched as he slid it on, transfixed by how amazing he looked.

As he walked toward me, I could hardly believe what was about to happen. We were really going to have sex. I waited for the anxiety or the fear to come but it never did. Actually, I felt completely comfortable with this decision. The other times I was with someone, it never really felt right.

He climbed back on top of me hesitantly, as if he was giving me time to stop him. I reached up and pulled him into a kiss. Seconds later, I felt him slide inside me and I had never felt so full. He began pumping slowly and deliberately. There was a time for gentle, but that was just not what I wanted. Right now I wanted raw sex.

"Faster," I demanded as I broke the kiss and yanked on his hair.

He smiled the crooked smile that haunted my dreams and picked up the pace. Now he was pounding into me hard and fast. It felt amazing as he hit my spot over and over again.

I was becoming short of breath as I felt the climax building up inside of me and I focused on it. Sometimes it was hard for me to hold on to it all the way through and it was really frustrating. David lifted my leg up in the air and pushed even deeper inside of me, and I didn't have to fight to keep the climax. It was rippling through my body.

He looked me straight in the eyes and I watched his pleasure overtake him. It was the most intimate experience I had ever had in my life and it terrified me. I wanted to look away but something kept me focused on him.

But just like that, he pulled out and went to grab some tissues to clean up.

I sat there on his desk and let what just happened sink in. I wasn't really sure where to go from here. It wasn't just that we couldn't take this moment back, but it also kind of brought us to a standstill. I definitely didn't want to be one of the girls in his little black book, but was I really ready to let this go? Could this be something more? Did I even want it to be more? He was leaving in a year, so if I got attached, I'd risk my heart breaking. But then again, the sex was mind blowing and I'd really be disappointed if I didn't get to do it again.

While I was pondering this, Berneli had gotten dressed. He walked back over to me and kissed me gently on the forehead. It was sweet and loving. I closed my eyes and when I opened them, he was staring deep into my soul. It was then that I realized I was holding my breath while waiting for some kind of grand declaration. Something appeared to be on the tip of his tongue but he seemed to shake himself out of the trance and walked to the door.

He simply said, "I will give you a moment to get yourself cleaned up." Then he unlocked the door and walked out.

I was a little hurt. It felt as if he used me and threw me away. I wasn't sure what I was expecting, or even what I wanted him to say. Maybe I was just one of the silly freshmen who fell under his spell. At least I had finally experienced good sex. I sighed and went to grab my clothes.

***

I walked out the door and saw David leaning against the wall next to his office. When he looked at me, he smiled. I tried to smile in return but I was a little hesitant. He took my hand and kissed the top of it.

"We should probably head back to the dance before people really start to wonder where we were."

My face went white. "Oh shit. I told my friends that I was going to the bathroom." I turned around and started for the main hallway. But he didn't let go of my hand, instead spinning me back into his chest. David dipped his head a little and kissed me one more time. It definitely was not a goodbye kiss. It was passionate and had almost too much tongue to handle. I loved it.

He gave me the impression this wouldn't be our last kiss.

Chapter 11

David had gone a different way so we wouldn't be seen emerging from some dark area of the school together. I finally made it back to the dance and tried to play it cool. Too bad Annabelle saw right through me.

"Where were you? Is everything okay?" she asked, a little more suspicious than concerned.

"Everything is fine. My mom is going through something so she wanted to talk again. She called me when I was leaving the bathroom." How many times could you lie to your best friend before you went to hell?

"That's funny since I have your phone." She held up my purse and gave me a knowing look. Then she leaned closer to me and whispered in my ear, "Plus, you have sex hair." Annabelle pursed her lips and raised her eyebrows at me.

"How do you know what sex hair looks like?"

"Not the point! What happened?" She reached out to smooth my hair a little.

"Okay, fine, but can we talk about it later? I

217

don't want anyone else to hear."

"Really? You can't tell me now?"

"I promise you, it'll be worth it." I tried to look as sincere as possible and watched the fight play out on her face. She clearly wanted to know everything now but decided to respect my wishes and wait.

"Fine, but it had better not have been with Trent." She gave me a warning look that could startle a full grown man.

"It wasn't Trent. I'm going to head back to my room to shower. When do you plan on leaving?" I was itching to get out of this dress since I felt like everyone could smell the sex on me.

"I'm ready. Clarissa said she doesn't want us to help clean since we set everything up. I need to say goodbye to everyone first." She looked back in the direction of the dance.

"Okay, then you should be done around the same time I get out of the shower. Just head over to my room when you're ready," I called as I started to walk out the door.

"Wait, what do you want me to tell Kyle and Jason?" she shouted to my back.

"Tell them that I didn't feel well and went back to the room." With that statement, I turned around and ran out the door before she could continue to question me.

The cold air felt good on my face. I probably needed a jacket, but I was so high on life that I doubted a winter storm could have cooled me off. I looked back up at David's office. The light was off but I knew he would be in there again. I smiled and headed to my dorm.

***

On the way there, I was stopped by a police officer. When he got closer, I realized it was Officer Finn. I tried to smile at him but I was too nervous. Did somebody already report us?

"Miss Carrington? Is everything okay?"

"Yes, why?"

"You look a little disheveled," he noted as he looked me up and down. I didn't know what it was but something about this made me a little uncomfortable. Maybe it was the way his eyes lingered a little too long on my breasts.

"I was at the dance and I began to feel a little sick. After some time in the bathroom, I decided it was best for me to head back to my dorm." Maybe the thought of me vomiting would help to turn him off.

"Is that because you were drinking?" he asked suspiciously.

"No! I think I have the stomach flu." I had only had that one mixed drink Patrick had given me and there was no way it was still in my system.

"No disrespect intended. There were some reports of underage drinking so we are trying to patrol. I should have known better than to think that about you," he said, looking apologetic.

"It's fine. I just had a long night and I'm ready to head to bed." I put on my best sick face. Apparently, it was too good. He reached over and grabbed my elbow.

"You look like you could use an escort." He started walking me toward the dorm.

"Really, I'm okay. Thank you though. I appreciate the help." I tried to step away from him but this didn't help as he then wrapped his arm around my waist in an effort to hold me better. This didn't feel right and I felt a bit of the same panic from the Trent issue begin to grab hold of my heart.

"I insist, it's my job."

He gripped my waist tighter and I spun away from him and just started to walk next to him.

"Thank you for your help." I decided it was better just to let him walk me to the dorm now that his hands weren't on me. It wasn't worth the fight.

"So, it was rude of your date not to take you back to your room. I should have a talk with him. Who were you with?"

"I went by myself." I started to walk a little faster. He was going incredibly slowly.

"A pretty girl like you? That's crazy. I wish I could have taken you. We would have had a great time but I had to work." He smiled brightly at me like his offer to take me to the dance was equivalent to an invitation from Orlando Bloom.

I forced a smile and we walked in silence for a minute. But really I was trying to build up enough courage to ask him the question that was burning a hole in my mind.

"What happens if a student is caught with a member of the staff, like a professor or a campus police officer?" I tried to sound casual and even smiled sweetly to possibly distract him.

"If any member of the staff was found with a student, well, there could be some serious problems. The staff member would be fired instantly and the student expelled. I mean, it's not like a young girl like you would get mixed up with a professor, right? I'd like to think you'd be more into the tough guy. Someone who could really protect his woman."

"I was just asking a question. I'm not actually interested in anyone." I pretended to cough to hopefully change the subject. He patted my back and then started to stroke it softly. Since I was in a halter dress, this meant that there was skin to skin contact and it freaked me out. I shrugged him off the best I could without seeming too rude.

"Well, give me a call if you ever need something. I'll drop whatever I am doing. If you're in trouble, I want to know. I have some pull at this school and I might be able to send it your way." He reached out and stroked my forearm. He seemed to try to be reassuring but it gave me chills, and not in a good way. I brushed his hand off lightly by pretending to shiver a little.

But then Finn reached into his bag and pulled out a pink lily. It was almost the same color as my dress.

"A pretty girl like you deserves a flower. My business card is tied to it." Finn winked at me as I accepted the lily.

"Thanks. I'll keep that in mind," I said, trying to smile. It really turned into a grimace.

"What's wrong? Is this the wrong type of flower?"

"No, lilies are beautiful."

"Is it your favorite, though?" he asked desperately.

"No, it's not," I admitted.

He cursed softly under his breath and turned and walked away.

I rushed up to my room and tossed the flower with the business card in the trash. It gave me a bad feeling. Was it a coincidence that this was the same color as my dress? Yes, he just happened to come across me as I was walking back to my room and he just happened to have a flower with him. It was a totally normal interaction. I repeated this mantra a few times but I had a hard time believing it, so I grabbed my shower stuff. Maybe the hot water would wash thoughts of him away.

***

I was brushing my hair when I heard a knock on the door. I got up and opened it to a very impatient Annabelle.

"Do not leave me alone with Janice again," she ordered, and walked in.

"Why? What happened?"

"She kept giving me all of these backhanded compliments. It was like she kept trying to compliment me but changed her mind halfway through." Annabelle sat down on my bed in a huff. She was still in her red dress and shoes.

"Like what?"

"'That dress is really pretty. I could never wear it because my waist is too small.' Or, 'I really like the moon you painted. It was meant to be abstract, right?' Like no, it's supposed to be realistic and you're being rude."

"Oh my god, did you say that to her?"

"No, give me some credit," she said, exasperated.

"It doesn't sound that bad. Maybe she just lacks a little tact."

"Just wait until you spend more than five minutes with her. Then we'll talk. Anyway, so that's off my chest. Who did you have sex with?"

"Okay, so, something has been going on that I haven't told you about because we just met and it's kind of frowned upon by the school, and maybe also society. So I was nervous to tell anyone since I may be kicked out of school. It's, like, really important it stays a secret."

"Stop, I am not going to tell anyone."

"I know. But I just get nervous and—"

"Violet, just tell me." Annabelle cut me off before I could continue rambling.

"Fine! Tonight, I was with Professor Berneli." I looked at her for her reaction.

"Oh." She stared at me for a second. "How did that start?"

"Remember, he was at casino night?"

"You hooked up with him at casino night and didn't tell me?" she shouted.

"No, that was just when we met. The first time was after the EET meeting when Trent stood me up. We just kissed. It happened two other times, but tonight we actually had sex," I said in a hushed tone, hoping she would mimic me and lower her voice a little.

"Oh," Annabelle uttered quietly, and seemed to ponder what she wanted to say. I waited patiently for her to find her words. "So, what are you two

223

doing? Is it, like, just a fun affair, or did you develop feelings for him?"

"I don't know. I mean, it has been happening so fast. Like, after I started really talking to Trent, I tried to ignore him. Then David saw me with the bandage on my hand and Trent with his black eyes. He figured out what happened and stood up for me. He actually threw Trent against the wall and threatened him. At first I was appalled at his aggression and then it turned into this unbelievably sexy moment. I don't know what I'm doing."

"Well, what happened tonight?"

I didn't know what to say at first. How could I explain that I sensed his presence? "I walked out of the gym to go to the bathroom, and as I headed there, I saw Berneli leave the gym out of the corner of my eye. For some reason I just walked over to an empty classroom and he followed. There was kissing and then we went up to his office and locked the door." I was only alluding to what happened. I had no problem talking about sex, but Annabelle's kiss with Kenny was her first kiss ever so I did not want to embarrass her.

"Remind me never to go see him for office hours," she teased, and I threw my pillow at her. Apparently she didn't embarrass that easily. "So, how was it?"

"It was amazing. I've been with a couple of guys before, but nothing like this. When he looked into my eyes, I felt special. I can't really explain it but it seemed real."

"What was that you were saying about not catching feelings?"

I rolled my eyes. "I just mean I don't know what to feel. This can never work. First, he is my professor, which is obviously a problem. Second, he will be headed back to England at the end of next semester so this has a time limit. Third, he is way older. Fourth, he may be seeing other students. My feelings aren't going to change any of those things," I said, feeling slightly defeated. It was the first time I had expressed these road blocks out loud. They seemed even more insurmountable and made my earlier actions seem even more reckless.

"Well, at least you know what you're getting in to. To be honest, I kind of suspected it may have been with him."

"I know you did. I saw it in your eyes. But do you think anyone else noticed? I ran into that cop again and he made an allusion to how much trouble you can get in for hooking up with a professor."

Annabelle reached out and grabbed my arm. "No, I don't think it's super obvious. I've noticed the way he looks at you. Plus, he took the rider away from Trent and insisted you continue to work with him. Not to mention, I'm your best friend. I also see the way you look at him."

"Do you think other people have noticed?" My stomach was turning and I felt sick.

"Definitely not. Everyone is so busy with their own drama that they don't have time to focus on yours," she said, waving her hand at me.

"But you noticed."

"I already knew you were attracted to him after casino night so I was looking to see how he felt. Really, it's been super subtle." She was trying to reassure me and I wanted it to work. I nodded but I wasn't sure if I believed her.

"I hope you're right."

***

I awoke early the next day and threw some clothes on. I decided it was time for a walk. Normally, I didn't go for walks as I found it stressed me out more since I usually got lost. But my emotions were a mess and I heard nature and quiet could help sort them out. I headed to the small lake at the back of the school. It was not so poetically named Lake Frank, but it was beautiful nonetheless.

All along the sides of it were bushes, small flowers, and some lazy trees reaching their overgrown branches into the water. I was told that during the spring, students took handmade canoes and wooden boats out to race across it. But today I was the only one there, or so I thought.

As I made my way to the other figure sitting on the bank, I realized I knew exactly who it was and I smiled. Jason was sitting with his brow furrowed in thought. He didn't realize I was there until I sat down right next to him.

"What are you doing here?" I asked as I extended my legs out just inches from the water. It was nice out but not warm enough to go in.

"Hey, I was just thinking." He smiled but it didn't seem to reach his eyes. "What are you doing here?"

"Same thing. I have some crazy things on my

mind and I thought a walk might help me sort them out."

"How is that going for you?"

"Probably about as good as you. What's going on? Is everything okay with Janice?" I watched his jaw tighten as I said her name. Whatever was bothering him clearly had a lot to do with her. He ran his fingers through his hair and I saw the struggle play out on his face as he debated telling me or not. After a few drawn out moments, he sighed and looked at me with real pain in his eyes.

"So, Janice and I have been together for two years now. Before college, I really thought I would be with her forever. When we are together, it is just comfortable, but lately I am not sure if that's enough. I don't know. There just is no excitement anymore. That probably sounds dumb." He threw some sticks into the water and sighed again.

"No, it doesn't. It just sounds like you're afraid of settling. There isn't anything wrong with wanting passion over comfort." I wanted to sound like I was talking to him instead of trying to convince myself. But Jason looked at me and he knew.

"So who are you feeling passionate with?" He gave me a suspicious look. I blushed, turning three shades pinker.

"Whoa! Let's not get excited here. We're just talking about you!" I gave his shoulder a little shove and then looked at him a bit more seriously. "What do you think you want to do?" I tried to steer the conversation back to him.

"I don't know. I love her and I know she loves me, but it may not be enough. It may not make sense, but I used to get butterflies just being around her—I haven't felt that way in a long time. I feel like we're just going through the motions." He hung his head for a second and I placed my hand on his forearm.

We sat there for a few minutes and just looked out into the water.

"Well, that's something to think long and hard about. I know couples go through dry spells and they come out fine. But if you think it is more than that, maybe it is time to end it." I hoped I could maintain an unbiased opinion. I wanted him to be happy but I also wanted Annabelle happy.

"Yeah, I know. I guess I'm just going to have to see how things go." We sat quietly for a few minutes before he spoke up again. "So what are you out here thinking about? Is the Trent thing still bothering you?"

I wanted to talk to him but I just didn't know if I was ready. He probably wouldn't report me, but would he judge me for it? Would it cause a rift between us?

"Basically. I just am trying to move on from it. I'm going to see him around and I can't be running off every time he comes close to me," I said, realizing that this was actually one of the things on my mind, just not the main issue.

"I'm here for you, Vi. I won't let anything happen to you," he promised, and wrapped an arm around my shoulder.

Things were a little too serious. "Can you just be my boyfriend? I feel like you and I would make the perfect match. Plus, I could give you tons of passion."

"Now that sounds exciting, but I worry that we'd explode with how much desire we have for each other," he said, and wagged his eyebrows at me.

I laughed and then we hugged for a second.

"Why don't we screw this walking and nature crap and go off campus for breakfast? My treat," Jason offered, and stood up, reaching a hand out to me.

"Well, only because you're paying, boyfriend." I smiled as he helped me stand up.

"Obviously, girlfriend. My momma raised me right." He tossed his arm over my shoulder and we walked to his car in silence. I was glad the serious moment was over but even happier it happened.

Even as I sat in his car, I didn't know where to start. Those obstacles I'd discussed with Annabelle weren't going anywhere, and neither were the feelings David was invoking. I did want to be with him again. I wanted it from the top of my head to the soles of my feet. But on the other hand, could my heart take it if I wasn't his only one? How would I say goodbye to him at the end of the year? My feelings were only going to grow. Then again, it's better to have loved and lost than to have never loved.

Okay, this may have been a little dramatic. I didn't love him, but I thought I could.

Breakfast was good. We spent the whole time talking about TV shows and movies we loved. The conversation did not dip into our romantic feelings for the people in our lives and the distraction helped for a minute.

I just couldn't help but think that the reason he was doubting Janice might have something to do with his growing feelings for Annabelle. Again, I didn't feel it was the right time to say something. The two of them needed to figure out their feelings before I told them what they were. Though I was not sure how much longer I could keep this to myself.

After we ate, Jason dropped me back off at my dorm, but not before he got a final word in.

"Whenever you are ready to talk about the other thing that is bothering you, let me know. But I understand if you aren't ready just yet." He honked the horn and left.

I couldn't help but smile.

***

I headed upstairs to work on some homework. It seemed like the best way to procrastinate dealing with my personal feelings. I wouldn't see Berneli until tomorrow in class and I had a feeling we wouldn't be having a big heart to heart there so I was in no rush to analyze my emotions.

I went to sleep feeling conflicted and emotionally drained. Unfortunately, I was woken up not long after turning off the light. I rolled out of bed and turned the light on. I opened the door and couldn't believe what I saw. Officer Finn was standing there.

"Violet, it's nice to see you again," he said as he looked me up and down. As I was in my pajamas and no bra, this made me feel a little uncomfortable.

Not to mention he was calling me Violet now and not Miss Carrington.

"What can I do for you, Officer?"

"We had another problem with Miss Lauren Zimmerman. Is she there?" He leaned forward, trying to look over my shoulder.

"No. I'm the only one here." I dropped my attitude and I instantly felt a bit of fear flow through me. I should have reported Tyler to the police. "Is everything okay? Is she okay?"

"There was an incident with Tyler Michaels and we are concerned for her safety but we can't find her. Do you know where she is?"

"I don't, but give me a minute. Let me call her." I closed the door and rushed over to my bed where my phone was sitting. As I started dialing, I heard the door open. I whipped around and saw Officer Finn walking into my room. He looked around and then came to stand next to me. It made me uneasy so I started pacing while the phone rang. Lola didn't answer so I sent her a text asking where she was and if she was all right.

"Sorry, I don't know where she is. Um, why are you in my room? How did you get in here? The door was locked from the inside," I said, forgetting Lola's issue for a second.

"I learned long ago how to pick the dorm room locks. Just in case something happens, I want to be able to get into any of the rooms on campus. It can create so many problems when you have to wait for a set of keys." He shrugged this off as not a big deal.

"I would prefer you wait for keys, if that is all

right."

"I'm not sure. I think we both know you need my help." He walked closer to me and I was boxed in between him and my nightstand. A pressure pushed on my chest and I needed him to move. Since he just stared down at me, I walked around him to the door.

"If I hear from her, I'll let you know." I opened the door, indicating that I was ready for him to walk out.

"Do you mind if I wait a few minutes? I'm hoping she will respond to the text." He was standing firm next to my bed.

"Sure, but let's go to the common room. I don't get the best service in here," I said, and grabbed my bathrobe. The common room was at the end of the hall and had three couches and some easy chairs. There was also a television on the wall for anyone to use, but most importantly, it was not my bedroom. I sat down in one of the easy chairs and Officer Finn sat down on the couch next to me.

"Are you feeling better?" he asked as he got comfortable.

"What?" I looked at him, confused.

"You were sick last night with the flu?" He stretched his legs out so that his knee was pressed up against my leg. I shifted uncomfortably but he kept moving so some part of his leg was touching mine. I pulled my knees into my chest and was finally out of his reach.

"Oh, turns out it wasn't the flu. I went to bed early and spent most of the day relaxing so I am feeling a lot better. Thanks."

"Good. I'm glad you are doing better. You certainly look a lot better," he said, and looked down toward my chest.

"Well, I haven't gotten a text from Lola so I'm going to go to bed. I have class first thing in the morning." I got up out of the chair and headed back to my room.

"Let me walk you to your door." He followed me down the hall and leaned in front of me to open the door for me. "Please let me know as soon as you hear from Lola. I think you know my number by now." He winked and then gently grazed my cheek with his knuckles.

I tried to close the door but he held onto it for a minute. He was too strong and I couldn't budge it. Finn leaned in closer and for a second I thought he was going to try to kiss me.

"Are you a rule breaker, Violet?"

I looked at him, confused. "What are you talking about?"

"I was thinking about our conversation last night. You asked what happens if a student is involved with a professor or a guard. That's kind of specific since there are several different types of staff members." Finn still had a vice grip on the door and the possessive way he looked at me was frightening.

"They were the first staff members to come to mind." My voice shook and I could tell he didn't believe me. He squinted his eyes and nodded.

"Right. Makes sense." Finn stared at me a minute longer. "'Cause if there is a specific professor bothering you or trying to date you, I could handle them for you."

"That isn't an issue."

Finn smiled big and let go of the door. "Then maybe there is a certain security guard who has caught your eye?"

"Like I said, there is no one I'm interested in."

He winked at me. "Right, keep it a secret. Good call!"

I quickly closed the door before he could say anything else. My heart raced and I couldn't escape that nagging feeling that he knew something. After a few deep breaths, I focused on the bigger problem at hand and called Lola again.

"Lola, are you okay?" I asked as soon as she answered.

"Yes, I went home to my mom's."

"What happened? The police came back and said something happened with Tyler."

"Well, Tyler and I got in a big fight over something stupid and he got mad and pulled a knife on me. But it was just a misunderstanding. Someone must have heard me scream and called the police. He uses steroids and just went into a rage. He didn't mean to. I just went to my mom's to give him time to cool off."

I couldn't believe she was trying to defend him.

"He pulled a knife? Like a big knife?" I was shocked. This was crazy!

"It was a pocket knife, so a small knife," she said as if it was made of plastic and not metal.

"Did he cut you?" I felt like this probably should have been one of my first questions but it was late at night.

"No, he just threatened me with it. It really

wasn't a big deal. I'm fine," she insisted, but she didn't sound as fine as she wanted to be.

"The campus police came to the door. They're looking for you. You may want to let them know that everything is fine." *Or, I don't know, maybe you should tell them that your boyfriend threatened you.*

"Well, I'm fine. They don't need to do anything."

I couldn't hold my tongue anymore. "Do you want to press charges or anything? This sounds kind of serious." I remembered what David had said about Trent. "It should at least be reported. What if something like this happens again?"

"No, no! It was a mistake. I just want to forget about it. Don't mention it to the police. Please, Violet, it really is not a big deal. I promise," she pleaded.

"Okay, if you insist that you're all right, then I'll let it go. Be safe." I hung up the phone and felt guilty for not calling the police, the real police. I didn't like the sound of being threatened with a knife. But at the same time, it wasn't my call to make. If Lola wanted to let it go, then I would have to do that. Besides, she probably would deny the whole thing happened.

Still, I decided that if anything else happened with Tyler, I would have to draw the line and alert the authorities. I just hoped I wouldn't be too late.

Chapter 12

I had a terrible time going to sleep. There were too many things on my mind and I couldn't shut my thoughts off. I was worried about Lola and Tyler, confused about David, and a little concerned about Officer Finn. Not to mention I didn't know what to do about Annabelle and Jason. I was beginning to think that the only way to make that happen would be a giant push from me.

When I finally fell asleep, I slept straight through my alarm. I finally woke up to a pounding on my door. I was really worried it was Officer Finn for a minute so I checked out the little peep hole. It was Annabelle.

"Um, hi. I could hear your alarm going off repeatedly and I figured you were either dead or still sleeping." She laughed a little as I yawned big.

"Yeah, I had a hard time sleeping." I stretched and looked at the clock. "Oh crap! I have class."

"No kidding! Get dressed." She followed me into my room and sat on the desk chair. We usually walked to class together so it was nice that she was waiting for me. I grabbed the first pair of jeans I came to and a plain t-shirt. Then I pulled my hair up into a low ponytail and grabbed my bag. Annabelle and I were halfway to class when I realized I was going to see David.

"Mother effer. I have Berneli's class first. I look like a scrub." I groaned and contemplated running back to my room.

"You look fine! Relax, he has already seen all of you. I'm pretty sure that showing up in a t-shirt and jeans isn't going to change his opinion of you." She laughed and I started breathing again.

"Okay, you're probably right about that. But does it look like I got the guy and now I don't care about my looks?"

"I think you are overreacting. If that connection you say you have is real, then it won't matter what you're wearing. And if that isn't the case, then wear your stripper heals to class on Wednesday."

"You make a good point." I laughed and we went our separate ways. Normally, I was pretty early to this class, but today I was exactly on time. I walked over to my desk and quickly sat down. Berneli was leaning against his desk and I felt butterflies flutter into my stomach.

He had his glasses off so I had nothing blocking my view deep into his soul. His button-down shirt was tailored so it fit his body like a glove. A flash of him walking toward me naked, in all of his manly glory, raced across my mind. I had to keep from fanning myself as heat soon raced through my body and forced its way into my core.

He was gorgeous and very clearly avoiding my

gaze. At first, I tried not to take it personally, but as the class went on, I couldn't help but notice that he didn't walk near my desk or call on me.

By the time the class was over I felt stupid. Obviously, he didn't feel the same way. It was just another lay for him. So I grabbed my things and began to hurry out the door before I could further embarrass myself. Just as I made it to the door, I heard my name.

"Miss Carrington, I have that extra credit report for you." He held up a big brown envelope and waved it in my direction. As I didn't turn in any extra credit report, I was confused. I walked over to him and took it. "Please go over my notes before your next assignment." He then returned to the students standing in front of him asking questions.

I turned around, puzzled, and headed out the door. Once I got out of the classroom, I went straight to the bathroom and into one of the stalls to look at the envelope. I had a feeling it was some kind of secret so I probably should open it in private. However, I was way too excited to go back to my room. It was simply too far away and I didn't have that kind of patience.

I opened the envelope and inside was a handwritten note.

Violet,

I thought of nothing but you all Sunday. All I wanted to do was find you and hold you in my arms again. I'm sorry for the way I probably treated you in class but I don't want to look like I'm giving you special treatment. Frankly, I'm even a little afraid to look at you because then everyone may see just how strongly you affect me. I have office hours set up for today at five and I'd love to see you then. I promise to keep my intentions honorable even if my thoughts are not.

Dreaming of a time when you and I can be together,

David

Was swooning still a thing? Because that was one hundred percent what I was doing in the bathroom stall. I should have planned this better. Swooning over a handwritten love note in a public bathroom stall was probably the least romantic moment of my life. Nonetheless, there I was, clutching the proof that the other night meant something to him as well. I texted Annabelle and told her that we needed to meet for lunch so I could show her the note. However, when I showed up, Jason and Kyle were there too.

"*Violet!*" Kyle yelled as he saw me.

"*Kyle!*" I tried to hide my disappointment because there was no way I could talk to Annabelle about this in front of the guys. "We can chat after lunch," I whispered to her.

She nodded and I sat down.

"I'm sorry you didn't get to spend more time

with Janice," Jason said to me.

"Yeah, I know. We should all get together another time," I insisted, and kicked Annabelle lightly under the table. I knew Janice was one of the last people she wanted to hang out with. But Jason was such a great guy that Janice couldn't be that annoying, right?

"I'll bring it up to her. She's crazy busy with school and some of her other clubs but as soon as she is free, I'll let you know."

This kind of frustrated me. How hard was it to find a couple of minutes to spend time with your boyfriend's friends? It seemed important to him that we got to know her, so why didn't she make the time?

"Can you believe Kenny?" Annabelle had broken my train of thought. "I mean, he flirts, dances, and kisses me, all while he has a girlfriend. Who does that?" We all looked at each other and gave a perceptive look.

"He was a jerk the whole time we knew him. I'm not surprised. I just feel bad for his girlfriend. She probably has no idea what an asshole he is." I never liked that jerk.

"Oh, she knows!" Kyle smiled brightly and looked at Jason. "Right, buddy?

"What?" Annabelle and I said in unison.

"Jason might have let it slip to her that he was fooling around with other girls very loudly while she was in earshot."

"Well, she needed to know, and I didn't like that he was messing around with Annabelle," Jason insisted, and dipped his head to try to hide the blush crawling across his face. But he couldn't hide it from me.

I smiled. It was sweet to watch Jason standing up for Annabelle.

"You didn't have to do that," Annabelle gushed as she gazed at her hero.

"I know. It's okay. I didn't like that he hurt you like that," Jason said, looking up at her. They kept eye contact for a second too long and then both looked away.

Kyle and I glanced at each other and looked very smug. Apparently, he was thinking the same thing about Jason and Annabelle that I was.

***

We all finished our meals while talking about the comedienne who would be coming next week. There was so much to do with EET and it was all really stressful, exciting but stressful. As the boys were getting ready to leave, Annabelle stuck around, pretending to still be eating one of the three french fries left on her plate. As soon as they were out of sight, she looked at me.

"So, what's going on? What did he say?"

"Well, he didn't talk to me or even look at me the whole class so I assumed he just wanted sex and was over it." I told her about the extra credit envelope and handed it to her. I sat there quite impatiently as I waited for her to finish reading.

"Oh my god! I cannot believe he wrote that to you! This is kind of intense. Are you going to see him later?"

241

"Of course! I don't know what to expect. He said that his intentions would be honorable. I mean, I don't expect to just bang it out in the middle of the day. Other people will be around, and what if someone comes in? No, someone would hear us—I'm not the quietest when I'm experiencing the most fulfilling sex ever."

"I'm confused. Weren't you in his office when you two banged the last time? What makes this different?" she asked accusingly.

"Okay, valid point. But it was late at night and not during his office hours. I don't think there were any other professors in their office but there probably will be this time. I'm definitely going, you know, I'm just nervous."

"It will be fine. Just make sure you come over right after and tell me all about it," she insisted as she packed up her stuff to leave.

"I will." I grabbed my stuff and followed her out of the cafeteria. "Wasn't it great how Jason stood up for you and made sure Kenny got what was coming to him?" I turned and watched her expression. She started to blush but quickly shook her head and it was gone almost as soon as it had appeared.

"Yeah, he is a good guy." She turned to look at something on the wall we were passing.

"But it seemed especially nice that he was looking out for you."

"I know, Violet. You just said that." She was still looking at the wall.

"I was just making conversation. It just seems interesting that even though he was at the dance with Janice, he was still trying to make sure you were doing all right. You know, he called me over to make sure I knew Kenny had a girlfriend. That was how I found out. He was going out of his way for you," I said, trying to beat a dead horse until she realized how big of a deal this was.

"Yeah, well, I cannot wait until you hang out with Janice and see what she is really like. After that, then we will see who you play footsie with under the table. I am pretty sure I have a bruise where you kicked me." She was changing the subject. Maybe she wasn't ready to talk about it anymore. I debated pushing her a little but decided against it. I came to her when I needed her and I was sure she'd do the same.

"Oh please, you're fine! Besides, Janice can't be that bad, right?" I didn't like the idea of Jason with anyone who would not treat him right.

"Just wait!" she insisted, and we parted ways to class.

My class went on for what seemed like forever. It finally ended but it was only four o'clock. I had an hour to kill before seeing David and no patience to wait. I thought about going back to my room to change into something more appealing and maybe putting some make-up on, but he'd seen me earlier, and if I changed, then I would definitely look like I was trying too hard. So I headed to a computer lab and decided to work on my statistics homework.

This week's lab was online so I could suffer through it without my book. After about thirty minutes and no correct answer, I decided to end the suffering and wound up on my social media page. Before I knew it, I was stalking Janice's page. It looked like she was involved in a lot of "save the earth" type clubs. She seemed really passionate about it and I had to smile. I could picture her and Jason in a third world country trying to feed the hungry and cure the sick. Crap, it was hard to hate her.

I got lost somewhere in her prom pictures. She and Jason looked really happy. It was easy to see the spark Jason was talking about. I wanted to see her and Jason together more to see if I could see that moment again.

It was almost time to meet with David, so I headed over to his office. It was a couple of minutes past five when I stood outside his door. I wondered if he was waiting for me. I took a deep breath and knocked. Before he answered it, I noticed a sign on the door. It said that his office hours were over at five. So, no one would be coming to meet with him now. I smiled to myself as the thought of being with him again left me feeling tingly all over.

The door opened and he invited me in. His glasses were off and I melted into his eyes. There was something about them that almost always caught my attention before the rest of him. This was, of course, surprising since he was so much taller. I really had to tilt my head to get a good look.

"Glad you could make it." He smiled and closed the door behind me.

I wasn't sure what to expect so I stood just inside his office, staring up at him, and he leaned against his bookshelf about three feet from me. I didn't know if he was going to kiss me. Should I go in for a hug, or maybe a kiss on the cheek? That was a

British thing, right?

I looked up at him and realized he was waiting for me to speak.

"Yeah, I wouldn't miss it."

I wasn't sure where to look, but if I continued to stare into his eyes, I had a feeling I would jump his bones. Then again, I did notice that David didn't lock the door like last time. Reluctantly, I decided to pull myself together.

"So, I wanted to talk about the other night," he told me as he appraised me from the bookshelf.

I knew the chair in front of his desk would be a heck of a lot more comfortable and probably safer than standing with him like this. But for some reason, I couldn't get my legs to head over there. He didn't move either.

I waited, barely breathing, to hear what he had to say. "I don't regret it. It was one of the best nights of my life."

A weight lifted off my chest. I couldn't believe it meant that much to him. "Mine too. We were like electricity."

"I'd like to do it again. Several more times, if I'm being honest. I feel as though we need some guidelines, though, like it should probably not happen in my office or even on school property."

I laughed. "Yeah, you're probably right about that. My dorm room would probably create a whole lot of problems too. Although my roomie would get a great show," I joked, trying to keep this conversation light. The truth was I was having a hard time keeping my hands off of him. He had rolled his sleeves up and his tan, muscled forearms were practically bursting out. I remembered how strong yet gentle they were when he held me. I longed to feel that again.

"That's what I think too. I guess we will have to make other arrangements and try to keep it together while we are at school."

"A lack of self-control has always been one of my faults," I admitted, trying not to notice the bulge in his pants. It would seem that just looking at me turned him on. I smiled, enjoying my power. Then I licked my lips and looked up at him. He definitely noticed.

"See, your games are not going to work because I have self-control and I'm proving it right now." He stuck his hands in his pockets and dropped his gaze from my eyes.

"I've seen your attempts at self-control and I've enjoyed shattering them," I insisted, and looked him up and down, making sure to stare at his growing member for just a second too long.

"That sounds like a challenge to me." He leaned in close. "I'm stronger than you think."

"If that's what you want to believe." I headed over to the chair and sat down, legs crossed. "Are you coming?" I asked without turning to look back at him. "If all we are going to do is stare at the other, then I would much prefer to do it in a chair." I placed my bag on the ground and Berneli walked to his desk and sat in the chair behind it. "What arrangements did you have in mind?" I was actually very curious. Clearly, he had taken time to think about this.

"I have a flat off campus and I've brought a good

portion of my library from England over. I don't think you would be bored spending some nights there. Obviously, I couldn't drive you to campus, but I'd be happy to pay cab fare to get you back." He said all of this like it was a business deal instead of a sexual proposition. It kind of irked me so I decided to continue teasing him.

"What makes you think there will be any time for reading if I were to come over to your bachelor pad?" I asked him, and leaned over his desk, letting my t-shirt dip a little so the girls were on display.

"Eventually, I'll wear you out."

"Now that sounds like a challenge." I inched my face closer to his. My heart was beating wildly in my chest and I was pretty sure he could hear it. I looked at his luscious lips and wanted to kiss him. No, I needed to kiss him. But I would wait. We were in a stalemate, and the first one to bend would surely lose. I did not lose.

"What are your plans for tonight?" he asked, and smiled the crooked smile that made me quiver and shake.

"You tell me. I do have this one professor who gave us this crazy assignment last week that is due on Friday. I should probably work on that."

"We both know you have already finished that paper and right now you probably are just checking on a few more sources. I think you have time."

I smiled because he was right. I actually liked the paper he had assigned and needed to finish editing it. I was thinking of adding another source but I had already gone a couple pages over the limit.

"Don't blame me when I ask for an extension."

247

"I think we will be able to work something out regarding that extension tonight. I have a feeling I know exactly how long it needs to be." He reached out and began to draw circles on the back of my hand. It felt delicious and I decided it was time to finish the cheesy innuendos.

"Well then, what time?"

"I'll send a cab for you around seven thirty. That should give you plenty of time to work on that paper."

"If you insist." I sat for a few extra seconds, enjoying the feeling of my hand in his. Then I got up and headed toward the door.

"Oh, and, Violet, call me crazy one more time and I will give you a whole new meaning for the word."

I didn't turn around and just shook my head. "What makes you think I don't like crazy?" I opened the door and headed out to the sound of him chuckling.

***

I hurried to the cafeteria and made a quick sandwich to eat as I ran to my room. Well, more accurately, to Annabelle's room because she was going to flip when I told her this. I had made it to our floor when I noticed Officer Finn was outside my door again. I sighed and slowed my pace.

"Officer, what's going on?" I had talked to Lola today so I knew she was not in any danger. At least she wasn't a few hours ago.

"Nothing. I'm just doing a follow-up. We heard

from Miss Zimmerman and she said there was a big misunderstanding. But girls say that a lot, so I wanted to make sure you are both doing fine." He was trying to sound noble but had managed to sound like an asshole.

"Well, I talked to her earlier and she assured me she was fine. She is visiting her mother right now so she isn't here." I hoped he would just walk away, but, of course, he didn't.

"Yes, she mentioned that. I also wanted to follow-up with you," he informed me as he stuck his chest out a bit. I heard birds did that when they were trying to attract a mating partner. Little did he know, I wasn't interested in his type of bird.

"I'm fine. No one is bothering me so you can go and check on someone else," I insisted, and went to unlock my door. He stepped in front of me and blocked my access.

"Are you sure? I don't mind hanging out here or escorting you anywhere you need to go. In fact, why don't I take you to dinner tonight? We could even go off campus if you'd like," he suggested with a giant grin on his face.

I lifted my sandwich and showed it to him. "I grabbed a quick dinner. I have a lot of homework and planned to spend the whole night in my room so I don't need to be escorted anywhere. But thanks for your offer. Good night, Officer." I said this with a strong emphasis on *officer*.

His smile faded for a second but then he found it again. "Anything for you. Since you said you weren't seeing anyone, I figured you would be free. Come on, a nice dinner out has got to be better than that sandwich." He was pushing me to accept his date but there was no way that was going to happen. I didn't want to be mean but I needed to be firm.

"I just don't think it's a good time for me to be involved with anyone. I need to focus on my school work." There, that sounded good.

"Like your literature class? I hear you have to work very hard for a good grade from that professor."

My eyes about popped out of my head and I felt my mouth instantly go dry but I kept my poker face. He clearly knew something about Berneli. This was too much of a coincidence. Besides, I had never mentioned to him that I was even taking a literature class.

"That is a hard class but I think I have a handle on it."

"I bet you do, have a handle on it." He smiled his creepy serial killer smile and pulled a white peony out of that ridiculous shoulder bag he seemed to always be carrying. He offered it to me but I didn't take it. "A single flower isn't enough to tempt you? I'll remember that for next time," Finn said, and finally let me walk into the room. I rolled my eyes and was about to drop my bag off and head over to Annabelle's room when her door opened.

"What the hell was that about? I heard noises outside and saw a campus security officer in front of your door. Wasn't that the guy from the urgent care center?" she asked, looking concerned.

"Ugh! Come on in. It is a bit of a long story," I said, and we settled on my bed. I told her about how he kept showing up and was always making slightly inappropriate comments but nothing too terrible to report. "I don't know. It's like every time I turn around, this guy is here watching me. I get that he might have a crush but it is getting a little creepy."

"Is there anyone you can report him to?" she asked, eating half of my sandwich.

"I don't know. He picked the lock of my room the other day and that really freaked me out. But I think he knows about Berneli and me. What if I report him and he then reports me?"

"What makes you think he would do that?" I saw the concern etched into her face.

"He drops little comments about me seeing a professor and how I could get kicked out of school for it. But just now, I told him I was staying in tonight to get school work done and he asked if it was for my literature class."

"That sounds ominous." Annabelle's face went a little whiter and I could tell she was a little freaked out for me.

"I know, so I don't want to report him in case he says something about David and me to someone important." I was trying to brush this whole thing under the rug and just tolerate his crap but it was taking its toll and I was exhausted.

"Well, I think you should say something, but that is just my opinion. If you do and he reports you, it will sound like he is just trying to get you back. I don't think anyone would take him seriously."

"I'll think about it." I couldn't help but think of Lola and the similarities in our situations. It was easy for me to tell her to report Tyler, but here I was in a situation much like hers and I was scared to report Finn.

"So, tell me what happened with Berneli," she practically squealed.

I explained how he wanted to meet off campus to continue the affair and how we were starting tonight.

"I really need my own car. It would make this so much easier," I said after I explained about the cabs.

"I don't know. It is kind of romantic to be picked up in a cab and whisked off to your lover's apartment," she uttered in a dreamy tone.

"I guess. I'll let you know. Anyway, I need to pack a bag. I have no idea what I'm going to wear. I mean, what do you wear to meet your lover at his apartment for the first time?" I got up and started going through my closet.

"Isn't the standard outfit a trench coat with lingerie underneath?" Annabelle teased while heading out the door.

"Ha-ha! Very funny," I sneered before saying goodbye. I had a few pieces of fun lingerie but they really weren't all that impressive, or at least not to a real adult. I was going to need to go shopping. For now, I would just have to settle for black matching bra and panties. I slipped those on with a pair of tight skinny jeans and a form fitting red blouse. Then I grabbed my high black heels to finish the look up.

I felt good about it. I headed to the bathroom and put a little make-up on. I didn't want to overdo it but I wanted to feel pretty. After my last swipes of mascara and some much needed hair gel, I was ready to meet him. I packed some clothes to wear tomorrow into my overnight bag, grabbed my backpack, and headed to the parking lot to wait for the cab.

***

I took a deep breath and climbed in the back of the car. As we drove off, I realized my hands were shaking. I couldn't figure out why. He and I had been together before, but maybe it was the idea of being with David again. Maybe being picked up in the cab was romantic and exciting. Maybe it was because I knew just how good we were together. Whatever it was, I needed to pull it together.

After about ten minutes in the cab, we pulled up to an apartment complex. It had sleek lines and was painted a dark grey color. There were floor-to-ceiling windows in the front with dark molding along the edges. It really was stunning. I was so impressed with the building that I almost didn't see him.

David came out of the complex and went straight to the cab. He opened the door for me and offered his hand to help me out. I slid my bags over my shoulder and accepted his hand. Then he stuck his head back in the car and paid the cabbie.

"Well, aren't you considerate," I gushed, batting my lashes ever so slightly at him.

"I try." David took my bags and my hand and then we headed to his apartment. When we entered the lobby, I looked around. There were glass tables with gorgeous flower bouquets and gold vases. They were practically spilling out they were so full.

I couldn't help but notice that they were violets. I knew he didn't put them there but it seemed like a sign to me. Yes, it was cheesy, but they were my favorite flower. My dad had brought a bouquet into the delivery room and my mom loved them so much that they decided to name me after them.

We headed to the gold elevator and up to the fourth floor. I felt like I should say something, but nothing came to mind that didn't sound like nervous babble. I kept quiet and so did he. I was getting a vibe that he was a little nervous too but that could have just been my nervous energy bouncing off of him. There was no reason for him to be nervous, right?

As he let me into his apartment, my mouth dropped. It was amazing. One of the other walls held a giant flat screen and the other had the same floor-to-ceiling windows as the lobby. There was a fluffy grey couch in the middle and it looked as if it was the most comfortable couch I had ever seen in my life. There were bookshelves stuffed with books filling two of the walls in his living room. They were all different sizes and colors and I was itching to browse.

"This is such a *Beauty and the Beast* moment," I uttered before I could stop myself.

"What are you talking about?"

"You know, in *Beauty and the Beast*, when the beast is looking for a way to win Belle's heart? He shows her the giant library and she starts to warm up to him." I walked over to one of the bookcases and began perusing the titles, running my finger down the spines gently.

"So does that mean you are warming up to me now?" he whispered, suddenly behind me.

"It depends. Are you a beast?"

"Be careful what you wish for."

I shivered as he wrapped his arms around me. I leaned my head into his shoulder and closed my eyes, just enjoying the feeling of being close to him. He smelled of clean water with a hint of some kind of musk. It was delicious.

"I've been waiting to hold you in my arms for days. I almost took you in my office earlier today. But I think you knew that, which is why you were teasing me. I also think it is about time I punish you for it." He nibbled a little on my ear before dropping to my shoulder, moving my shirt slightly so he could kiss the bare skin.

"It doesn't really feel like punishment to me. But if you insist." I giggled as I placed my hands on the bookshelf in front of me.

"Oh, it will be. I'm going to bring you to just shy of absolute pleasure and then I'm going to stop. We'll see how many times I have to do it before you apologize." He pulled the ponytail holder out of my hair, ran his fingers through it, and lightly massaged my scalp.

"I don't think you're going to be able to just stop. I have ways to make you finish."

He pressed his body against mine and I felt his excitement. "Remember, I have self-control." He spun me around and I looked up at him. I saw carnal lust in his eyes and it was exhilarating to know that I provoked such feelings in this man.

"Remember, I have none." I reached my arms

around his neck and pulled him into a kiss. He opened his lips for me and I dove in. He picked me up and pressed me against the wall next to the bookcase. His kisses were passionate and filled with a yearning that I was only too happy to satisfy. Maybe he would forget about the teasing punishment.

He dipped his head and kissed my neck while moving his hand under my blouse and on top of my black bra. He cupped my breast and ran his thumb over my nipple. They had already grown hard and David recognized this.

"Easy, love, you always get so excited so fast," he joked in his gruff voice. When he spoke to me in that low, throaty voice, I could feel myself grow damp. He started to kiss me again and slid his hand from my breast to my back, where he unhooked my bra.

David then reached back around to my breast and cupped it again. When he gently pulled on my nipple, I let out a moan. I didn't mean to, but it felt so good. I leaned my head back against the wall when he started to stroke my other breast and I pushed my chest out, forcing more of it into his hand.

"You're so responsive to me. It's going to be very easy to punish you," he warned in his throaty voice.

"What?" My eyes shot open. "You were serious about that?" I asked, breathless. He was already building me up to a climax and my pants and shirt were still on. I had a bad feeling about this, or maybe too good a feeling.

"Teasing is not nice. By the time I'm done, you will be begging for my forgiveness. And only then will I consider allowing you to come," he threatened while stroking and lightly plucking my nipple.

I was going to respond, but when I opened my mouth, another moan escaped. David swallowed that moan and kissed me hard. He removed his hand from my breast and moved to my butt. He gripped it hard and picked me up, carrying me to his bedroom. David threw me on the bed and I reached down to take my shoes off when his hands stopped me.

"No, I like them." He smiled that crooked smile and bit his bottom lip.

"I had a feeling you might when I put them on."

"I like that you thought of me when you got dressed. I want to be on your mind constantly."

"Well, keep up what you're doing, and I won't be able to push you from my thoughts."

He climbed on the bed toward me, pulled off my shirt, and then made quick work of unhooking my bra. I lifted my arms over my head and he held them down against the bed. David dipped his head and began to suck on my nipple. It was gentle at first and then the intensity picked up. I started to feel an insatiable pressure between my legs. I began to shift and twist my legs, desperate for some kind of relief.

"No, no, love. You don't get any kind of relief yet." He climbed on top of me and held my legs down with his hips. I couldn't move but I kind of liked it. Then he blew ever so lightly on my wet nipples. The sensation made me shake all over and left tingles down to my toes. "Are you ready to

257

apologize yet?" he asked as he nibbled on my ear.

"I don't know what you want me to apologize for," I purred back.

"If that's the way you want to play it, then so be it." He reached down to unbutton my jeans and then slid them down my hips to show my panties. "Black is really a good color on you," he said as he slid his finger under the elastic band and then yanked them down with his teeth.

David started slow and slid a finger inside me, feeling my arousal. It was almost gentle as he went in and out. While it felt amazing, it wasn't meeting my needs. The pressure inside of me had reached a boiling point and I was going to explode. I raised my hips off the bed in an effort to have him fill me deeper but he was not having it.

"David. Stop playing with me," I demanded fiercely.

He chuckled and slowly took his finger out. "I haven't heard an apology yet. I can promise you that I will not let you reach climax until I do." He slid two fingers inside, his pace picking up a little but it was still not enough. I groaned in frustration. David removed his fingers again and dipped his head, blowing slightly. The rush of cold air caught me off guard and I was having problems breathing. Then he slipped his tongue inside.

"Holy crap!" I screamed. The truth was that no guy had ever done that to me before and it felt amazing. I could feel my release coming closer and closer when he stopped.

"Say my name," he commanded loudly.

"David," I whispered, begging for him to

continue.

"Now say, 'David, I'm sorry.'" He then continued to lick. I was quiet for a moment too long when he found my bud. He started to suck on it and I exploded.

"I'm so sorry. I'll never tease you again," I screamed, hoping he wouldn't stop. David picked up the pace and within a matter of seconds, I was shaking as the orgasm hit me hard.

"That's a good girl." He chuckled and wiped his mouth with a tissue from the night stand. I looked at him and laughed. Of course he was still in his button-down shirt with the sleeves rolled up and his perfectly pressed slacks. Meanwhile, I was lying stark naked on the bed with my jeans at my ankles, my fancy heels still on.

At first I felt a little vulnerable, but then I realized the excitement. For some reason, I didn't mind it. Well, at least for a little while. I reached down and removed my shoes and my jeans.

It seemed to be a crime to cover up that perfect figure. I sat up on my knees and reached out to him. He looked down at me and smiled.

"You are so beautiful." There was so much sincerity in his voice and I didn't feel the need to try to cover myself up.

I began unbuttoning his shirt, kissing his skin as it became free of fabric. As I got to the end, I reached down and took his belt off. David stood with his hands by his sides, not touching me, but watching everything I did with a longing in his eyes that both scared and excited me. I unbuttoned his pants and then slid them off. I leaned back for a second and admired his muscles glistening in the soft moonlight shining through the bedroom window. But I wanted more. I pulled his boxers off and was pleased to see that he was primed and ready for me.

I reached out and took him, sliding my hand up and down gradually. We maintained eye contact and I watched his eyes light up. But I craved more. I leaned down and took him in my mouth. I started with gentle strokes at his tip and then slowly took more and more of him. When I had all of him I could manage, I began to suck. David's knees buckled a little and he let out a raspy moan. He then placed his hands on my shoulders for balance. His grip tightened as he fought the battle to control his feelings.

I continued and took him in and out at a quicker pace, randomly sucking and caressing with my tongue. I felt him tense up and he broke. Berneli let out a loud groan of satisfaction and I took it all. When he had finished, he handed me the box of tissues so I could wipe my mouth. Almost as soon as I was done, David took my face in his hands and kissed me hard. He pushed me down and then climbed on top of me.

His hands soon found my breasts and he began to feel, pluck, and squeeze with his strong hands. From between his legs, I could feel that he was already excited and ready for more. Now he was focused on getting me there and he knew exactly what to do to push my buttons.

Finally, David reached between my legs and found that I was soaking wet. Pleasing him had really done a number on me. I enjoyed it almost as much as he did and he started to kiss my neck. It soon became too much for me.

"Please, get a condom," I commanded breathlessly, and he obliged.

He went into his bedside table and slipped it on. David looked me in the eyes and I could see the fire ready to erupt from him but he still stopped all the same.

"Ready, love?" he asked, and grabbed my hips.

I nodded, not sure if I could speak. He slid inside me, slowly at first, and then I soon felt him fill me up. I let out a moan and ran my fingers through David's hair. The pace was still too slow for me and my core was pounding.

I needed more. I grabbed a handful of hair and yanked it. He moaned loudly, biting my shoulder in response. But his pace quickened and he pushed even deeper inside me. This already felt amazing, and then he hit my spot. I let out a loud yell of delight and lifted my hips up to try to take him deeper. I could feel my climax coming and I gripped onto it, afraid I'd lose it again. But so far, David wasn't about to let that happen.

Within seconds I was screaming his name as the relief hit me and left my body shaking with aftershocks. Apparently, my excitement was too much for David as his climax shortly followed mine. I had heard stories about couples finishing together but it had always seemed like something out of a novel. Especially since most of the guys I'd been with finished way before I was ready. But David wasn't most guys.

He kissed me gently and then slid out of me and walked to the bathroom. I lay there on his bed, trying to catch my breath. David came back to the bed and engulfed me in a giant embrace.

We lay there like that for a minute while I listened to his heartbeat. It was almost more intimate than the acts we'd just completed. David kissed the top of my head and then gave me a quick squeeze.

"Are you hungry?" he asked sweetly.

"I'm a little hungry." I remembered that Annabelle had eaten half of my sandwich.

"I'll make us some supper," he said, letting me go and heading to his mahogany dresser. David slipped on a pair of shorts and a white t-shirt and then looked at me and smiled. He tossed me a t-shirt and shorts to put on.

While David headed to the kitchen, I grabbed the clothes and headed to the bathroom. After a little clean-up, I splashed water on my face and put his clothes on. I took an extra couple of seconds just breathing in his scent off the shirt.

***

There were some sounds from the kitchen and I went to check it out. David was standing over a cutting board slicing some onions. I sat on the barstool across from where he was working.

"Can I help with something?" I asked, pretending I knew what to do in the kitchen. The truth was that I was a menace whenever I attempted to cook. My mother had tried to teach me but I didn't have a knack for it.

"No, it's my treat to you. I intend to satisfy you in all ways humanly possible. One of those includes your stomach." He looked up from the cutting board and winked.

"I like this plan. What are you making?" I asked, looking at the ingredients on the counter.

"Pasta. I make a great red sauce. I didn't know what you liked but I figured pasta was a safe bet."

"Pasta is actually one of my favorite meals."

"Then score one for me. I have some soft drinks in the fridge if you want some. Cups are in the cabinet next to it." He tilted his head toward the fridge. I walked over and grabbed two cups.

"Did you want some?" I asked as I grabbed two sodas out of the fridge.

"Yeah, sounds lovely."

I added some ice to the cups and then poured the soda. I placed the cup near him, but not too close that he would knock it over. Then I took my cup over to one of the bookcases. There were so many books that I had never heard of and I was dying to check them out. David seemed to also have a soft spot for murder mystery novels. I picked a couple off the shelf and looked at their summaries.

"Any take your fancy?" he shouted from the kitchen.

"Only about twenty. I'm a big murder mystery fan too."

"You can take any one you like," he offered, and poured some pasta into a pot.

"Thanks." I grabbed one of the books and headed to the comfy couch where I settled in with my feet tucked underneath me.

It was very peaceful. I sat on the couch, reading and listening to David hum while he cooked. I breathed in the aromas coming from the kitchen and started to lose myself in the story of a young girl murdered in a parking lot. Eventually, I heard David walking toward me. He leaned over the couch and kissed me on the cheek.

"The grandmother did it."

"*What?* Why would you tell me that?" I groaned.

"I'm kidding. Relax, there is no grandmother in the book. Supper is ready." He tapped my nose and headed back to the kitchen.

"Ha-ha. It smells good." I followed him to the breakfast bar and David slid a plate in front of me. The pasta was piled high, looked incredible, and smelled even better. He grabbed his own plate and sat down next to me. I took my first bite and couldn't help but sigh.

"This is amazing!" There was such a difference between that crappy sauce they served in the cafeteria. The taste of fresh ingredients burst on my tongue and it was one of the best things I'd ever tasted.

"Thank you. My mother owns a restaurant in England so she has had me cooking since I was little. She thought it was one of the most important things you can learn." He practically beamed as he said this and I noticed the pride in his voice when he talked about her.

"My mom tried to teach me to cook but I'm kind of hopeless," I confessed as I grabbed a piece of bread.

"And you were going to try to help with dinner tonight?" he asked incredulously.

"Well, I didn't want to be rude." I blushed a little.

"It's okay. I can teach you a couple things," he offered, and stroked my cheek gently. "Did you like that book?"

"I just started but I liked the sound of it. I mean, can you really go wrong with a spy novel and the murder of an art gallery worker? Clearly there is going to be fraud and fencing stolen goods with some deception," I said, getting excited. It really did seem like a good book.

"Clearly. It actually is a good book. I think you are going to like it." He grabbed some more bread. We spent the next hour talking about books and finishing all of the pasta. It turned out we read a lot of the same books but we had vastly different opinions about them.

I insisted on cleaning the dishes while David went to the bookshelf and grabbed a few other books. The next few hours flew by. We curled up on the couch and continued the book conversation. There were many books that we both liked, but what really connected us was the fact that we could debate them. There was something sexy about an intelligent conversation.

Normally, this would be annoying or frustrating, but with David it was comfortable. I didn't get frustrated or annoyed when he explained his point of view. He made some valid arguments and actually listened to what I had to say. A first for me since I tended to ignore contradicting opinions, but

David made me want to listen. Before we knew it, I checked the clock and it was after one in the morning.

"Oh man! I have got to get to sleep." I stretched my arms and fought a yawn.

"Let me help you," he offered, and picked me up. David carried me to his bed. We set an alarm and settled into each other. My heart was racing and I was having a hard time calming it. It was the first time I had spent the night in a guy's bed. I wanted to be here but a million thoughts were going through my mind. What happened in the morning? What happened if he snored, or worse, what happened if I snored? Would I even be able to sleep in this unknown place?

As if sensing my unrest, Berneli reached up and began stroking my hair. It was comforting and somehow slowed my brain down. I focused on his heartbeat and before long I was asleep.

Chapter 13

The alarm went off far too early. Apparently, David was a heavy sleeper because he didn't even move. I tried to slip out from under his arm but he held on tighter.

"Nope, too early." He pulled me back into his embrace and locked his arms.

"We have to get to class. I need to shower, catch a cab, and get breakfast." I was pretending to fight his grasp but I was fine lying there for a few more minutes.

"Shower, huh?" he asked, growling in my ear. "I'm ready for the shower."

"I bet you are." I noticed that morning wood seemed to be a real phenomenon and not a rumor.

"What? It would go twice as fast if someone is helping you," he insisted as we both climbed out of bed.

"I have a feeling that it would take twice as long." I grabbed my bag and headed to the shower.

"What if I wrote you a note? *Dear Professor, Violet was late for class today because she was busy helping her other professor in the shower. No, I don't share. Thank you for your consideration. Signed, David Sex Slave Berneli.* I think it could work." He pulled me into the bathroom and I fought the urge to giggle.

"Sex slave, huh?" I asked as he started to help me out of my clothes, well, his clothes.

"Oh yeah. Let me serve you." He turned the shower on and it was more than the warm water that eased my tension.

As it turned out, showering together did take twice as long so I had to skip breakfast. Luckily, my cab got to David's pretty quickly so I wasn't late for my first class. As I had that big paper to turn in, it was a good thing.

***

I sat in class trying to pay attention but all I could think about was the perfect night I'd spent with David. The sex was good, obviously, but it was more than that. I felt at home with him and completely at ease. This just created more trouble because my feelings were growing.

I met up with Annabelle outside the coffee shop after our first class and she about ran me over.

"So, how was it?" She grabbed a table and leaned forward eagerly.

I was famished so I was shoving my pastry into my mouth. It was truly an attractive sight.

"It was a perfect night. I mean, yeah, we had sex, and I still think he is a god, but it's more than that. We spent most of the night arguing about books and authors. I can just speak my mind and he takes it and responds however he wants. We don't worry about hurting each other's feelings or what the other will think. It's just two people discussing things they're passionate about. It was nice," I said, reminiscing.

It was hard not to smile as the thought of lying with my feet in his lap on the couch while we discussed Peter Pan, Oliver Twist, and, unfortunately, Anna Karenina.

"There is no judgement," I continued. "And he is considerate. He made me this huge dinner and had even set up the cab the night before. He planned the whole night and it was amazing. Dates from this moment forward will forever have to live up to last night." I was trying to put my feelings into words but they didn't seem to match the level of perfection.

"I hate you! That sounds amazing. He sounds amazing. I never would have guessed he was like that. In all the EET meetings, he seems so stuffy and boring. I mean, even his jokes are dry," she said, stealing a few bites of my pastry. I was definitely going to have to do something about her food stealing habit.

"I think it's a British thing, that dry humor. I actually really like it." I ate the rest of my pastry before Annabelle could take any other bites.

"So, you officially have feelings?" she asked, looking at me with a smile.

"I mean, I don't think it will ever be more than just some fun. Sure, he is leaving in a year, but a lot can happen between now and then. We could be broken up in a month. Why worry now?" I said, hoping I sounded more convinced than I actually was. I was trying to keep the feelings pushed down inside. Denial was the perfect solution.

"Sounds like a load of crap to me."

My mouth fell open as I stared at her. "What?"

"You just looked at me with so much passion in your eyes, so I'm calling bullshit. You care about him a lot more than you're willing to admit. If you need to lie to me to keep this façade going, that's fine, I just hope you aren't lying to yourself too."

I closed my eyes and then looked at her, all kidding aside. "Yeah, okay. I have feelings for him. I think about him constantly and it feels amazing to be with him. But it can't go anywhere and I know that. At this point, I just want to enjoy it while I can and pretend tomorrow doesn't exist."

"Well, I'm all for you enjoying your time together. And I'll be here when tomorrow does come." She reached her hand out and held mine just for a second. I smiled at her and we had a moment. "But are you going to tell him about Finn?"

"Probably not. I don't want to worry him. I'm really just overreacting. There is no way Finn can know about it." If I said it out loud enough, maybe it would prove to be true.

"I feel like he would want to know. Isn't he risking his job? Shouldn't he be the one making the decision?"

"We talked about it once. He said that he would worry about it. Besides, he could probably just go back to his job in England." I tried to ignore the terrible feeling in my gut. It was possible that I was being a little selfish. "Maybe I'm afraid that if I tell him, he will want to end it." I looked down, averting Annabelle's judgmental gaze.

"It sounds to me like he already knows his job is on the line. At least make him aware so that both of you dive in with your eyes open."

"Fine, I will bring it up the next time I see him." She was right, but I didn't feel any better about this.

"Good. I need my own pastry and a giant cup of coffee now." She went over to the cash register and left me to my thoughts.

Last night, David and I had finally exchanged numbers. We had to be delicate about it though. I even changed his name to Hercules in my phone just in case. Okay, that was also for my amusement but it still served a purpose.

He hadn't texted me yet, probably because he just got out of his own class, but I didn't want to text him first this morning. Somehow, even after all the passion, we'd managed to forget, or at least overlook, setting up another night. I had no reason to think we wouldn't, but I was a worrier like that.

Annabelle headed back to the table and handed me my own pastry that she promised not to eat. I needed to change the subject before she realized just how neurotic this man could make me.

"Are you ready for the comedienne this weekend?" I asked, knowing Annabelle had been working hard on this.

"Yes! I am ready for this to be over!"

"Okay, I think that is a little dramatic."

"It is just a lot of work, especially since Trent is not doing anything anymore."

"Well, give me some more work. Right now all I am doing is dealing with the rider." I was feeling a little guilty. It was kind of my fault that Trent was not around anymore.

"You'll regret you said that." She got out some notes from her EET binder. "So the biggest issue right now is that we have not sold nearly enough tickets. People are not signing up to sell tickets and we need to hang up some flyers and do some fun advertising," Annabelle said, going over those notes.

"What if we got some chalk and wrote on the sidewalk outside the dorms and the apartments about the comedienne?" I was partially kidding, partially serious.

"Um, I don't know how I feel about it. Part of me loves the idea and the other part thinks it is silly."

"At least it would cost, like, no money," I said, trying to sound hopeful.

"Actually, I am pretty sure we have chalk in the EET office so it would be totally free. This is starting to sound better and better. I mean, if it doesn't work, then it is not that big of a deal, right? What are you doing after the EET meeting? Are you meeting with him again?" she asked as she downed her coffee.

Then, all of a sudden, my phone went off. I jumped about three feet in the air and dropped my phone on the ground. "My bad!" I was blushing a deep pink.

"I guess we know who texted you. I'll chat with you at EET." Annabelle got up and headed to her next class.

"Bye, babe," I said, and opened his text.

David: Hey, beautiful. I've been thinking about u all morning. How was ur day?

Me: Good so far. I'm excited to see you at the meeting but obviously I can't jump your bones.

David: I have work 2night, hoping you could come over tomorrow. We have to get the rider ready and then we can work on ur self-control. I have some ideas.

Me: I think I can make some time for you in my schedule. I have some ideas of my own.

David: Can't wait.

I closed my phone and headed to my next class with a smile I could no longer contain.

***

After class, I went to the computer lab to wait for the EET meeting. I had just started to get in a stride when Annabelle came running in.

"Uh, hi," I said as she ran up to me.

"You have to come to the EET board meeting." She was talking very fast.

"Why?" I asked looking confused.

"Never mind why. Just get your stuff and hurry up," she ordered, and actually grabbed my phone to

273

ensure I followed her.

I logged out of the computer and grabbed my things. I had no idea why I was needed at this meeting. My chalk idea really was not that big of a deal and I felt like if something was going on with David, Annabelle would have told me. I walked into the meeting and everyone looked at me. It seemed a little weird but I waved anyway.

"So, Annabelle has been telling us about your ideas and how you have the time to be on the board. Obviously, you know that Trent has backed out of the position and we have an opening," Clarissa said with a huge smile on her face. "We would like to extend the position of late night entertainment chair to you."

"Thank you! Yes, I accept." I actually was really excited.

"Great! You will need to meet with us before the meetings and you will be in charge of some of the smaller late night events, but we can go over that after the comedy show." Nat handed me a handbook and gave me a bright smile.

She continued to talk about the comedienne and what needed to be done. Annabelle was vigorously taking notes and I felt a little out of place. I looked around the room and my eyes fell on David. He smiled slightly, the corners of his mouth perking up, and winked at me. I looked down to hide my blush and then it hit me. I really hoped that our relationship had nothing to do with this decision. Annabelle looked at me and smiled big. Really, my relationship with Annabelle probably had more to do with this job than my relationship with Berneli.

They announced my joining the EET board in the actual meeting and we went over more information for the comedienne. The meeting went pretty well and no one seemed to question my new position. Well, at least no one questioned it to my face.

David and I had to sit and work together because we needed to plan out the rider. We decided to go out tomorrow after his last class and then privately decided to head to his place after. I was really excited. Sitting across from each other knowing that I couldn't touch him only seemed to make my need worse. It was exhilarating. I left with Annabelle feeling even more turned on than I had been this morning.

Annabelle and I went to the dorms with the chalk and began to decorate. It was surprisingly more fun than I had initially thought. You could even say it was therapeutic. I wasn't the most artistic person but I could color within the lines that Annabelle drew. Apparently, Clarissa was really artistic so she came with us.

I really liked her. She was a very real person and didn't hesitate to tell you like it is. The three of us went to dinner after we finished coloring and spent hours talking. Clarissa had always been nice to me but this was the first time I was actually getting to know her.

When we finished, I headed back to my room. My computer class had a huge project due this week and I had just barely started. With the comedienne coming this weekend, I knew I needed to finish it ahead of time. As I dropped my stuff on my desk, I noticed something that didn't belong. There was a bouquet of violets in a vase on my desk. I didn't have a vase, and I damn sure didn't have fresh flowers.

My heartbeat sped up as I looked at the card.

Maybe a different type of flower is enough to please you, baby. If not, I'll keep trying.

Love,

Your Protector

"Finn," I mumbled. Then I realized a bigger problem. My door was locked. Finn had broken into my room to leave these flowers. I felt a tear fall down my cheek as the fear and frustration took over. How could this man who was supposed to protect me take away any semblance of safety I once felt?

I grabbed the flowers and ran outside. My pulse raced as I rushed toward the woods behind the dorm building. I ignored the path and pushed forward as low hanging leaves whipped at my face. Finally, when I couldn't see my dorm anymore, I hurled the flowers at a tree and watched as the vase shattered into a million pieces.

My knees gave out and I fell to the hard ground, barely registering the pain that shot through my legs. I fought for control, forcing my breathing to return to normal. If Finn wouldn't take a hint, then I would spell it out for him. I'd make it clear as day that we weren't ever going to be together. He would have to accept it and leave me alone, right? I pushed the doubt away and then returned to my room and went to sleep.

I woke up terrified and gasping for air. There was a sound and for a second I thought it was Finn.

"Sorry, did I wake you up?" Lola asked as she crept in wearing what looked an awful lot like a walk of shame dress. Things must have still been going well with Tyler.

"No, I mean, yeah, you woke me up, but my alarm was just about to go off so no worries." I rubbed my face and tried to get ahold of myself. Once I talked to Finn today, it would all be over and I wouldn't have to worry about this panic. He would be free to find someone who shared his feelings.

I got dressed and headed to David's class. I didn't expect any attention from him so I brought my homework for some of my other classes. I figured he would not care too much since my project for him was already done. I could always make it up to him later.

The class was uneventful. If he noticed I was working on other homework, he didn't say anything. Another student was doing their presentation and that took up most of the class. David decided to let us out early to work on our papers. I was headed to the library when I got a text from Annabelle about selling tickets. I had completely forgotten that I had agreed to do that with her so I turned around and headed to the table she had set up in one of the hallways.

"So what's the plan?" I asked, sitting down next to her.

"I mean, it is pretty self-explanatory. We sit here and ask people if they want to buy tickets," she said, and grabbed a bunch of flyers. "I thought we could hand these out to people so maybe they can think it over if they don't want to buy tickets straight away."

"Okay, I can do that for a couple minutes. Then do you mind if I put some finishing touches on my project?" I asked, hoping she would not get irritated.

"Yeah, its fine. I really just wanted the company. No one else was available for this time slot." She had just pulled out her sign-up sheet.

"How were you? Don't you have class during this time too? I was only free because I got out of class early."

"My first class was a test so I asked the teacher if I could take it early because I had EET stuff that had to be done; David wrote me a note. Apparently, teachers do not care that much about taking the test early. It's when you take it late that they get irritated. Anyway, I took it last Friday."

"Well, aren't you dedicated," I teased.

"Shut up." She rolled her eyes and we went on to pass out flyers when classes let out. After about fifteen minutes, the halls started to clear up as people went to their next classes and we were generally alone. We had sold about twenty tickets, which Annabelle said was really good, and we had given out a lot of flyers. I sat down to work on my homework but Annabelle was not having it.

"So when are you seeing him again?"

"Tonight. That's why I'm trying to get all of my

homework done in advance. This way I can have no distractions when we're together," I said, trying to ignore the blush creeping up my face.

"Good thinking. I would hate for homework to interrupt your booty call."

"Stop, it's more than that."

"I know, I'm kidding."

About a half an hour went by and I was just closing my laptop. My computer project was done and all I was doing at this point was nitpicking and I needed to stop. I put my computer away in my bag and went to the sandwich stand to grab Annabelle and me a small lunch. On my way back, I noticed him. It was Officer Finn. I tried not to make eye contact and headed back to the table with Annabelle.

"Hey, Violet," Officer Finn yelled, and came over to the table.

I gave a forced smile and introduced him to Annabelle.

"Nice to meet you," he said, and returned his attention to me. "So, how have things been since that threat against you and your roommate?"

"What threat?" Annabelle asked, looking white as a ghost.

"It wasn't a threat against me. Lola and her boyfriend got in a fight and there was some confusion about a knife. I was not even there and she said it's all fine," I said, trying to explain to Officer Finn that I wasn't the one in danger.

"Right, but you two live together, so if he threatened her, then you could also be in danger," he said with an air of condescension.

"I'm not in danger, but thank you for your concern," I said, and started to eat my lunch.

"You've said that before and yet here I am." He was standing tall and pushing his chest out. The effect was not impressive but rather pathetic. All this macho man act did was make me feel uncomfortable.

"Like I said before, I'm fine," I commented sternly, hoping he would hear me, but doubting he would listen.

"I would think that after last night you'd be more than fine, Violet." Finn winked at me. He must have not thought that the flowers were creepy.

"Actually, now that you mention it. Can I talk to you, over here?" I stood up and walked away from Annabelle. He quickly followed, probably assuming I was thrilled about the flowers. Boy, was he in for his own surprise.

"So, did I hit the nail on the head? Beautiful violets for Violet. But you know, none of those flowers are anywhere near as pretty as you are." He reached his hand out to try to stroke my cheek but I jerked away from him.

"No, I don't like violets. I think they're super cheesy. I'm more concerned about the fact that you broke into my room," I lied, hoping he'd just back off.

"We talked about this, I was just trying to make sure that guy with the knife wasn't waiting for you. I'm just thinking about your safety. I'm always thinking about your safety." Finn nodded as if this were obvious.

I felt the frustration begin to boil inside of me

and I exploded. "Look, I'm not interested in you. I don't want you anywhere near my room, I don't want you to continue to give me flowers, and I don't want your help!"

Finn's face barely moved. It was like he had botox or something because only his eye twitched slightly. "Let me get this straight, you're breaking up with me? I can get you different flowers. Sunflowers, yeah, sunflowers seem more your thing," Finn decided, wagging his finger in my face.

"I don't know how I can make this any clearer, back off or—"

"Or what? Relationships between staff and students, or even professors and students, are forbidden. We wouldn't want someone to find out about you, would we? I'd watch what you say to me if I were you," Finn whispered as he stepped into my personal space. He was now inches from my face and it took everything inside me to keep from shaking. That was what he wanted, to see my fear. Well, I wasn't going to give him the satisfaction.

"First of all, don't you dare threaten me! Second, Finn, we were never a thing. We will never be a thing. So leave me the hell alone." I walked away, leaving him standing against the wall. At first I thought he was going to follow me, but he just walked away.

"What was that about?" Annabelle had closed her laptop, and much to my dismay, she was focusing on me.

"He just doesn't seem to understand the word 'no,' or anything close to it." I wanted to brush it off and pretend like everything was over. He was going to stop bothering me and I didn't need to worry about him saying anything about David.

"What's he doing?"

I should have known she wasn't going to just let this go. "He keeps giving me flowers, and when I asked him to stop, he assumed it was because I didn't like the type of flower. Well, last night, he broke into my room and gave me a bouquet of violets. So—"

"Wait a minute," Annabelle shouted, cutting me off. "What do you mean he broke into your room?"

"That's just it. My room was locked, and when I unlocked the door and went inside, the flowers were sitting on my desk."

"Violet, you need to report this to campus safety, like, right now." Annabelle started packing her things up.

"It's fine. I talked to him and told him to back off. Before, I was being too nice, but I was very clear this time. Plus, he keeps hinting that he knows about Berneli and me. What if he reports me?" I said, dread pouring out of me.

"And what if he kills you? He broke into your room. What's to stop him from breaking into someone else's? He's a freakin' cop! As for Berneli, if he really had proof, then he probably would have done something already."

"Annabelle, I've—"

"No, we're going." Annabelle got up and grabbed my bag. She rushed out of the building and headed straight for the campus security office. I had no choice but to follow her.

I caught up to Annabelle just as she reached the

building. "Geez, these doors are heavy," she groaned as she struggled with opening the door against the wind.

"Seriously, you took my bag?" I asked her as she handed it to me.

"You just needed proper motivation," she gloated, and then shoved me to the front desk.

There was a woman, maybe a couple years older than us, who was messing around on her phone. "What can I help you with?" she asked me without looking up.

"I have an issue with one of the officers. Um, specifically Officer Finn."

Her head shot up and she looked at me wide-eyed. "What's the problem with Officer Finn, is he all right?"

"Uh, yeah, he's fine but I'm not. He snuck into my dorm room last night and left me flowers."

"Okay…and…?" she said, waiting for me to continue.

"He's been following me around campus and I think he has crossed the line. I'm uncomfortable." My face flushed as she looked at me, confused, again. I felt the heat all along my neck and straight to my roots. Was I really making a big deal out of nothing?

"I'm sure he is just trying to protect you. Officer Finn is a really good police officer. Plus, have you really looked at him? He's fine! I certainly wouldn't be complaining if he broke into my room." The secretary fluffed her brown hair and stood up a little straighter as she spoke about him. It was almost like he could see her and she wanted to impress him.

"Well, I don't feel comfortable with him breaking into my room. It isn't right." I was trying to steer the conversation back to his crimes.

"You're right. Who would want a sexy guy to sneak into their room and leave them flowers? The horror!" The secretary started laughing at me and I felt tears start to well up but I fought to keep them from showing. Luckily, I wasn't alone.

Annabelle slammed her fist on the desk and the secretary jumped about three feet in the air. "Look, it's not sweet, it's creepy. I know it's against the rules for him to be in her room without probable cause, which Violet did not provide. It is her right to complain about this and we want to file an incident report with the department, now," Annabelle demanded loudly.

My mouth fell open as I looked at her. She was always so mild and quiet, but here she was showing what a badass she could be. While I loved the attitude shift, the secretary clearly didn't. She opened her mouth to respond, but then shut it quickly.

"Listen, we are a real police station and don't have time for this kind of nonsense. Has Finn hurt you?"

"No, but he just threatened me."

"Did he say he was going to hurt you?"

"No, it was implied."

"I'm going to level with you, sweetie," she said, and patted my hand. "I could go get the chief and let him know that you want to complain about one of our most decorated officers on the force because he is bringing you flowers and he 'implied' a threat to you, or I can let the chief deal with more pressing matters. Your choice."

The condescension dripping from her voice was so thick I couldn't handle it. I was embarrassed and I needed to get out of there. It was my word versus the cop's. Why did I ever think they'd believe me? Plus, I'd tossed the flowers out. Those were the only evidence I had.

I ran out of the security center and fought to keep my tears at bay.

Chapter 14

After Annabelle and I left campus security, I refused to talk about it. She tried to tell me that I wasn't being overdramatic but I wouldn't listen. The secretary had completely humiliated me and I didn't want to deal with this anymore. I told Finn to back off and he would. That was what I decided.

My class went by pretty quickly, which suited me just fine. I was meeting with Berneli at six to go get the stuff on the rider for the comedienne this weekend and I wanted to run by my room to get a jacket and pack a bag.

David texted that he was going to pick me up in the parking lot near the dorms. I was waiting by the curb for about five minutes before a black Mercedes pulled up in front of me. The window lowered and I saw David's face.

"Looking for a date?" I asked, smiling. He laughed and unlocked the door. I climbed in and gasped. This may have been the nicest car I had ever seen. The leather was beautiful and it still smelled like a new car. The radio had all sorts of fancy buttons and a touch screen. Not to mention it had amazing speakers.

"This is a fun car." I looked at him in awe, all efforts to act cool and collected gone as I started pushing random buttons.

"Cheers. I leased it for my time here. It's a real smooth drive."

"Plus, it's pretty," I exclaimed.

"So are you," he said, and then handed me a sheet of paper. "Here is a list of all the things we need to get for the rider. We have a deal with a catering company so most of the main food is covered, but we need to get some snacks and a couple other things."

"Okay, this doesn't look too bad." I stole a look at him as I handed him back the rider. He was wearing his glasses today and his curls were pushed back off of his face. His cream button-down shirt was rolled up over his elbows and he was wearing a grey vest on top. He looked like Hercules was dressed by a hipster. I loved it.

"So, did you finish your paper today in class?" he asked, and I turned bright red.

"What are you talking about?"

"Do you really think I didn't notice you working awfully hard in class today?"

"I finished your paper the other night. I just needed to finish a paper for another class."

"Uh-huh," he said judgmentally.

"Well, it's due tomorrow and I knew that I was going to see you tonight but I didn't have time to get it all done. I knew someone was presenting today so I paid enough attention to think of a couple questions if needed. But I finished it."

"Appreciate it. I have a lot planned for you tonight so I doubt you would have had time to finish the paper anyway."

"Just trying to be proactive," I mumbled, trying to control my blush. We had been together multiple times but I just couldn't keep the blush off of my face. Berneli must have noticed. He reached over and took my hand and then brought it to his mouth, placing a gentle kiss on it, but didn't let go.

That was what messed with my feelings. I didn't want to be with someone who I got used to. I wanted to feel the jitters when he kissed me, and the exhilaration as his hands caressed me. Without those feelings, what would I have?

I looked out the window and took a couple deep breaths. Before anything happened tonight, I needed to tell him about Finn.

"Okay, so I don't really know how to say this so I'm just going to come out with it. There is this campus police officer, the one who was following me around that day? Well, he has been stalking me kinda and he keeps dropping hints that he may know about us." I sat there, unmoving, waiting to hear what he had to say.

"He has been stalking you? Have you reported it?" David looked at me and was horrified. It was the same look he gave me when he heard about the first Tyler incident.

"I tried, but the secretary made it seem unimportant. He hasn't done anything but I'm more worried that he knows about us." I didn't want to tell him about the flowers. David would freak out and that wouldn't help any of us.

"Sod that! He doesn't have any proof. You have a stalker and you're worried he might tattle on us?" David had pulled the car over to the shoulder and he turned to look at me with nothing but concern. It kind of infuriated me. Why couldn't he understand I was trying to look out for him?

"What about your job? I know you have a job back in England, but what if they hear about this?"

"There will always be another job. Stop worrying about it."

"I don't want to be the reason you lose your job." I ran my fingers through my hair to try to ease the shaking.

"Well, I don't want you being expelled from school."

"So what are you saying? You want to stop whatever this is?" I felt tears coming and I forced them down. No, I was living this day by day. If it was over, then I'd accept it. This was never going to be permanent.

"I don't want to stop this." David was serious and he looked deep into my eyes. He reached up and wiped away the tear that had escaped my clutches.

"I don't either."

"Let me know if this officer bothers you again."

"David, I—"

"No, Violet. Tell me."

I nodded, knowing that I wouldn't tell him but hoping he didn't pick up on it.

David looked at me for a few moments, as if trying to size me up. He then turned to the road and said, "Then let's forget about it and go to the shops." He started the car again and pulled back into traffic.

I started thinking about what I had just said. We never really defined what "this" was. It could have been the physical relationship or it could have been more. Did he want it to be something more? Did he already think it was an actual relationship? What did I even think? Was he seeing other girls? Nat always seemed to be around him. I was dying to talk to him about it but I decided to wait. We definitely didn't need another serious talk like the one we just had. I was living day by day, and today, he was with me.

We drove to the store with my hand in his while we talked about the comedienne and what we needed to do. For the rest of the drive, we kept things strictly business.

***

"Have you eaten?" he asked, looking over at me as we headed back to his apartment.

"Yeah, I had some pizza before meeting up with you. I didn't want to assume you would be cooking again and I know we really can't go out to eat or anything," I said, hoping he didn't have a big dinner planned.

"That was a good idea. I had a late burger for lunch so I'm not hungry either. I was just looking out for you," he said, and winked at me. "I did, however, buy some ice cream the other night. I remembered you said that cookie dough was your favorite, so we could have some dessert."

"Sounds good to me," I said, and looked at him. I liked to be in charge and I loved planning things, but for some reason, it was relaxing to have someone else thinking ahead.

When we got inside, he placed the bags near the door and then pulled me in for a kiss. It was soft and gentle, not begging for sex. The kiss said *I missed you*, and I believed him. He broke the kiss and looked down at me. "Would you like some ice cream now?"

"Yes," I exclaimed, and we went to the kitchen.

David grabbed two bowls and then got the ice cream out of the freezer. We both settled down at the kitchen bar. This lasted about three minutes before we shoved the bowls aside and started making out. Berneli moved the bowls to the floor, picked me up, and placed me on the kitchen bar. This was not an *I miss you* kiss anymore. It was an *I need you now* kiss, and I let him have it. The kiss became hurried as he explored my mouth with his tongue. The intensity amplified with every passing second.

As his hands traveled my body, I began unbuttoning his vest and then his shirt. It was a little frustrating how many layers he was wearing right now but I wanted to feel his abs. My fingers were shaking but I managed to get all of the buttons undone and I slipped his shirt and vest off his sturdy shoulders. I ran my fingers over them and then down his defined pecs to his rock hard abs. I grew wet and the look in my eyes must have been feverish.

David unbuttoned my jeans and yanked them and my panties off in one fluid motion. He reached into his wallet and pulled a condom out. Then I helped him pull his pants down. They had barely reached the floor when I felt him push inside me. I let out a moan of pleasure as his fast pace started to build up the pressure I felt inside. He grabbed my shoulders and used them to push deeper and deeper. At this point I was practically crying it felt so good.

"Say my name," he demanded breathlessly.

"David. Take me, David," I begged, feeling the orgasm within my grasp. I noticed a hitch in his breath as he drove into me. Then he let out a pained moan. The sound pushed me over the edge. I closed my eyes and rode the orgasm out. My body was pulsating and my toes curled up. It would seem that my excitement got to him because I felt him go right after me.

We sat there for a moment trying to catch our breath.

"Is that what you had planned for me?" I asked when I remembered how to breathe in and out.

"No, that was spontaneous. You were eating your ice cream like a porn star." He wiped pretend ice cream off my lip.

"Wait, what? I was not eating my ice cream like a porn star. How do you even eat ice cream like a porn star?" I was only trying to be a little obnoxious this time.

"You were licking the spoon and sucking on it and being overly dramatic with your bites," he insisted as he walked over to the bathroom to handle his clean up.

"I wasn't. That's how you use a spoon," I claimed, and went to the bedroom bathroom. Okay, I may have been laying it on thick for him but clearly it worked.

"If that is how you use a spoon, then can I request you don't use one in public?"

"Jealous?" I came out of the bathroom and gave him a little kiss.

"I don't get jealous."

"Sounds like a challenge." I leaned into him but didn't kiss him yet.

"Oh, love, you do not want to start that challenge," he purred, and leaned further into me.

"Says the man who was jealous of Trent," I reminded him, and wrapped my arms around his neck.

"I was not jealous of Trent," he insisted, shaking his head.

"You kicked him off working on the rider so you could work with me."

"No, the rider was important and I wanted it done right, and Trent is an idiot," he maintained, and started to pull away from me, but I grabbed onto him and started to kiss his neck.

"You were a little jealous. Admit it!" I continued to kiss his neck and went down to his collarbone.

"You're cheating," he accused me hoarsely.

"You're avoiding the question." I ran my fingers over his chest and then down to the inside seem of his boxers.

"I was a little jealous," he admitted softly.

"He has nothing on you." I kissed him hard and wrapped my arms around his back. We broke the

293

kiss and stood there hugging for a moment.

"Okay, so do you want to try to eat your ice cream like a normal person or should we forget about it?" he asked, joking.

I hit him on the arm. "That's rude. I eat ice cream like a normal person." I sulked off to the freezer to help myself to another scoop.

Later we put a movie on. It turned out he was a big fan of *The Matrix* and I had never seen it. At first I was really confused. There was so much going on and I honestly couldn't follow it. David was pausing the movie and explaining it for the first half hour. After that, I figured it out. Once the movie ended, I couldn't handle what I had just watched.

"That was crazy! We have to watch the second one." I was completely hooked.

"The second one isn't on."

"So we are going to the store to pick it up," I suggested, and began putting my shoes on.

"Whoa. Where do you think you are going?" He was still sitting on the couch.

"We need to go to the store and get the second one." Why wasn't he moving?

"Love, it is ten o'clock at night. You want to go to the shop and pick up a movie and then watch it when we get back? Don't you sleep?" he asked me while stretching out on the couch.

"Oh, I'm sorry, is it past the old man's bedtime?" I asked, teasing him.

"What did you say?" He shot up.

"I asked if it was past the old man's bedtime," I reiterated, walking toward him.

He came at me and started to tickle me. Fun fact, I was very ticklish. I was howling and kicking to try to break free. But his strong arms held onto me until I started crying.

"I'm sorry! I'm sorry!" I screamed, trying to make him stop.

"What are you sorry for?" he asked, giving me a small reprieve.

"I am sorry for calling you an old man," I grunted.

He leaned down and kissed me on the forehead. This apology thing was getting annoying.

"I will pick the next two movies up and we can have a marathon the next time you are over." He pulled me back down to the couch and I fought him a little.

"There are two more?"

"Yep, and the third one makes no sense at all. Fair warning," he said, and I cuddled against him. We turned the channel and watched some new crime show for a few minutes. But all of a sudden his hand slipped under my shirt and he was on my breast. He was slowly caressing me through my bra. I didn't say a word and pretended not to notice at first. Then, as he started to stroke my nipple, I shifted to give him a better angle. Within seconds of this I was wet and trying to suppress the need to moan.

He had enough of the subtle motions and pulled me onto his lap. He unhooked my bra and pulled my shirt off. He started to suck on my nipple and I leaned my head back, arching into him. I slowly started to grind against him and I felt his erection growing underneath me. I was a little sore since I was not used to all of this action but decided it was worth it.

After a few more moments, David picked me up and carried me to the bedroom. He had never put his shirt back on but had put on some sweatpants. They were easy enough to get off. I reached over to his bedside table for a condom and slid it on him. This time it was my turn. I climbed on top of Berneli and positioned myself just over him. I came down slowly at first, barely taking him in. With each thrust I took more and more until he was fully inside me. I kept it slow and controlled. He seemed to want to play a bigger role but I was not having it.

"I'm in control," I commanded, and pulled him out up to the tip.

"I just want to help." He was looking pained and I kind of enjoyed it. I slammed down hard on top of him and watched his eyes nearly burst out of his head. Then I leaned forward and started pounding hard and fast.

"I said, I'm in control," I demanded again in a firmer voice. Then I stopped suddenly. "Say it! Say I'm in control," I screamed.

"You are in control," he moaned.

I took his hands and placed them on my hips. I leaned back this time and began to move fast, taking him deep. Every once in a while I mixed things up and spun my hips into a circle. I kept the fast pace until I was panting from effort but it was worth it. David was losing it. He screamed my name as he came and I followed him with my own moan of ecstasy. I leaned forward and lay down on top of him.

"Holy shit. What just happened?" he asked, running his fingers through his sweat slicked hair.

"I showed you why you don't have to be jealous," I said, still panting a little as I fought to catch my breath.

"After that I am going to be jealous every time you even look in another man's direction."

"Do I have a reason to be jealous?" I asked while trying to control my breathing.

"Of course. I can't keep the EET girls off me." David chuckled and then rolled over.

As I listened to his breathing even out, I couldn't shake the feeling that he wasn't kidding. I flat out told him that he didn't need to be jealous and then he told me that I should be. Maybe this was his way of saying that we weren't exclusive. It wasn't like we spent every night together. He definitely had more than enough time to see another girl. Maybe he was with someone last night.

I rolled over and watched David as he slept. It seemed that with each breath, a knife was being pushed further and further into my heart. What if this was all part of his game? I was risking my future on this man, a man I thought I could depend on. Now I didn't know what to think. It was time to do what was right for me.

Gently, I slipped out of bed and felt around the room for my clothes. I couldn't find my panties and I didn't want to risk turning the light on or the flashlight on my phone. *Screw it*, I thought, and I grabbed my bag to go. Before I left the bedroom, I turned around one last time and took this moment in. We'd had a lot of good times together and I was going to miss him.

A lone tear slid down my cheek and I let it. As much as I tried to push them away, the feelings I had for David were real. I was tired of pretending otherwise. I knew he didn't share those real feelings, but that was okay. It would be okay.

I headed out of the apartment and called a cab to take me back to the dorm.

Chapter 15

As I was walking to my class, my phone buzzed in my back pocket. Naturally, it was David. I had to turn in my computer project so I didn't have time to answer him. At least that was what I told myself. If I were being honest, I just didn't want to talk to him. There was a good chance he would talk me back into his bed and I'd be right back in the same cycle I was in before. I couldn't do that to myself or to my future. We were done.

***

The rest of the week went by pretty fast, especially since I continued to avoid talking to David, about David, or even really looking in his direction. In class, I just kept my head down and rushed out before he had the chance to corner me. Luckily, with the comedienne coming on Saturday, I didn't have time to see David again. I was nervous but I was determined not to be alone with him. If I kept with the plan, then maybe I could get through it.

Saturday started pretty late in the afternoon. At around four, two people were needed to sell tickets so Jason and I volunteered to go to the box office. Annabelle had things she needed to handle in the EET office so she sent us on our way.

"She's getting bossy!" Jason laughed and then looked at me. I forced a smile but Jason frowned. "What's been going on with you? You've been quiet and moping for the last couple of days."

"It's nothing. Let's just sell the tickets," I said as we walked into the ticket office in front of the auditorium.

"We can do this the hard way or the easy way. But just remember that we will be here for the next two hours and I can be unbelievably annoying," Jason teased, and gave me a playful shove.

"There is just a lot to get into and some of it kinda breaks a lot of school rules."

"I'm waiting," Jason said, and sat back in his chair, relaxed.

"Fine. I may have been having a relationship with someone I wasn't supposed to and it got complicated. I ended it and that sucks. So, see, lots of complications."

"Maybe you could fill in some more of those details because it sounds like you got back together with Trent, and if you did, I'll kill him if he touched you again." Jason looked at me hard and serious.

"No, you're sweet, but I'm not seeing Trent. Um, okay, so don't freak out, please," I begged, and prepared myself to tell him.

300

"Let's go. Out with it."

"All right, I've been seeing Professor Berneli." I winced and waited.

Jason didn't respond at first but then he nodded and smiled wide. "I'm not gonna lie, I had a feeling you were doing something you shouldn't with him." He laughed and shook his head. "I even asked Annabelle about it a couple times but she denied it."

My heart raced and panic began to set in. "Was it that obvious? Do you think other people know?" I dropped my head and squeezed my eyes shut. What did I do?

"Well, I figured something was up when he took Trent off the rider. Plus, you've been pretty absent most nights. No one has that much homework."

"Great. What if other people noticed? I could get kicked out of school." Regret flew through me and it felt like ice searing through my veins.

"Whoa, whoa, relax," he said. "Okay, I'm sure people were pissed about the rider because a lot of people wanted to do it, but that doesn't mean anything. And why would anyone else know you've been gone almost every night? So what if they have some kind of idea, there is no proof."

"Proof, yeah, I guess the only way people would know is if there was a camera in his apartment or his office. Okay, that helps."

"His office, really?" Jason teased, giving me a judgmental look.

"Shut up."

"All right, so tell me what the issue is."

"I tried to ask him what we are, like in a relationship or exclusive or, you know, just fuck buddies."

"Language, princess!" Jason's hand flew to his chest and he acted shocked.

"Oh, so sorry! Well, I tried to ask and he didn't want to label it or anything. So I asked if I had a reason to be jealous and he made a joke about it. I think he might be seeing other students and it's just not worth it. Like, what would I be risking everything for? Sex? Well, okay, it was amazing, but that's not what I need. I just wanted someone to be with, you know?" My lips started to quiver a little and Jason quickly pulled me into a hug.

"Shhh, it's okay."

"No, no, it's not okay. I thought I was special and meant something to him. But now I think he may have just been using me for sex. Am I being dramatic here? I keep wondering if maybe he did feel something and I left too soon."

He gently stroked my back and held me tight. "As much as I want to tell you I think he cares, if he did, then I feel like he'd say it. Now, I'm not saying it's because he's seeing other girls, but he is leaving next year. Maybe he's trying to keep from getting involved too deeply." Jason let go of me and handed me a tissue.

I hadn't started crying yet but I could feel it welling up inside of me.

"So you agree with me?" Somehow hearing that I wasn't crazy helped me relax a little.

"Well, I probably would have kept going for the sex," Jason teased, and smiled at me.

"Ha-ha. What, Janice isn't giving you enough?"

Jason looked at me and smiled. "Actually, we're

both virgins."

"Oh, now I didn't see that coming."

"Look, I have always thought that sex was supposed to be this special thing between people who love each other. I'm not ready until I know I love the person I'm with. Those are just my beliefs. I'm not judging you or anything," he said as he reached out and touched my shoulder.

"So, you don't love Janice?" I was really confused. I thought that was why they were together.

"I do love her but I'm not sure if she's the one. But you already know that. Just like I already knew you were seeing someone. We know each other and I know you're really hurting inside. Do you think he is as broken up?"

"No. He called me a couple times after I left him without a word but it's not like he's banging down my door to make up," I said with a heavy heart. Part of me did want him to fight for me. Maybe prove that those feelings existed. But apart from those few calls, it had been nothing but radio silence.

"Then I think you have your answer. When a guy wants to be with a girl, he's not going to just let her leave. If it makes you feel better, I'll buy you ice cream again."

I giggled for a minute and gave him another hug. "I'll be all right. If you keep buying me ice cream when I'm upset, you'll be broke and I'll be fat. I just need to move on and be single for a little while."

"Sounds like a plan. Now, show a little leg, we need to sell the rest of these tickets." Jason opened the windows to the ticket booth and we got to business.

***

I headed over to the green room with Jason so we could announce the good news about the tickets.

"We have officially sold out," Jason declared to the room.

But my heart stopped when I saw him again. I couldn't celebrate with everyone else because it took everything inside me to keep my heart from breaking into little pieces. I looked at the corner of the room where David was standing and swooned a little. He looked amazing. Instead of the slacks he always wore, he was wearing a pair of dark jeans. They were a little loose but I could still make out the amazing curve of his ass. He was wearing his EET Staff shirt under a dark blue vest that was unbuttoned. He looked up at me and our gaze held for a moment longer than was appropriate. I looked away and Annabelle gave me a sweet smile.

"Great! Now let's hope she shows up," Nat said from the green room couch. Clarissa had spent the last half hour on the phone with the comedienne's driver, who was lost. So at this point it was anyone's guess as to when she would get here.

I walked over to Jason and Annabelle and we sat around the table of amazing-looking food that we were not allowed to touch.

"You look cute!" Annabelle nodded to my jean skirt.

"Thanks, babe. I try just for you," I flirted, and

winked at her.

"What? I thought it was for me!" Jason held his hand to his heart, pretending to be wounded.

"You caught me. I am madly in love with you, Jason. I've been trying to keep it together but you are too much man for me." I pretended to swoon.

"It's okay, Vi. I get this problem a lot. Through extreme therapy you just may be able to get by." He patted me on the shoulder and winked.

Annabelle kicked him under the table.

"Everyone be quiet. Her manager is calling again," Clarissa screamed. After a couple of nondescript comments, Clarissa said goodbye and hung up the phone. "Okay, they found us. They just pulled into the parking lot. Professor Berneli, Nat, and I are going to go greet her and bring her here."

Nat smiled at Berneli and stroked his shoulder. I locked my jaw to keep from running over there and punching her in the face.

"Everyone else, make a single file line outside and we will do the meet and greet before the show starts. We have reserved seats in the orchestra pit of the auditorium so you don't need to worry about finding seats," she said, and the three of them headed out.

We all got up and headed outside to get in line.

"Jason, where's Janice?" I asked, confused. I just realized she wasn't here.

"Oh, she wanted to sit with her friends so I already gave her the ticket," he said, and shrugged his shoulders.

"Is it me, or does she try to avoid us?" I looked at Annabelle and she nodded in agreement.

"I don't know anymore. She said she liked you guys, but I don't know what's up." He shook his head and stared at the floor.

Annabelle quickly changed the subject to the comedienne when David, Nat, and Clarissa walked into the hallway, escorting her. While Clarissa was mooning over the star, Nat had her hooks into David. She had her arm in his and was laughing hysterically at something he said. She must have been faking it. He really wasn't that funny.

I wanted to go over there and break her hand off but I couldn't. This just seemed to solidify my decision. Why didn't he brush her hand off? Was he seeing her too? Had he been seeing her this whole time?

I pushed all of this from my mind and tried to be excited to meet a famous person for the first time.

***

Once the meet and greet was over, we headed down to take our seats. We had two opening acts that would be performing for about seven minutes each and then the star attraction was coming.

The opening acts were two students who had auditioned for the EET board before I was on it. They had been picked out of a group of about six. From what Annabelle said they were pretty funny. Turned out one of them, Greg, had really bad stage fright and managed to screw up most of his jokes. That was quite painful to watch. The student after him, though, Jeff, was a natural. He got everyone warmed up.

The comedienne we picked was hysterical. She tailored her jokes to college campuses and seemed to relate really well to everyone. At one point I was crying from laughing so hard. It truly was a success. After the show was over, we took a large group photo of everyone in EET and all three comedians.

Then the EET board headed to the green room to clean up after the comedienne and her people. It was a disaster so this was going to take a while. I needed to go to the bathroom so I headed around the corner. All of a sudden David cut me off.

"What is going on? You don't return any of my calls or text messages and then you avoid me all day?" he asked me. His glasses were in his pocket and nothing was blocking his devastated stare.

"I just don't want to do this. What am I risking my education for? Just sex?" I tried to walk around him but he quickly cut off my escape with his body.

"I understand, we wouldn't want you risking anything for just sex." He glowered at me.

"Right, so just let me be. I'm sure there are other club members eager to crawl on top of your desk."

"Is that what you think of me?"

"I saw the way you were with Nat. She was all over you," I said, and rushed into the bathroom, locking the door behind me. Part of me wanted him to pound on the door and beg me to open it. Of course he didn't. The tears threatened to come and I pushed them away. I looked in the mirror and forced a smile on my face.

"Listen," I said, pointing at my reflection. "Just get through the rest of the night and then you can cry tonight. Do not let that man see how much he is affecting you. You're a hell of a lot stronger than this." I nodded at myself and opened the door.

Luckily, David wasn't there waiting for me. Maybe it would have made a small difference if he had tried a little harder. But then again, what would that matter? Then I would be back in the same position I was just in.

***

As I was leaving to go to my room, I groaned. Leaning against the wall next to my dorm building was Officer Finn. I tried not to acknowledge him but he blocked my entrance.

"So where were you tonight, Violet?" He crossed his arms in front of him and looked like a dad ready to chastise his daughter for missing curfew.

"I was at the show."

"You shouldn't be walking alone this late. It's not safe," he said, and his voice sounded a little threatening.

A shiver went down my spine but I stood tall. He was done scaring me. "I'm fine. I have tried to be nice but this is not okay anymore. I don't need your protection, nor do I want it. Stop bringing me flowers, don't leave them for me, and definitely don't go to my room."

"Is that because you're too busy with your literature professor? That's right, I know about him." He sounded angry and I could smell alcohol on his breath. I took a step back and looked around. The courtyard was completely empty.

"I don't know what you're talking about. I'm

single." I took a step to the side and leaned against the wall of the dorm, trying to be subtle. If I could get to the door, I could lock him out for a few minutes and call the police. He couldn't be that fast with picking a lock.

"If you're single, then you should have no problem being with me."

"I'm not sure how many different ways I can say that I'm not interested in you. Now let me pass or—"

Finn cut me off and leaned in close. "Or what?" he whispered. "Is that professor going to come and save you?" He winked at me and then grabbed me by the waist. I gasped and tried to fight his hold but he quickly put me over his shoulder. Finn was headed to the parking lot.

"I wouldn't be with you if you were the last man on the planet," I shouted.

"We'll see about that." Finn carried me behind the building and slammed me into the grass. Then he climbed on top of me and I panicked. I started kicking and screaming. Someone had to hear me. When he didn't get off, I let out a loud shriek.

Then Finn took out his cuffs and forcefully handcuffed me.

"Listen, I'm not the enemy here. You had better behave or I'll have to be the bad guy, and I don't want to be the bad guy," he warned, and held my hands above my head with one hand and covered my mouth with his other. We were behind the main dorm building so I kept hoping that someone would look out their window and see me struggling.

"Now let me see. You have such a pretty figure

under these clothes. That is one of the main reasons you're unsafe. I have seen the way men look at you and it is disgusting. You need a man to protect you from all of that filth. Do you think your professor can do that? You need me!" He ripped my shirt open, leaving my bra on display.

Sweat dripped down my face and I searched my mind for something to do. I noticed that while he was looking at my stomach, his hand on my mouth shifted a little and I bit down hard.

"You bitch," he shouted, and slapped me across the face. I let out a piercing scream as my vision came in and out. "Don't you dare do that to me again! There will be consequences," he warned, and repositioned his hand over my mouth. "Now, I am going to move my hand, but if you scream, I will hit you even harder. Do you understand?"

I nodded. He moved his hand and shifted his position. He put his hand on the hem of my skirt and began to raise it a little higher. His fingers stroked my panties. Goose bumps spread out across my body as my adrenaline kicked into overdrive.

I was not going to sit here and get raped. Finn was on my hips so I tried to shift and kick my legs so that I could break free. This didn't work. But it did cause him to loosen his grip on my hands while he was trying to pin my legs down. I moved quickly and got them loose, so I slammed them hard onto his head, making sure the metal of the cuffs hit him first.

He let out a loud curse and swung at me with his flashlight, but the force of the movement knocked him a little off balance. I capitalized on this and shoved him off me. Finn fell to the side and I got up and ran.

The security office was only a few feet away, and if I could just get there, then they could help me. I could hear his ragged breathing behind me and I pushed my legs faster. The door was in my grasp when I heard his voice.

"What the hell is going on here?"

"Stay out of this, Professor, or I'll show them all my evidence of your affair," Finn said as I whipped around.

"I don't care what you do, just keep your hands off her," David begged as he finally reached us.

Finn grabbed his shoulders and tried to shove him away. David quickly overpowered him and wrestled him to the ground.

David looked at me and I saw rage in his eyes. "Violet, go get someone from inside."

I pulled at the heavy doors and made it inside.

"Help, I was just attacked by Officer Finn. One of the professors was passing by and he broke it up, but we need help," I screamed, slamming my hands down on the desk.

An officer didn't hesitate and rushed outside while calling for back up on his walkie-talkie. He quickly took over for David and had Finn in cuffs almost instantly, and then quickly undid the cuffs scraping up my wrists.

David rushed over to me. "What can I do?" he asked, holding my face in his hands.

"Get Annabelle," I begged, handing him my phone from my pocket.

It felt like I was in a tunnel. I could hear him

311

explaining what happened to Annabelle but he seemed really far away. He hung up the phone and I slipped it back in my pocket.

"She will be right out. Love, are you okay?" He looked at the bruises I felt forming on my face and then noticed my ripped shirt. David slid out of his jacket and draped it over my shoulders.

"Everything hurts," I managed to say. I was about to lean into him when I heard one of the officers call his name.

"Professor, do you mind giving a statement?" He beckoned David to head over to him.

I didn't want him to leave me and he didn't seem to want to go. What saved us was Annabelle. I smiled when I saw her. She was wearing leggings and a long t-shirt with a robe flying behind her. Her wet hair clung to her face and she nearly tripped in her shower flip-flops. David let go of my hand and backed up. It was good because she threw herself on me in a huge hug.

"I got this, Professor," she assured him, and he headed over to the officer. Annabelle was amazing. She didn't ask any questions but held me and stroked my hair as I finally broke down in tears. I heard my name being called by an unfamiliar voice and looked up. He introduced himself as Chief Johnson, the head of the police force on campus. I instantly felt relieved to see him.

"Miss Carrington, why don't we go to my office and talk? It is a little chilly out here. Your friend can come." He nodded at Annabelle and they both helped me up.

"I'd like to come too. I'm her faculty advisor for

EET. She was injured leaving my event so I believe I need to be present." David spoke with an air of authority. I needed him there so I hoped the officers would listen.

"Okay, Professor," the chief said, and we all followed him to the campus security office.

I was still shaking and I clung to David's jacket. It smelled like him and provided some small level of comfort.

When I was seated in the captain's office, I took a couple of deep breaths and tried to ignore the panic that was quickly starting to take hold. The adrenaline was wearing off and the magnitude of what almost happened was sinking in.

Chapter 16

After I finished telling my story, Chief Johnson asked David to explain what he saw.

"I was walking from my office to my car when I thought I heard someone scream. I headed toward where I thought I heard the sound coming from," he explained, and balled his fists up. Even telling the story was clearly frustrating him.

"I saw Officer Finn on top of a young woman. I didn't know it was Miss Carrington at the time, but I rushed over to help her." He looked at me for a split second and then continued. "I watched her fight him off but then he pursued her as she ran to this office for help. I told him to leave her alone but he came at me so I had to restrain him." He ran his fingers through his hair and I noticed they were shaking and that his knuckles had blood on them. I hoped it wasn't his own.

"Thank you, Professor," the chief said as he finished making notes. "We are a full police force here and have arrested Andrew Finn for attempted rape and assault. He will be incarcerated until he is arraigned. In case he gets out on bail, a restraining order has been issued. He will not be allowed within one hundred feet of the campus or Miss Carrington," he assured, and then looked at me.

"Miss Carrington, I wanted to express my deepest apologies for what happened to you tonight. I just have one question. If you felt that this man was a danger to you, why didn't you report him to us earlier?"

There was a moment of silence as I pondered this. "I did. I spoke to the secretary and told her about Finn breaking into my room and stalking me. She insisted I was being overdramatic and talked me out of speaking to an officer."

"Miss Carrington, I can guarantee you that all of our staff are extensively trained to take these matters very seriously. It should have been escalated to either an officer or me so that we could determine if there was any danger. We will investigate your claim and work from there. But I urge you not to let someone like that talk you out of reporting a serious matter like someone breaking into your room. You were correct in thinking he was dangerous. I only wish we'd known," the chief said with a deep sadness in his eyes and a splash of guilt in his voice as if he blamed himself for this incident.

"Thank you, Chief," I whispered quietly. I knew it wasn't his fault and I didn't blame him. The truth was that I never thought Finn would be violent. I just wanted him to leave me alone.

"Can we take you back to your dorm?" Chief Johnson asked me.

"No, that's okay. I am going to take her to my house. I think staying here tonight will be too much," Annabelle said, and helped me stand up.

I nodded at the chief and headed out of the office.

***

Annabelle, David, and I walked toward the parking lot. "What do you want to do, Violet?" Annabelle asked when we were all alone. "We really can go to my house for the weekend."

"Or you can come with me. Please, Violet, I can't bear the thought of you being out of my sight right now." David took my hands and kissed the knuckles. There were tears in his eyes as he looked at me. "I lied in there. As soon as I heard the scream, I knew that was you. My heart was broken at the thought of him hurting you."

"David…" I started before he quickly cut me off.

"No, Violet, it's you. I need to be with you. There is nothing going on with Nat, or any other girl for that matter. I didn't realize you needed me to say it. Since I saw you at Casino Night no other woman has even crossed my mind. Please come back to my flat tonight. Let me take care of you, and not just for the night."

"Okay," was all I managed to say before the tears started flowing again. He reached out and gently brushed the tears away with his soft thumb.

"Well, Violet, give me your key and I'll get you some overnight stuff."

I handed Annabelle my wristlet and smiled at

her.

She turned to David. "Thank you for finding her. Take good care of my friend," she ordered, and I was so grateful I'd made friends with the shy girl across the hall.

"Thanks for coming," I said, and tried to keep from crying.

"Oh stop. Of course I'm here. Let me know if you need me for anything." She turned to David again and then hugged him tightly.

"I will, Annabelle. I'll have her text you later to let you know she is doing all right." He helped me into the car.

I jumped a little when he started the engine. I was a little on edge.

We just sat there in silence for a few minutes while Annabelle packed me a bag. She returned quickly and we said goodbye. Then David stepped on the gas and we drove in silence.

***

We walked up to his apartment and David let us in without a word. He pulled me into a deep hug and kissed my hair over and over. Finally, he pulled away.

"What do you want to do, love?" he asked, putting my bag on a kitchen barstool.

"I want to forget," I said and looked out the window.

"Okay, I can help you do that. I purchased the three *Matrix* movies and there are two containers of ice cream in the freezer. I even promise not to say anything if you eat it like a porn star." He forced a laugh and I appreciated the effort.

I smiled and turned to look at him. This was the man who had rescued me. He made me feel safe, and right now I needed to feel safe. I went to David and kissed him.

At first it was a hurried kiss where I was pushing the intensity up, but then I slowed down. I kissed him passionately and wrapped my arms around him. He pulled me close and held me against him. I melted instantly. He pulled away from the kiss for a second.

"Are you sure?" he asked tenderly.

"I need to feel safe again. Make me feel safe," I pleaded, and kissed him. That was all he needed. He picked me up and carried me into the bedroom. He placed me on the bed and then climbed on top of me. I panicked for a moment because this the was position I was in when Finn had attacked me. Sweat began to build up on my upper lip and my breathing grew hard.

David seemed to pick up on this and then pulled me on top of him. I bent down to kiss him and he responded. He was careful not to take me by surprise and slowly slid his hand under my shirt and unhooked my bra. I sat up and pulled his jacket off, and then proceeded to remove my shirt and bra. Then I got David to sit up and took his shirt off. I fell into him, begging to be held. Feeling his skin against mine made me start to cry. He kissed the tears away, holding me tightly.

We stayed like that for a few minutes until I reached down and unbuttoned his jeans. He lifted his hips up and helped me pull them off. It was my turn but I did not want him going up my skirt so I took it off myself. I slid my panties off and tossed them aside. David seemed to realize that I needed to be in charge tonight so he followed my lead.

I reached for a condom in the bedside table and slipped it on him. Then I climbed on top of him and tried to slide him inside me but I could not do it. David picked me up off of the bed and placed me against the wall. He wrapped my legs around his waist and pressed inside me. I held on tightly and started to feel the pressure building up. I started to moan and my head fell back against the wall. Instead of joining my whimpers, he started whispering in my ear.

"I'm here, love. Nothing can happen to you tonight. I will keep you safe. I'm not going anywhere. It is all going to be okay." He repeated this over and over again until I felt the orgasm wash over me. I let it take me over the edge and closed my eyes. When I opened them again, I saw him staring back at me. He had done it. I felt safe, and maybe even loved.

***

I wanted to clean up but I was definitely not ready to go in alone. Before I could even express this concern, David was there. He carried me to the bathroom and turned the water on. I felt the hot steam start to rise and I took it in. My muscles still were not relaxing though. I looked up at David and he met my gaze.

"I can come in and help you or you can take a minute to yourself. Whatever you want," he said, kissing my forehead. I took his hand and held it close to my chest.

"Don't leave me," I insisted, and pulled him into the shower with me. We had sex again under the steaming hot water in almost complete silence. I wanted to replace the memory of Finn with a better one of David and that was exactly what we did. I knew that the memory was not gone forever but at least for now it was. There was no way I was going to let Finn ruin sex for me. David was reminding me how good it felt to have a man touch me. A man who I wanted to touch me. A man who would never raise a hand to me.

We dried off and climbed into bed. Tonight had been one of the worst days of my life. I had never been so scared, but here I was lying with a man who always defended me, even when I was not his to defend.

David kissed the inside of my palm and interrupted my thoughts. "I realize that my timing may be awful but there is something I need to ask you. Winter holiday is coming up and I was hoping you would spend it with me in England. This is more than just sex to me. I have been thinking that we need to give this a real go with no rules or police looking over our shoulders. In England, there are no restrictions on us being together. I'm buying my ticket soon and I was hoping I could get you one as well." He smiled, meeting my gaze. "If this is too much, we can discuss it another time, but I just didn't think I could look at you a moment longer without at least bringing it up."

I took a deep breath and went over the options. This would be a really big step for us. It would mean defining the relationship and choosing to risk my education, my future, and my heart. I thought that was the real reason I was scared to dive into my feelings. If I loved him and he left, I would be devastated.

I closed my eyes for a second and imagined walking the streets of London hand in hand. I thought about what it would feel like to sit across from him in a restaurant, or to laugh with him at the movies. There would be no sneaking around or secret cabs. We could just be together. It was a no-brainer.

If I didn't give this relationship a try, I would regret it for the rest of my life. I had real feelings for him. It may have been a little too early to know if it was love or not, but it could be. Ignoring those feelings was no longer an option for me. If we were careful, there would be no reason to risk my education. I could have both.

"Yes, I want to take this step with you," I said, and he kissed me softly and talked all about his hometown. It sounded perfect. I drifted off to sleep dreaming of a time when Berneli and I could actually be together. This time it was possible.

***

The rest of the semester went on with very little excitement. David and I managed to keep our relationship a secret. I was spending four or five

321

nights a week at his place and he even let me have two drawers.

The first time he found a pack of tampons in the bathroom, though, he did freak out for a few minutes. I just reminded him about the benefits he experienced when I visited and he calmed right down. Plus, the tampons meant I wasn't pregnant.

We decided to live each day as it came. There would be a time when he would leave Elton Hall University for good and I would stay here. But today, he was mine, and that was all I needed. However, David was right, I didn't understand the third *Matrix* movie.

Elton Hall Chronicles:

SECOND SNOWFALL

Chapter 1

Annabelle

He had a girlfriend. It was what I told myself on an almost daily basis. It was what my best friend, Violet, liked to remind me. Though I thought she did it more to see my reaction than out of true concern. Nevertheless, Jason and I had spent a lot of time together over winter break.

Violet was in England, and each time I invited Janice to hang out, there was always an excuse as to why she could not go. I really didn't like her. In fact, I wasn't even sure Jason liked her. But as long as they were together, I would not knowingly cross that line. That very thin line that Jason and I grew closer and closer to as the days went on.

This next semester was going to be an interesting one.

Acknowledgements

I'd like to thank Kelsey McKnight. You're not only one of my best friends but one of my biggest fans and supporters. You've been there for me since I first told you about the story and you've read every draft. I wouldn't be here without you.

I'd also like to thank Limitless Publishing and my editor Gillian Leonard for bringing Elton Hall University to life.

About the Author

Always the avid reader, Sarah Fischer found it frustrating that there were so few books following the struggles and joys that a typical college student faces. While recovering from surgery, she decided to write one. *Elton Hall Chronicles: First Semester* is based on real events that happened to Sarah and her friends over the years. When she isn't unveiling long held secrets or working as a government drove, Sarah likes to go to the movies with her husband and spend time with her three furbabies.

Facebook:
https://www.facebook.com/sarah.elizabeth.129

Twitter:
https://twitter.com/SarhAlexander7